Henry Morley, Thomas Churchyard, George Cavendish

The Life of Cardinal Wolsey

To which is added Thomas Churchyard's tragedy of Wolsey - With an introd. by

Henry Morley

Henry Morley, Thomas Churchyard, George Cavendish

The Life of Cardinal Wolsey
To which is added Thomas Churchyard's tragedy of Wolsey - With an introd. by Henry Morley

ISBN/EAN: 9783337270865

Printed in Europe, USA, Canada, Australia, Japan

Cover: Foto ©Raphael Reischuk / pixelio.de

More available books at **www.hansebooks.com**

THE LIFE

OF

CARDINAL WOLSEY

BY

GEORGE CAVENDISH

HIS GENTLEMAN-USHER

TO WHICH IS ADDED THOMAS CHURCHYARD'S
TRAGEDY OF WOLSEY

WITH AN INTRODUCTION BY HENRY MORLEY

LL.D., PROFESSOR OF ENGLISH LITERATURE AT
UNIVERSITY COLLEGE, LONDON

LONDON
GEORGE ROUTLEDGE AND SONS
BROADWAY, LUDGATE HILL
NEW YORK: 9 LAFAYETTE PLACE
1885

MORLEY'S UNIVERSAL LIBRARY.

" Marvels of clear type and general neatness."

Daily Telegraph.

INTRODUCTION.

GEORGE CAVENDISH, a gentleman of Wolsey's household, who continued loyal to the Church of Rome
after his master's death, told in this book, from his
own knowledge, his master's life. From a reference
in the book to King Philip as " now our sovereign
lord," we learn that it was written between the
25th of July 1554 and November 1558. But a
reference near the close of the book to a Mr. Radcliffe,
as son and heir to the Lord Fitzwalter and now
Earl of Sussex, places the writing of the book before
the 17th of February 1557, when that Earl of
Sussex died. A life of Wolsey by one who had no
goodwill to the dissolution of the monasteries or
respect for Anne Boleyn could not be printed in
Elizabeth's reign. The original manuscript is said
to have been in the hands of the Pierrepoint family,
but the interest of such a narrative from one who
lived in Wolsey's household, and was an eyewitness
of much that he tells, caused a demand for copies.
More than a dozen of them are now known: two
are in the British Museum ; two are in the library at

...nbeth Palace; one is in the Bodleian Library at ...ford, one is in the University Library at Cam-...ridge; and it is evident that, from some one of the [S. copies in circulation, Shakespeare had read Cavendish's Life of Wolsey before he wrote his play of King Henry VIII.

The book was first printed in 1641. It was issued for party purposes, with omissions and interpolations, having been called forth by the great argument of that year against Episcopacy. It was the year of Milton's pamphlets on Church Discipline. This first edition was entitled " The Negotiations of Thomas Woolsey, the Great Cardinall of England . . . . composed by one of his own Servants, being his Gentle-man-Usher." The book was a quarto of 118 pages. The next edition was a duodecimo of 157 pages, published in 1667, with a portrait of Wolsey by Marshall, and entitled " The Life and Death of Thomas Woolsey, Cardinal . . . . written by one of his own Servants, being his Gentleman-Usher." The third edition was an octavo published in 1706 as " The Memoirs of that great Favourite Cardinal Woolsey," &c. The next publication was by Joseph Grove in his " History of the Life and Times of Cardinal Wolsey," published in four volumes in 1742–4; but Grove reproduced the garbled edition of 1641, and when he found how untrustworthy that was, he caused a few copies of a private edition in 8vo from a trustworthy MS. to be printed in 1761.

The biography, which is one of the most interesting in our language, was included in the Harleian Miscellany (1744–6). Dr. Christopher Wordsworth, brother of the poet, included it also, in 1810, in his "Ecclesiastical Biography."

In 1814, the Rev. Joseph Hunter, of Bath, author of the "History of Hallamshire" and of other good antiquarian works, published a pamphlet on the question, "Who Wrote Cavendish's Life of Wolsey?" In this he finally proved that the author was George Cavendish, of Glemsford, and not his more successful brother William, to whom it had been ascribed in the "Biographia Britannica." In 1815, Mr. Samuel Weller Singer published, in two octavo volumes, "Cavendish's Life of Cardinal Wolsey and Metrical Versions from the Original Autograph Manuscript, with Notes and other Illustrations." There was a second edition of it in one volume in 1827, and this is the text of Cavendish here given. Mr. Singer prefixed to his book, which was rich in good illustrative matter, Mr. Hunter's essay.

Thomas Cavendish, Clerk of the Pipe in the Exchequer, married the daughter and heiress of John Smith, of Padbrook Hall, in Suffolk, and died in 1524, leaving two sons, George and William. William, the younger, was born in Suffolk in 1505, he lived to be knighted by Henry VIII. and to become an officer in the court erected for the augmentation of the king's revenue by the sequestration of ecclesiastical

property.   He built the great house at Chatsworth
out of the crumbs of the spoil that fell to his own
share.   Sir William married, in the first year of the
reign of Edward VI., Elizabeth Hardwick, daughter
of John Hardwick of Hardwick in Derbyshire.   She
then was the young widow of Robert Barlow of
Barlow in the same county.   This lady helped Sir
William to advance his fortunes, and after he died,
leaving her a widow with six children, she advanced
her own fortunes by marrying twice again; her last
husband was George Talbot, sixth Earl of Shrewsbury, whom she outlived by seventeen years.   Helped
by his wife Elizabeth, Sir William throve.   He was
continued by Queen Mary in the offices of Treasurer
of the Chamber and Privy Councillor which he had
held under Edward VI., but he was one of the
Derbyshire gentlemen who refused the Queen a loan
of a hundred pounds in aid of the French war.
For, while his brother George held by the old way,
Sir William, as far as the care of his income
allowed, went with the Reformers.

Sir William died in 1557, leaving three sons and
three daughters.   The second son was created Earl
of Devonshire in 1618, and a son of the third son
became that Duke of Newcastle whose life, by his
wife Margaret, was a book dear to Charles Lamb.
The eldest daughter was married to Henry Pierrepoint; the next to Charles Stuart, Earl of Lennox;
the third to Gilbert Talbot, Earl of Shrewsbury.

Thus Sir William Cavendish became the patriarch to a great tribe of peers.

George Cavendish, of Glemsford, in Suffolk, the elder brother, born about 1500, had entered Wolsey's service, "abandoning," as Wolsey said of him, "his own country, wife and children, his house and family, his rest and quietness, only to serve me." He had done this at least as early as 1527, which was seven years before the birth of the first child of his brother William, in 1534. After the Cardinal's death, on the 28th of November 1530, George Cavendish, about thirty years old, retired to his own estate with a present from the king of six cart-horses to carry his furniture to Suffolk, and five marks for his cost homeward ; to which there were added ten pounds wages due, and twenty pounds for a reward. So he went home to his wife Margery—who was a niece of Sir Thomas More's, and daughter to William Kemp of Spainhall in Essex—and lived at home in peace until his death in 1561 or 1562.

George Cavendish had a son William, who owned, after his father's death, the manor of Cavendish, and that son William had a son William who became a mercer in London and sold Cavendish in 1579. History is silent about other descendants.

This was the George Cavendish who, in the reign of Queen Mary, looking back upon what he had known thirty years before, with the reflection of ripe years to soften all, made of it one harmonious picture of the vanity of that ambition through which, perhaps, he had himself partly learnt the blessedness of being little.   Old memories of love and duty temper the religious spirit in which Wolsey's faithful servant, grey with years that had slipped by since his master's death, shaped what he had known into a picture of life so single and so true that the direct suggestion to Shakespeare of his play of King Henry VIII. may have come from the reading of George Cavendish's Life of Wolsey.   Apart from the direct suggestion of particular passages in the play, there is a likeness in the main suggestion that "Man walketh in a vain shadow and disquieteth himself in vain, he heapeth up riches and cannot tell who shall gather them.   And now, Lord, what is my hope ?   Truly, my hope is in thee."

I have appended to George Cavendish's book the tragedy of Wolsey contributed to "The Mirror for Magistrates," by Thomas Churchyard, a poet born at Shrewsbury about 1520, whose activity began with the beginning of Elizabeth's reign, and for whose epitaph these lines were written:

" Poverty and Poetry his tomb doth inclose;
Wherefore, good neighbours, be merry in prose."

H. M.

April, 1885.

THE

LIFE OF CARDINAL WOLSEY.

THE PROLOGUE.

MESEEMS it were no wisdom to credit every light tale,
blasted abroad by the blasphemous mouth of the rude
commonalty. For we daily hear how, with their
blasphemous trump, they spread abroad innumer-
able lies, without either shame or honesty, which
primâ facie showeth forth a visage of truth, as though
it were a perfect verity and matter indeed, whereas
there is nothing more untrue. And amongst the wise
sort so it is esteemed, with whom those babblings be of
small force and effect.

Forsooth I have read the exclamations of divers
worthy and notable authors, made against such false
rumours and fond opinions of the fantastical commonalty, who delighteth in nothing more than to hear
strange things, and to see new alterations of authorities;
rejoicing sometimes in such new fantasies, which afterwards give them more occasion of repentance than of
joyfulness. Thus may all men of wisdom and discretion understand the temerous madness of the rude

commonalty, and not give to them too hasty credit of every sudden rumour, until the truth be perfectly known by the report of some approved and credible person, that ought to have thereof true intelligence. I have heard and also seen set forth in divers printed books some untrue imaginations, after the death of divers persons, which in their life were of great estimation, that were invented rather to bring their honest names into infamy and perpetual slander of the common multitude, than otherwise.

The occasion therefore that maketh me to rehearse all these things is this; for as much as I intend, God willing, to write here some part of the proceedings of Legate and Cardinal Wolsey, Archbishop of York, and of his ascending and descending from honorous estate; whereof some part shall be of mine own knowledge, and some of other persons' information.

Forsooth this cardinal was my lord and master, whom in his life I served, and so remained with him, after his fall, continually, during the term of all his trouble, until he died; as well in the south as in the north parts, and noted all his demeanor and usage in all that time; as also in his wealthy triumph and glorious estate. And since his death I have heard diverse sundry surmises and imagined tales, made of his proceedings and doings, which I myself have perfectly known to be most untrue; unto the which I could have sufficiently answered according to truth, but, as me seemeth, then it was much better for me to suffer, and dissemble the matter, and the same to remain still as lies, than to reply against their untruth, of whom I might, for my boldness, sooner have kindled a great flame of displeasure, than to quench one spark of their malicious untruth. Therefore I commit the truth to Him who knoweth all things. For, whatsoever any man hath conceived in him when he lived, or since his death, thus much I dare be bold to say; without displeasure to any person, or of affection, that in my judgment I never saw this realm in better order, quietness, and obedience, than it was in the time of his authority and rule, nor justice better ministered with indifferency; as I could evidently prove, if I should not be accused of too much affection, or else that I set forth more than truth. I will therefore here desist to speak any more in his commendation, and proceed farther to his original beginning and ascending by fortune's favour to high honours, dignities, promotions, and riches.

Finis quod G. C.

TRUTH it is, Cardinal Wolsey, sometime Archbishop of York, was an honest poor man's son, born in Ipswich, within the county of Suffolk ; and being but a child, was very apt to learning ; by means whereof his parents, or his good friends and masters, conveyed him to the University of Oxford, where he prospered so in learning, that, as he told me in his own person, he was called the boy-bachelor, forasmuch as he was made Bachelor of Arts at fifteen years of age, which was a rare thing, and seldom seen.

Thus prospering and increasing in learning, he was made Fellow of Magdalen College, and after appointed, for his learning, to be schoolmaster there; at which time the Lord Marquess Dorset had three of his sons there at school with him, committing as well unto him their virtuous education, as their instruction and learning. It pleased the said marquess against a Christmas season, to send as well for the schoolmaster as for his children, home to his house, for their recreation in that pleasant and honourable feast. They being then there, my lord their father perceived them to be right well employed in learning, for their time : which contented him so well, that he having a benefice in his gift, being at that time void, gave the same to the schoolmaster, in reward for his diligence, at his departing after Christmas upon his return to the University. And having the presentation thereof he repaired to the ordinary for his institution and induction ; then being fully furnished of all necessary instruments at the ordinary's hands for his preferment, he made speed without any farther delay to the said benefice to take thereof possession. And being there for that intent, one Sir Amyas Pawlet, knight, dwelling in the country thereabout, took an occasion of displeasure against him, upon what ground I know not : but, sir, by your leave, he was so bold to set the schoolmaster by the feet during his pleasure ; the which was afterward neither forgotten nor forgiven. For when the schoolmaster mounted the dignity to be Chancellor of England, he was not oblivious of the old displeasure ministered unto him by master Pawlet, but sent for him, and after many sharp and heinous words, enjoined him to attend upon the council until he were by them dismissed, and not to depart without license, upon an urgent pain and forfeiture : so that he continued within the Middle Temple, the space of five or six years, or more ; whose lodging there was in the gate house next the street, which he re-edified very sumptuously, garnishing the same, on the outside thereof, with cardinals' hats and arms, badges and cognisaunces of the cardinal, with divers other devices, in so glorious a sort, that he thought thereby to have appeased his old unkind displeasure.

Now may this be a good example and precedent to men in authority, which will sometimes work their will without wit, to remember in their authority, how authority may decay; and those whom they punish of will more than of justice, may after be advanced in the public weal to high dignities and governance, and they based as low, who will then seek the means to be revenged of old wrongs sustained wrongfully before. Who would have thought then, when Sir Amyas Pawlet punished this poor scholar, that ever he should have attained to be Chancellor of England, considering his baseness in every condition. These be wonderful works of God, and fortune. Therefore I would wish all men in authority and dignity to know and fear God in all their triumphs and glory ; considering in all their doings, that authorities be not permanent, but may slide and vanish, as princes' pleasures do alter and change.

Then as all living things must of very necessity pay the due debt of nature, which no earthly creature can resist, it chanced my said Lord Marquess to depart out of this present life. After whose death this schoolmaster, considering then with himself to be but a small beneficed man, and to have lost his fellowship in the College (for, as I understand, if a fellow of that college be once promoted to a benefice he shall by the rules of the house be dismissed of his fellowship), and perceiving himself also to be destitute of his singular good lord, thought not to be long unprovided of some other succour or staff, to defend him from all such harms, as he lately sustained.

And in his travail thereabout, he fell in acquaintance with one Sir John Nanphant, a very grave and ancient knight, who had a great room in Calais under King Henry the Seventh. This knight he served, and behaved him so discreetly, and justly, that he obtained the especial favour of his said master; insomuch that for his wit, gravity, and just behaviour, he committed all the charge of his office unto his chaplain. And, as I understand, the office was the treasurership of Calais, who was, in consideration of his great age, discharged of his chargeable room, and returned again into England, intending to live more at quiet. And through his instant labour and especial favour his chaplain was promoted to the king's service, and made his chaplain.

And when he had once cast anchor in the port of promotion, how he wrought, I shall somewhat declare.

He, having then a just occasion to be in the present
sight of the king daily, by reason he attended, and said
mass before his grace in his private closet, and that
done he spent not the day forth in vain idleness, but
gave his attendance upon those whom he thought to
bear most rule in the council, and to be most in favour
with the king, the which at that time were Doctor Fox,
Bishop of Winchester, then secretary and lord privy
seal, and also Sir Thomas Lovell, knight, a very sage
counsellor, and witty ; being master of the king's wards,
and constable of the Tower.

These ancient and grave counsellors in process of
time after often resort, perceived this chaplain to have
a very fine wit, and what wisdom was in his head,
thought him a meet and an apt person to be preferred
to witty affairs.

It chanced at a certain season that the king had an
urgent occasion to send an ambassador unto the emperor
Maximilian, who lay at that present in the Low Country
of Flanders, not far from Calais. The Bishop of Winchester, and Sir Thomas Lovell, whom the king most
highly esteemed, as chief among his counsellors (the king
one day counselling and debating with them upon this
embassy), saw they had a convenient occasion to prefer
the king's chaplain, whose excellent wit, eloquence, and
learning they highly commended to the king. The king
giving ear unto them, and being a prince of an excellent
judgment and modesty, commanded them to bring his

chaplain, whom they so much commended, before his grace's presence. At whose repair thither to prove the wit of his chaplain, the king fell in communication with him in matters of weight and gravity: and, perceiving his wit to be very fine, thought him sufficient to be put in authority and trust with this embassy ; and commanded him thereupon to prepare himself to this enterprise and journey, and for his depeche, to repair to his grace and his trusty counsellors aforesaid, of whom he should receive his commission and instructions. By means whereof he had then a due occasion to repair from time to time into the king's presence, who perceived him more and more to be a very wise man, and of a good entendment. And having his depeche, he took his leave of the king at Richmond about noon, and so came to London with speed about four of the clock, where then the barge of Gravesend was ready to launch forth, both with a prosperous tide and wind. Without any farther abode he entered the barge, and so passed forth. His happy speed was such that he arrived at Gravesend within little more than three hours ; where he tarried no longer than his post horses were provided ; and travelling so speedily with post horses, that he came to Dover the next morning early, whereas the passengers were ready under sail displayed, to sail to Calais. Into which passengers without any farther abode he entered, and sailed forth with them, so that he arrived at Calais within three hours, and having there post horses in a readiness, departed incontinent, making such hasty speed, that

he was that night with the emperor ; who, having
understanding of the coming of the King of England's
ambassador, would in no wise defer the time, but sent
incontinent for him (his affection unto King Henry the
Seventh was such, that he rejoiced when he had an
occasion to show him pleasure). The ambassador
having opportunity, disclosed the sum of his embassy
unto the emperor, of whom he required speedy expedition, the which was granted ; so that the next day
he was clearly dispatched, with all the king's requests
fully accomplished. At which time he made no
farther tarriance, but with post horses rode incontinent that night towards Calais again, conducted thither
with such number of horsemen as the emperor had
appointed, and was at the opening of the gates there,
where the passengers were as ready to return into
England as they were before in his advancing ; insomuch that he arrived at Dover by ten of the clock
before noon ; and having post horses in a readiness,
came to the court at Richmond that night. Where
he taking his rest for that time until the morning,
repaired to the king at his first coming out of his
grace's bedchamber, toward his closet to hear mass.
Whom (when he saw) he checked him for that he
was not past on his journey. " Sir," quoth he, " if it
may stand with your highness' pleasure, I have already ·
been with the emperor, and dispatched your affairs, I
trust, to your grace's contentation." And with that
delivered unto the king the emperor's letters of credence.· The king, being in a great confuse and wonder

of his hasty speed with ready furniture of all his proceedings, dissimuled all his imagination and wonder in
that matter, and demanded of him, whether he encountered not his pursuivant, the which he sent unto
him (supposing him not to be scantly out of London)
with letters concerning a very necessary cause, neglected in his commission and instructions, the which
the king coveted much to be sped. "Yes, forsooth,
Sire," quoth he, " I encountered him yesterday by the
way : and, having no understanding by your grace's
letters of your pleasure therein, have, notwithstanding,
been so bold, upon mine own discretion (perceiving that
matter to be very necessary in that behalf) to dispatch
the same.   And for as much as I have exceeded your
grace's commission, I most humbly require your gracious
remission and pardon."   The king rejoicing inwardly
not a little, said again, " We do not only pardon you
thereof, but also give you our princely thanks, both
for the proceeding therein, and also for your good
and speedy exploit," commanding him for that time to
take his rest, and to repair again to him after dinner,
for the farther relation of his embassy.   The king
then went to mass ; and after at convenient time he
went to dinner.

It is not to be doubted but that this ambassador
hath been since his return with his great friends, the
Bishop of Winchester, and Sir Thomas Lovell, to
whom he hath declared the effect of all his speedy
progress ; nor yet what joy they conceived thereof.
And after his departure from the king in the morning,

his highness sent for the bishop, and Sir Thomas
Lovell ; to whom he declared the wonderful expedition
of his ambassador, commending therewith his excellent wit, and in especial the invention and advancing
of the matter left out of his commission and instructions. The king's words rejoiced these worthy
counsellors not a little, for as much as he was of their
preferment.

Then when this ambassador remembered the king's
commandment, and saw the time draw fast on of his
repair before the king and his council, he prepared
him in a readiness, and resorted unto the place assigned
by the king, to declare his embassy. Without all
doubt he reported the effect of all his affairs and proceedings so exactly, with such gravity and eloquence
that all the council that heard him could do no less
but commend him, esteeming his expedition to be
almost beyond the capacity of man. The king of his
mere motion, and gracious consideration, gave him at
that time for his diligent and faithful service, the
deanery of Lincoln, which at that time was one of the
worthiest spiritual promotions that he gave under the
degree of a bishoprick. And thus from thenceforward
he grew more and more into estimation and authority,
and after was promoted by the king to be his almoner.
Here may all men note the chances of fortune, that
followeth some whom she listeth to promote, and even
so to some her favour is contrary, though they should
travail never so much, with all the urgent diligence
and painful study, that they could devise or imagine ;

whereof, for my part, I have tasted of the experience.

Now ye shall understand that all this tale that I have declared of his good expedition in the king's embassy, I received it of his own mouth and report, after his fall, lying at that time in the great park of Richmond, I being then there attending upon him; taking an occasion upon divers communications, to tell me this journey, with all the circumstances, as I have here before rehearsed.

When death (that favoureth none estate, king or keiser) had taken that prudent prince Henry the Seventh out of this present life (on whose soul Jesu have mercy!) who for his inestimable wisdom was noted and called, in every Christian region, the second Solomon, what practices, inventions, and compasses were then used about that young prince, King Henry the Eighth, his only son, and the great provision made for the funerals of the one, and the costly devices for the coronation of the other, with that virtuous Queen Catherine, then the king's wife newly married. I omit and leave the circumstances thereof to historiographers of chronicles of princes, the which is no part mine intendment.

After all these solemnities and costly triumphs finished, and that our natural, young, lusty and courageous prince and sovereign lord, King Henry the Eighth, entering into the flower of pleasant youth, had taken upon him the regal sceptre and the imperial diadem of this fertile and plentiful realm of England (which at that time flourished in all abundance of wealth and riches, whereof he was inestimably garnished and furnished), called then the golden world, such grace of plenty reigned then within this realm. Now let us return again unto the almoner (of whom I have taken upon me to write), whose head was full of subtil wit and policy, and perceiving a plain path to walk in towards promotion, he handled himself so politicly, that he found the means to be made one of the king's council, and to grow in good estimation and favour with the king, to whom the king gave a house at Bridewell, in Fleet Street, sometime Sir Richard Empson's, where he kept house for his family, and he daily attended upon the king in the court, being in his especial grace and favour, having then great suit made unto him, as counsellors most commonly have that be in favour. His sentences and witty persuasions in the council chamber were always so pithy that they, always as occasion moved them, assigned him for his filed tongue and ornate eloquence, to be their expositor unto the king's majesty in all their proceedings. In whom the king conceived such a loving fantasy, and in especial for that he was most earnest and readiest among all the council to advance the king's only will and pleasure, without any respect to the case ; the king, therefore, perceived him to be a meet instrument for the accomplishment of his devised will and pleasure, called him more near unto him, and esteemed him so highly that his estimation and favour put all other ancient counsellors out of their

accustomed favour, that they were in before ; insomuch
that the king committed all his will and pleasure unto
his disposition and order.   Who wrought so all his
matters, that all his endeavour was only to satisfy the
king's mind, knowing right well, that it was the very
vein and right course to bring him to high promotion.
The king was young and lusty, disposed all to mirth
and pleasure, and to follow his desire and appetite,
nothing minding to travail in the busy affairs of this
realm.   The which the almoner perceiving very well,
took upon him therefore to disburden the king of so
weighty a charge and troublesome business, putting
the king in comfort that he shall not need to spare
any time of his pleasure, for any business that should
necessarily happen in the council, as long as he, being
there and having the king's authority and commandment, doubted not to see all things sufficiently furnished and perfected ; the which would first make the
king privy of all such matters as should pass through
their hands before he would proceed to the finishing
or determining of the same, whose mind and pleasure
he would fulfil and follow to the uttermost, wherewith
the king was wonderly pleased.   And whereas the
other ancient counsellors would, according to the office
of good counsellors, diverse times persuade the king to
have sometime an intercourse in to the council, there
to hear what was done in weighty matters, the
which pleased the king nothing at all, for he loved
nothing worse than to be constrained to do any thing
contrary to his royal will and pleasure ; and that

knew the almoner very well, having a secret intelligence of the king's natural inclination, and so fast as the other counsellors advised the king to leave his pleasure, and to attend to the affairs of his realm, so busily did the almoner persuade him to the contrary; which delighted him much, and caused him to have the greater affection and love to the almoner. Thus the almoner ruled all them that before ruled him; such things did his policy and wit bring to pass. Who was now in high favour, but Master Almoner? Who had all the suit, but Master Almoner? And who ruled all under the king, but Master Almoner? Thus he proceeded still in favour; at last, in came presents, gifts, and rewards so plentifully, that I dare say he lacked nothing that might either please his fantasy or enrich his coffers; fortune smiled so upon him; but to what end she brought him, ye shall hear after. Therefore let all men, to whom fortune extendeth her grace, not trust too much to her fickle favour and pleasant promises, under colour whereof she carrieth venomous gall. For when she seeth her servant in most highest authority, and that he assureth himself most assuredly in her favour, then turneth she her visage and pleasant countenance unto a frowning cheer, and utterly forsaketh him: such assurance is in her inconstant favour and sugared promise. Whose deceitful behaviour hath not been hid among the wise sort of famous clerks, that have exclaimed her and written vehemently against her dissimulation and feigned favour, warning all men* thereby, the less to regard her, and to have her in small estimation of any trust or faithfulness.

This almoner, climbing thus hastily on fortune's wheel, that no man was of that estimation with the king as he was, for his wisdom and other witty qualities, he had a special gift of natural eloquence, with a filed tongue to pronounce the same, that he was able with the same to persuade and allure all men to his purpose.   Proceeding thus in fortune's blissfulness, it chanced the wars between the realms of England and France to be open, but upon what occasion I know not, in so much as the king, being fully persuaded, and resolved in his most royal person to invade his foreign enemies with a puissant army, to delay their hault brags, within their own territory : wherefore it was thought very necessary, that this royal enterprise should be speedily provided and plentifully furnished in every degree of things apt and convenient for the same; the expedition whereof, the king's highness thought no man's wit so meet, for policy and painful travail, as his wellbeloved almoner's was, to whom therefore he committed his whole affiance and trust therein.   And he being nothing scrupulous in any thing, that the king would command him to do, although it seemed to other very difficile, took upon him the whole charge and burden of all this business, and proceeded so therein, that he brought all things to a good pass and purpose in a right decent order, as of all manner of victuals, provisions, and other necessaries, convenient for so noble a voyage and puissant army.

All things being by him perfected, and furnished, the king, not minding to delay or neglect the time appointed, but with noble and valiant courage advanced to his royal enterprise, passed the seas between Dover and Calais, where he prosperously arrived; and after some abode there of his Grace, as well for the arrival of his puissant army royal, provisions and munitions, as to consult about his princely affairs, marched forward, in good order of battle, through the Low Country, until he came to the strong town of Terouanne. To the which he laid his assault, and assailed it so fiercely with continual assaults, that within short space he caused them within to yield the town. Unto which place the Emperor Maximilian repaired unto the king our sovereign Lord, with a puissant army, like a mighty and friendly prince, taking of the king his Grace's wages, as well for his own person as for his retinue, the which is a rare thing seldom seen, heard, or read, that an emperor should take wages, and fight under a king's banner. Thus after the king had obtained the possession of this puissant fort, and set all things in due order, for the defence and preservation of the same to his highness' use, he departed from thence, and marched towards the city of Tournay, and there again laid his siege; to the which he gave so fierce and sharp assaults, that they within were constrained of fine force to yield up the town unto his victorious majesty. At which time he gave the almoner the bishoprick of the same See, for some part of recompense of his pains sustained in that journey And when the king had

established all things there agreeable to his princely
pleasure, and furnished the same with noble valiant
captains and men of war for the safeguard of the town
against his enemies, he returned again into England,
taking with him divers worthy persons of the peers of
France, as the Duke of Longueville, and Countie Cler-
mont, and divers other taken there in a skirmish most
victoriously.   After whose return immediately, the See
of Lincoln fell void by the death of Doctor Smith, late
bishop of that dignity, the which benefice and promotion his Grace gave unto his almoner, Bishop elect of
Tournay, who was not negligent to take possession
thereof, and made all the speed he could for his conse-
cration : the solemnization whereof ended, he found the
means to get the possession of all his predecessor's goods
into his hands, whereof I have seen divers times some
part thereof furnish his house.   It was not long after
that Doctor Bambridge, Archbishop of York, died at
Rome, being there the king's ambassador unto the Pope
Julius ; unto which benefice the king presented his new
Bishop of Lincoln ; so that he had three bishopricks in
one year given him.   Then prepared he again of new
as fast for his translation from the See of Lincoln, unto
the See of York.   After which solemnization done, and
he being in possession of the Archbishoprick of York,
and *Primas Angliœ*, thought himself sufficient to compare
with Canterbury ; and thereupon erected his cross in the
court, and in every other place, as well in the presence of
the Archbishop of Canterbury, and in the precinct of his
jurisdiction as elsewhere.   And forasmuch as Canterbury

claimeth superiority and obedience of York, as he doth of
all other bishops within this realm, forasmuch as he is
primas totius Angliæ, and therefore claimeth, as a token
of an ancient obedience, of York to abate the advancing
of his cross, in the presence of the cross of Canterbury;
notwithstanding York, nothing minding to desist from
bearing of his cross in manner as is said before, caused
his cross to be advanced and borne before him, as well
in the presence of Canterbury as elsewhere. Wherefore Canterbury being moved therewith, gave York a
certain check for his presumption; by reason whereof
there engendered some grudge between Canterbury and
York. And York perceiving the obedience that Canterbury claimed to have of York, intended to provide some
such means that he would rather be superior in dignity
to Canterbury than to be either obedient or equal to
him. Wherefore he obtained first to be made Priest
Cardinal, and *Legatus de latere;* unto whom the Pope
sent a Cardinal's hat, with certain bulls for his authority
in that behalf. Yet by the way of communication ye
shall understand that the Pope sent him this hat as a
worthy jewel of his honour, dignity, and authority, the
which was conveyed hither in a varlet's budget, who
seemed to all men to be but a person of small estimation. Whereof York being advertised, of the baseness
of the messenger, and of the people's opinion and
rumour, thought it for his honour meet, that so high a
jewel should not be conveyed by so simple a messenger;
wherefore he caused him to be stayed by the way, immediately after his arrival in England, where he was

newly furnished in all manner of apparel, with all kind
of costly silks, which seemed decent for such an high
ambassador.   And that done, he was encountered upon
Blackheath, and there received with a great assembly
of prelates, and lusty gallant gentlemen, and from thence
conducted and conveyed through London, with great
triumph.   Then was great and speedy provision and
preparation made in Westminster Abbey for the confirmation of his high dignity ; the which was executed
by all the bishops and abbots nigh or about London, in
rich mitres and copes, and other costly ornaments ;
which was done in so solemn a wise as I have not seen
the like unless it had been at the coronation of a mighty
prince or king.

Obtaining this dignity he thought himself meet to
encounter with Canterbury in his high jurisdiction
before expressed ; and that also he was as meet to bear
authority among the temporal powers, as among the
spiritual jurisdictions.   Wherefore remembering as well
the taunts and checks before sustained of Canterbury,
which he intended to redress, having a respect to the
advancement of worldly honour, promotion, and great
benefits, he found the means with the king, that he
was made Chancellor of England ; and Canterbury
thereof dismissed, who had continued in that honourable room and office, since long before the death of
King Henry the Seventh.

Now he being in possession of the chancellorship,
endowed with the promotion of an Archbishop, and
Cardinal Legate *de latere*, thought himself fully furnished

with such authorities and dignities, that he was able to
surmount Canterbury in all ecclesiastical jurisdictions,
having power to convocate Canterbury, and other
bishops, within his precincts, to assemble at his convo-
cation, in any place within this realm where he would
assign; taking upon him the correction of all matters
in every diocese, having there through all the realm
all manner of spiritual ministers, as commissaries,
scribes, apparitors, and all other officers to furnish his
courts; visited also all spiritual houses, and presented
by prevention whom he listed to their benefices. And
to the advancing of his Legatine honours and jurisdictions, he had masters of his faculties, masters Cere-
moniarum, and such other like officers to the glorifying
of his dignity. Then had he two great crosses of silver,
whereof one of them was for his Archbishoprick, and
the other for his Legacy, borne always before him
whithersoever he went or rode, by two of the most
tallest and comeliest priests that he could get within
all this realm. And to the increase of his gains he had
also the bishoprick of Durham, and the Abbey of St.
Albans *in commendam;* howbeit after, when Bishop
Fox, of Winchester, died, he surrendered Durham into
the king's hands, and in lieu thereof took the Bishoprick
of Winchester. Then he held also, as it were *in ferme,*
Bath, Worcester, and Hereford, because the incumbents
thereof were strangers, born out of this realm, continuing always beyond the seas, in their own native
countries, or else at Rome, from whence they were
sent by the Pope in legation into England to the king.

And for their reward, at their departure, the prudent
King Henry the Seventh thought it better to reward
them with that thing, he himself could not keep, than
to defray or disburse any thing of his treasure.   And
then they being but strangers, thought it more meet
for their assurance, and to have their jurisdictions con-
served and justly used, to permit the Cardinal to have
their benefices for a convenient yearly sum of money
to be paid them by exchanges in their countries, than
to be troubled, or burdened with the conveyance thereof
unto them : so that all their spiritual promotions and
jurisdictions of their bishopricks were clearly in his
domain and disposition, to prefer or promote whom he
listed unto them.   He had also a great number daily
attending upon him, both of noblemen and worthy gentlemen, of great estimation and possessions, with no
small number of the tallest yeomen, that he could get
in all this realm, in so much that well was that nobleman and gentleman, that might prefer any tall and
comely yeoman unto his service.

Now to speak of the order of his house and officers,
I think it necessary here to be remembered.   First ye
shall understand, that he had in his hall, daily, three
especial tables furnished with three principal officers ;
that is to say, a Steward, which was always a dean or
a priest ; a Treasurer, a knight ; and a Comptroller,
an esquire ; which bare always within his house their
white staves.   Then had he a cofferer, three marshals,
two yeomen ushers, two grooms, and an almoner.   He
had in the hall-kitchen two clerks of his kitchen, a
clerk comptroller, a surveyor of the dresser, a clerk of

his spicery. Also there in his hall-kitchen he had two master cooks, and twelve other labourers, and children as they called them; a yeoman of his scullery, and two other in his silver scullery; two yeomen of his pastry, and two grooms.

Now in his privy kitchen he had a Master Cook who went daily in damask satin, or velvet, with a chain of gold about his neck; and two grooms, with six labourers and children to serve in that place; in the Larder there, a yeoman and a groom; in the Scalding-house, a yeoman and two grooms; in the Scullery there, two persons; in the Buttery, two yeomen and two grooms, with two other pages; in the Pantry, two yeomen, two grooms, and two other pages; and in the Ewery likewise: in the Cellar, three yeomen, two grooms, and two pages; beside a gentleman for the month: in the Chaundery, three persons: in the Wafery, two; in the Wardrobe of beds, the master of the wardrobe, and ten other persons; in the Laundry, a yeoman, a groom, and three pages: of purveyors, two, and one groom; in the Bakehouse, a yeoman and two grooms; in the Wood-yard, a yeoman and a groom; in the Garner, one; in the Garden, a yeoman and two labourers. Now at the gate, he had of porters, two tall yeomen and two grooms; a yeoman of his barge: in the stable, he had a master of his horse, a clerk of the stable, a yeoman of the same; a Saddler, a Farrier, a yeoman of his Chariot, a Sumpter-man, a yeoman of his stirrup; a Muleteer; sixteen grooms of his stable, every of them keeping four great geldings: in the Almeserie, a yeoman and a groom.

B

Now I will declare unto you the officers of his chapel, and singing men of the same. First, he had there a Dean, who was always a great clerk and a divine ; a Sub-dean ; a Repeater of the quire; a Gospeller, a Pisteller ; and twelve singing Priests : of Scholars, he had first, a Master of the children; twelve singing children ; sixteen singing men ; with a servant to attend upon the said children. In the Revestry, a yeoman and two grooms : then were there divers retainers of cunning singing men, that came thither at divers sundry principal feasts. But to speak of the furniture of his chapel passeth my capacity to declare the number of the costly ornaments and rich jewels, that were occupied in the same continually. For I have seen there, in a procession, worn forty-four copes of one suit, very rich, besides the sumptuous crosses, candlesticks, and other necessary ornaments to the comely furniture of the same. Now shall ye understand that he had two cross bearers, and two pillar bearers : and in his chamber, all these persons ; that is to say : his high Chamberlain, his Vice Chamberlain ; twelve Gentlemen ushers, daily waiters ; besides two in his privy chamber ; and of Gentlemen waiters in his privy chamber he had six ; and also he had of Lords nine or ten, who had each of them allowed two servants ; and the Earl of Derby had allowed five men. Then had he of Gentlemen, as cup-bearers, carvers, sewers, and Gentlemen daily waiters, forty persons ; of yeomen ushers he had six ; of grooms in his chamber he had eight ; of yeomen of his chamber he had forty-six daily to attend upon his person ; he had also a priest there which was his Almoner, to attend upon his table at dinner. Of doctors and chaplains attending in his closet to say daily mass before him, he had sixteen persons : and a clerk of his closet. Also he had two secretaries, and two clerks of his signet ; and four counsellors learned in the laws of the realm.

And for as much as he was Chancellor of England, it was necessary for him to have divers officers of the Chancery to attend daily upon him, for the better furniture of the same. That is to say : first, he had the Clerk of the Crown, a Riding Clerk, a Clerk of the Hanaper, a Chafer of Wax. Then had he a Clerk of the Check, as well to check his Chaplains, as his Yeomen of the Chamber ; he had also four Footmen, which were apparelled in rich running coats, whensoever he rode any journey. Then had he an Herald at Arms, and a Sergeant at Arms ; a Physician ; an Apothecary ; four Minstrels ; a Keeper of his Tents, an Armourer ; an Instructor of his Wards ; two Yeomen in his Wardrobe ; and a Keeper of his Chamber in the court. He had also daily in his house the Surveyor of York, a Clerk of the Green Cloth ; and an Auditor. All this number of persons were daily attendant upon him in his house, down-lying and up-rising. And at meals, there was continually in his chamber a board kept for his Chamberlains, and Gentlemen Ushers, having with them a mess of the young Lords, and another for gentlemen. Besides all these, there was never an officer and gentleman, or any other worthy person in

his house, but he was allowed some three, some two
servants; and all other one at the least; which
amounted to a great number of persons. Now have I
showed you the order of his house, and what officers
and servants he had, according to his checker roll,
attending daily upon him; besides his retainers, and
other persons being suitors, that most commonly were
fed in his hall. And whensoever we shall see any
more such subjects within this realm, that shall maintain any such estate and household, I am content he
be advanced above him in honour and estimation.
Therefore here I make an end of his household;
whereof the number was about the sum of five hundred
persons according to his checker roll.

You have heard of the order and officers of his
house; now I do intend to proceed forth unto other of
his proceedings; for, after he was thus furnished, in
manner as I have before rehearsed unto you, he was
twice sent in embassy unto the Emperor Charles the
Fifth, that now reigneth; and father unto King Philip,
now our sovereign lord. Forasmuch as the old Emperor
Maximilian was dead, and for divers urgent causes
touching the king's majesty, it was thought good that
in so weighty a matter, and to so noble a prince,
that the Cardinal was most meet to be sent on so
worthy an embassy. Wherefore he being ready to
take upon him the charge thereof, was furnished in all
degrees and purposes most likest a great prince, which
was much to the high honour of the king's majesty,
and of this realm. For first in his proceeding he was

furnished like a cardinal of high estimation, having
all things thereto correspondent and agreeable. His
gentlemen, being in number very many, clothed in
livery coats of crimson velvet of the most purest colour
that might be invented, with chains of gold about their
necks; and all his yeomen and other mean officers
were in coats of fine scarlet, guarded with black velvet
a hand broad. He being thus furnished in this
manner, was twice sent unto the emperor into Flanders,
the emperor lying then in Bruges; who entertained our
ambassador very highly, discharging him and all his
train of their charge; for there was no house within
all Bruges, wherein any gentlemen of the Lord Ambassador's lay, or had recourse, but that the owners of the
houses were commanded by the emperor's officers, that
they, upon pain of their lives, should take no money
for any thing that the cardinal's servants should take
or dispend in victuals; no, although they were disposed
to make any costly banquets : furthermore commanding
their said hosts, to see that they lacked no such thing
as they desired or required to have for their pleasures.
Also the emperor's officers every night went through
the town, from house to house, where as any English
men lay or resorted, and there served their liveries for
all night; which was done after this manner: first,
the emperor's officers brought in to the house a cast of
fine manchet bread, two great silver pots, with wine,
and a pound of fine sugar; white lights and yellow;
a bowl or goblet of silver, to drink in ; and every night
a staff torch. This was the order of their liveries

every night. And then in the morning, when the officers came to fetch away their stuff, then would they accompt with the host for the gentlemen's costs spent in that night and day before. Thus the emperor entertained the cardinal and all his train, for the time of his embassy there. And that done, he returned home again into England, with great triumph, being **no** less in estimation with the king than he was before, but rather much more.

Now will I declare unto you his order in going to Westminster Hall, daily in the term season. First, before his coming out of his privy chamber, he heard most commonly every day two masses in his privy closet; and there then said his daily service with his chaplain: and as I heard his chaplain say, being a man of credence and of excellent learning, that the cardinal, what business or weighty matters soever he had in the day, he never went to his bed with any part of his divine service unsaid, yea not so much as one collect; wherein I doubt not but he deceived the opinion of divers persons. And after mass he would return in his privy chamber again, and being advertised of the furniture of his chambers without, with noblemen, gentlemen, and other persons, would issue out into them, apparelled all in red, in the habit of a cardinal; which was either of fine scarlet, or else of crimson satin, taffety, damask, or caffa, the best that he could get for money: and upon his head a round pillion, with a noble of black velvet set to the same in the inner side; he had also a tippet of fine sables

about his neck; holding in his hand a very fair orange, ...
whereof the meat or substance within was taken out,
and filled up again with the part of a sponge, wherein
was vinegar, and other confections against the pestilent
airs; the which he most commonly smelt unto, passing
among the press, or else when he was pestered with
many suitors. There was also borne before him first,
the great seal of England, and then his cardinal's hat, by
a nobleman or some worthy gentleman, right solemnly,
bareheaded. And as soon as he was entered into his
chamber of presence, where there was attending his
coming to await upon him to Westminster Hall, as
well noblemen and other worthy gentlemen, as noblemen and gentlemen of his own family; thus passing
forth with two great crosses of silver borne before
him; with also two great pillars of silver, and his
pursuivant at arms with a great mace of silver gilt.
Then his gentlemen ushers cried, and said: "On, my
lords and masters, on before; make way for my Lord's
Grace!" Thus passed he down from his chamber
through the hall; and when he came to the hall door,
there was attendant for him his mule, trapped all
together in crimson velvet, and gilt stirrups. When
he was mounted, with his cross bearers, and pillar
bearers, also upon great horses trapped with fine
scarlet. Then marched he forward, with his train
and furniture in manner as I have declared, having
about him four footmen, with gilt pollaxes in their
hands; and thus he went until he came to Westminster
Hall door. And there alighted, and went after this

manner, up through the hall into the chancery; howbeit he would most commonly stay awhile at a bar,
made for him, a little beneath the chancery on the
right hand, and there commune sometime with the
judges, and sometime with other persons. And that
done he would repair into the chancery, sitting there
till eleven of the clock, hearing suitors, and determining of divers matters. And from thence, he would
divers times go into the star chamber, as occasion did
serve; where he spared neither high nor low, but
judged every estate according to their merits and
deserts. .

He used every Sunday to repair to the court, being
then for the most part at Greenwich, in the term;
with all his former order, taking his barge at his privy
stairs, furnished with tall yeomen standing upon the
bayles, and all gentlemen being within with him; and
landed again at the Crane in the vintry. And from
thence he. rode upon his mule, with his crosses, his
pillars, his hat, and the great seal, through Thames
Street, until he came to Billingsgate, or thereabout;
and there took his barge again, and rowed to Greenwich, where he was nobly received of the lords and
chief officers of the king's house, as the treasurer
and comptroller, with others; and so conveyed to the
king's chamber: his crosses commonly standing for
the time of his abode in the court, on the one side of
the king's cloth of estate. He being thus in the court,
it was wonderly furnished with noblemen and gentlemen, much otherwise than it was before his coming.

And after dinner, among the lords, having some consultation with the king, or with the council, he would depart homeward with like state : and this order he used continually, as opportunity did serve.

Thus in great honour, triumph, and glory, he reigned a long season, ruling all things within this realm, appertaining unto the king, by his wisdom, and also all other weighty matters of foreign regions, with which the king of this realm had any occasion to intermeddle. All ambassadors of foreign potentates were always dispatched by his discretion, to whom they had always access for their dispatch. His house was also always resorted and furnished with noblemen, gentlemen, and other persons, with going and coming in and out, feasting and banqueting all ambassadors diverse times, and other strangers right nobly.

And when it pleased the king's majesty, for his recreation, to repair unto the cardinal's house, as he did divers times in the year, at which time there wanted no preparations, or goodly furniture, with viands of the finest sort that might be provided for money or friendship. Such pleasures were then devised for the king's comfort and consolation, as might be invented, or by man's wit imagined. The banquets were set forth, with masks and mummeries, in so gorgeous a sort, and costly manner, that it was a heaven to behold. There wanted no dames, or damsels, meet or apt to dance with the maskers, or to garnish the place for a time, with other goodly disports. Then was there all kind of music and harmony set forth, with excellent voices both of men and children. I have seen the king suddenly come in thither in a mask, with a dozen of other maskers, all in garments like shepherds, made of fine cloth of gold and fine crimson satin paned, and caps of the same, with visors of good proportion of visnomy; their hairs, and beards, either of fine gold wire, or else of silver, and some being of black silk; having sixteen torch bearers, beside their drums, and other persons attending upon them, with visors, and clothed all in satin, of the same colours. And at his coming, and before he came into the hall, ye shall understand, that he came by water to the water gate, without any noise; where, against his coming, were laid charged many chambers, and at his landing they were all shot off, which made such a rumble in the air, that it was like thunder. It made all the noblemen, ladies, and gentle-women, to muse what it should mean coming so sud-denly, they sitting quietly at a solemn banquet; under this sort : First, ye shall perceive that the tables were set in the chamber of presence, banquet-wise covered, my Lord Cardinal sitting under the cloth of estate, and there having his service all alone; and then was there set a lady and a nobleman, or a gentleman and gentle-woman, throughout all the tables in the chamber on the one side, which were made and joined as it were but one table. All which order and devise was done and devised by the Lord Sands, Lord Chamberlain to the king; and also by Sir Henry Guilford, Comptroller to the king. Then immediately after this great shot

of guns, the cardinal desired the Lord Chamberlain,
and Comptroller, to look what this sudden shot should
mean, as though he knew nothing of the matter. They
thereupon looking out of the windows into Thames,
returned again, and showed him, that it seemed to
them there should be some noblemen and strangers
arrived at his bridge, as ambassadors from some foreign
prince. With that, quoth the Cardinal, "I shall
desire you, because ye can speak French, to take the
pains to go down into the hall to encounter and to
receive them, according to their estates, and to conduct
them into this chamber, where they shall see us, and
all these noble personages sitting merrily at our banquet,
desiring them to sit down with us, and to take part of
our fare and pastime." Then they went incontinent
down into the hall, where they received them with
twenty new torches, and conveyed them up into the
chamber, with such a number of drums and fifes as I
have seldom seen together, at one time in any masque.
At their arrival into the chamber, two and two together, they went directly before the cardinal where he
sat, saluting him very reverently ; to whom the Lord
Chamberlain for them said : " Sir, forasmuch as they
be strangers, and can speak no English, they have desired me to declare unto your Grace thus : they, having
understanding of this your triumphant banquet, where
was assembled such a number of excellent fair dames,
could do no less, under the supportation of your good
grace, but to repair hither to view as well their
incomparable beauty, as for to accompany them at

mumchance, and then after to dance with them, and
so to have of them acquaintance. And, sir, they
furthermore require of your Grace licence to accomplish the cause of their repair." To whom the
cardinal answered, that he was very well contented
they should so do. Then the maskers went first and
saluted all the dames as they sat, and then returned
to the most worthiest, and there opened a cup full of
gold, with crowns, and other pieces of coin, to whom
they set divers pieces to cast at. Thus in this
manner perusing all the ladies and gentlewomen, and
to some they lost, and of some they won. And thus
done, they returned unto the cardinal, with great
reverence, pouring down all the crowns in the cup,
which was about two hundred crowns. "At all,"
quoth the cardinal, and so cast the dice, and won
them all at a cast; whereat was great joy made.
Then quoth the cardinal to my Lord Chamberlain, " I
pray you," quoth he, " show them that it seemeth me
that there should be among them some noble man,
whom I suppose to be much more worthy of honour
to sit and occupy this room and place than I ; to
whom I would most gladly, if I knew him, surrender
my place according to my duty." Then spake my
Lord Chamberlain unto them in French, declaring my
Lord Cardinal's mind, and they rounding him again in
the ear, my Lord Chamberlain said to my Lord
Cardinal, " Sir, they confess," quoth he, " that among
them there is such a noble personage, whom, if your
Grace can appoint him from the other, he is contented

to disclose himself, and to accept your place most worthily." With that the cardinal, taking a good advisement among them, at the last, quoth he, " Me seemeth the gentleman with the black beard should be even he." And with that he arose out of his chair, and offered the same to the gentleman in the black beard, with his cap in his hand. The person to whom he offered then his chair was Sir Edward Neville, a comely knight of a goodly personage, that much more resembled the king's person in that mask, than any other. The king, hearing and perceiving the cardinal so deceived in his estimation and choice, could not forbear laughing ; but plucked down his visor, and Master Neville's also, and dashed out with such a pleasant countenance and cheer, that all noble estates there assembled, seeing the king to be there amongst them, rejoiced very much. The cardinal eftsoons desired his highness to take the place of estate, to whom the king answered, that he would go first and shift his apparel ; and so departed, and went straight into my lord's bedchamber, where was a great fire made and prepared for him ; and there new apparelled him with rich and princely garments. And in the time of the king's absence, the dishes of the banquet were clean taken up, and the tables spread again with new and sweet perfumed cloths ; every man sitting still until the king and his maskers came in among them again, every man being newly apparelled. Then the king took his seat under the cloth of estate, commanding no man to remove, but sit

still, as they did before. Then in came a new
banquet before the king's majesty, and to all the rest
through the tables, wherein, I suppose, were served
two hundred dishes or above, of wondrous costly meats
and devices, subtilly devised. Thus passed they forth
the whole night with banqueting, dancing, and other
triumphant devices, to the great comfort of the king,
and pleasant regard of the nobility there assembled.

All this matter I have declared at large, because ye
shall understand what joy and delight the cardinal
had to see his prince and sovereign lord in his house
so nobly entertained and pleased, which was always
his only study, to devise things to his comfort, not
passing of the charges or expenses. It delighted him
so much, to have the king's pleasant princely presence, that no thing was to him more delectable than
to cheer his sovereign lord, to whom he owed so much
obedience and loyalty ; as reason required no less, all
things well considered.

Thus passed the cardinal his life and time, from
day to day, and year to year, in such great wealth, joy,
and triumph, and glory, having always on his side the
king's especial favour ; until Fortune, of whose favour
no man is longer assured than she is disposed, began
to wax something wroth with his prosperous estate,
and thought she would devise a mean to abate his
high port ; wherefore she procured Venus, the in-
satiate goddess, to be her instrument. To work her
purpose, she brought the king in love with a gentlewoman, that, after she perceived and felt the king's

good will towards her, and how diligent he was both to please her, and to grant all her requests, she wrought the cardinal much displeasure ; as hereafter shall be more at large declared. This gentlewoman, the daughter of Sir Thomas Boleyn, being at that time but only a bachelor knight, the which after, for the love of his daughter, was promoted to higher dignities. He bare at divers several times for the most part all the rooms of estimation in the king's house ; as Comptroller, Treasurer, Vice-Chamberlain, and Lord Chamberlain. Then was he made Viscount Rochford ; and at the last created Earl of Wiltshire, and Knight of the noble Order of the Garter ; and, for his more increase of gain and honour, he was made Lord Privy Seal, and most chiefest of the king's privy council. Continuing therein until his son and daughter did incur the king's indignation and displeasure. The king fantasied so much his daughter Anne, that almost all things began to grow out of frame and good order.

To tell you how the king's love began to take place, and what followed thereof, I will even as much as in me lieth, declare unto you. This gentlewoman, Mistress Anne Boleyn, being very young was sent into the realm of France, and there made one of the French queen's women, continuing there until the French queen died. And then was she sent for home again ; and being again with her father, he made such means that she was admitted to be one of Queen Katharine's maids, among whom, for her excellent gesture and behaviour, she did excel all other; insomuch, as the king began to kindle the brand of amours; which was not known to any person, nor scantly to her own person.

Insomuch as my Lord Percy, the son and heir of the Earl of Northumberland, then attended upon the Lord Cardinal, and was also his servitor; and when it chanced the Lord Cardinal at any time to repair to the court, the Lord Percy would then resort for his pastime unto the queen's chamber, and there would fall in dalliance among the queen's maidens, being at the last more conversant with Mistress Anne Boleyn than with any other; so that there grew such a secret love between them that, at length, they were ensured together, intending to marry. The which thing came to the king's knowledge, who was then much offended. Wherefore he could hide no longer his secret affection, but revealed his secret intendment unto my Lord Cardinal in that behalf; and consulted with him to infringe the precontract between them : insomuch, that after my Lord Cardinal was departed from the court, and returned home to his place at Westminster, not forgetting the king's request and counsel, being in his gallery, called there before him the said Lord Percy unto his presence, and before us his servants of his chamber, saying thus unto him. "I marvel not a little," quoth he, "of thy peevish folly, that thou wouldest tangle and ensure thyself with a foolish girl yonder in the court, I mean Anne Boleyn. Dost thou not consider the estate that God hath called thee unto in this world ? For after the death of thy noble father, thou art most like to inherit and possess one of the most worthiest earldoms of this realm.   Therefore it had been most meet, and convenient for thee, to have sued for the consent of thy father in that behalf, and to have also made the king's highness privy thereto ; requiring therein his princely favour, submitting all thy whole proceeding in all such matters unto his highness, who would not only accept thankfully your submission, but would, I assure thee, provide so for your purpose therein, that he would advance you much more nobly, and have matched you according to your estate and honour, whereby ye might have grown so by your wisdom and honourable behaviour into the king's high estimation, that it should have been much to your increase of honour.   But now behold what ye have done through your wilfulness.   Ye have not only offended your natural father, but also your most gracious sovereign lord, and matched yourself with one, such as neither the king, nor yet your father will be agreeable with the matter.   And hereof I put you out of doubt, that I will send for your father, and at his coming, he shall either break this unadvised contract, or else disinherit thee for ever.   The king's majesty himself will complain to thy father on thee, and require no less at his hand than I have said ; whose highness intended to have preferred Anne Boleyn unto another person, with whom the king hath travailed already, and being almost at a point with the same person, although she knoweth it not, yet hath the king, most like a politic and prudent prince, conveyed the matter in such sort, that she, upon the king's motion, will be (I doubt not) right glad and agreeable to the same." "Sir," quoth the Lord Percy, all weeping, "I knew nothing of the king's pleasure therein, for whose displeasure I am very sorry. I considered that I was of good years, and thought myself sufficient to provide me of a convenient wife, whereas my fancy served me best, not doubting but that my lord my father would have been right well persuaded. And though she be a simple maid, and having but a knight to her father, yet is she descended of right noble parentage. As by her mother she is nigh of the Norfolk blood: and of her father's side lineally descended of the Earl of Ormond, he being one of the earl's heirs general. Why should I then, sir, be any thing scrupulous to match with her, whose estate of descent is equivalent with mine when I shall be in most dignity? Therefore I most humbly require your Grace of your especial favour herein; and also to entreat the king's most royal majesty most lowly on my behalf for his princely benevolence in this matter, the which I cannot deny or forsake." "Lo, sirs," quoth the cardinal, "ye may see what conformity and wisdom is in this wilful boy's head. I thought that when thou heardest me declare the king's intended pleasure and travail herein, thou wouldest have relented and wholly submitted thyself, and all thy wilful and unadvised fact, to the king's royal will and prudent pleasure, to be fully disposed and ordered by his Grace's disposition,

as his highness should seem good." " Sir, so I would,"
quoth the Lord Percy, " but in this matter I have gone
so far, before many so worthy witnesses, that I know
not how to avoid myself nor to discharge my conscience." " Why, thinkest thou," quoth the cardinal,
" that the king and I know not what we have to do in
as weighty a matter as this ? Yes (quoth he), I warrant thee. Howbeit I can see in thee no submission
to the purpose." " Forsooth, my Lord," quoth the Lord
Percy, " if it please your Grace, I will submit myself
wholly unto the king's majesty and your Grace in this
matter, my conscience being discharged of the weighty
burthen of my precontract." " Well then," quoth the
cardinal, " I will send for your father out of the north
parts, and he and we shall take such order for the
avoiding of this thy hasty folly as shall be by the king
thought most expedient. And in the mean season I
charge thee, and in the king's name command thee,
that thou presume not once to resort into her company,
as thou intendest to avoid the king's high indignation."
And this said he rose up and went into his chamber.

Then was the Earl of Northumberland sent for in
all haste, in the king's name, who upon knowledge of
the king's pleasure made quick speed to the court.
And at his first coming out of the north he made his
first repair unto my Lord Cardinal, at whose mouth he
was advertised of the cause of his hasty sending for ;
being in my Lord Cardinal's gallery with him in secret
communication a long while. And after their long
talk my Lord Cardinal called for a cup of wine, and

drinking together they brake up, and so departed the earl, upon whom we were commanded to wait to convey him to his servants. And in his going away, when he came to the gallery's end, he sat him down upon a form that stood there for the waiters some time to take their ease. And being there set called his son the Lord Percy unto him, and said in our presence thus in effect. " Son," quoth he, " thou hast always been a proud, presumptuous, disdainful, and a very unthrift waster, and even so hast thou now declared thyself. Therefore what joy, what comfort, what pleasure or solace should I conceive in thee, that thus without discretion and advisement hast misused thyself, having no manner of regard to me thy natural father, nor in especial unto thy sovereign lord, to whom all honest and loyal subjects bear faithful and humble obedience ; nor yet to the wealth of thine own estate, but hast so unadvisedly ensured thyself to her, for whom thou hast purchased thee the king's displeasure, intolerable for any subject to sustain ! But that his Grace of his mere wisdom doth consider the lightness of thy head, and wilful qualities of thy person, his displeasure and indignation were sufficient to cast me and all my posterity into utter subversion and dissolution : but he being my especial and singular good lord and favourable prince, and my Lord Cardinal my good lord hath and doth clearly excuse me in thy lewd fact, and doth rather lament thy lightness than malign the same ; and hath devised an order to be taken for thee ; to whom both thou and I be more bound than we be able well to consider. I pray to God that this may be to thee a sufficient monition and warning to use thyself more wittier hereafter; for thus I assure thee, if thou dost not amend thy prodigality, thou wilt be the last earl of our house. For of thy natural inclination thou art disposed to be wasteful prodigal, and to consume all that thy progenitors have with great travail gathered together and kept with honour. But having the king's majesty my singular good and gracious lord, I intend (God willing) so to dispose my succession, that ye shall consume thereof but a little. For I do not purpose, I assure thee, to make thee mine heir; for, praises be to God, I have more choice of boys who, I trust, will prove themselves much better, and use them more like unto nobility, among whom I will choose and take the best and most likeliest to succeed me. Now, masters and gor‾ ntlemen," (quoth he unto us), " it may be yo‧‧ ·s hereafter, when I am dead, to see the proof of these things that I have spoken to my son prove as true as I have spoken them. Yet in the mean season I desire you all to be his friends, and to tell him his fault when he doth amiss, wherein ye shall show yourselves to be much his friends." And with that he took his leave of us. And said to his son thus: "Go your ways, and attend upon my lord's grace your master, and see that you do your duty." And so departed, and went his way down through the hall into his barge.

Then after long debating and consultation upon the Lord Percy's assurance, it was devised that the same

should be infringed and dissolved, and that the Lord
Percy should marry with one of the Earl of Shrewsbury's daughters; (as he did after) ; by means whereof
the former contract was clearly undone.   Wherewith
Mistress Anne Boleyn was greatly offended, saying,
that if it lay ever in her power, she would work the
cardinal as much displeasure ; as she did indeed after.
And yet was he nothing to blame, for he practised
nothing in that matter, but it was the king's only
device.   And even as my Lord Percy was commanded
to avoid her company, even so was she commanded to
avoid the court, and sent home again to her father for
a season ; whereat she smoked : for all this while she
knew nothing of the king's intended purpose.

But ye may see when Fortune beginneth to lower,
how she can compass a matter to work displeasure by
a far fetch.   For now, mark, good reader, the grudge,
how it began, that in process of time burst out to the
utter undoing of the cardinal.   O Lord, what a God
art thou ! that workest thy secrets so wonderfully,
which be not perceived until they be brought to pass
and finished.   Mark this history following, good reader,
and note every circumstance, and thou shalt espy at
thine eye the wonderful work of God, against such
persons as forgetteth God and his great benefits ! Mark,
I say, mark them well !

After that all these troublesome matters of my Lord
Percy's were brought to a good stay, and all things
finished that were before devised, Mistress Anne Boleyn
was revoked unto the court, where she flourished after

in great estimation and favour; having always a privy
indignation unto the cardinal, for breaking off the precontract made between my Lord Percy and her, supposing that it had been his own device and will, and none
other, not yet being privy to the king's secret mind,
although that he had a great affection unto her. Howbeit, after she knew the king's pleasure, and the great
love that he bare her in the bottom of his stomach
then she began to look very hault and stout, having all
manner of jewels, or rich apparel, that might be gotten
with money.   It was therefore judged by-and-bye
through all the court of every man, that she being in
such favour, might work masteries with the king, and
obtain any suit of him for her friend.

And all this while, she being in this estimation in
all places, it is no doubt but good Queen Katharine,
having this gentlewoman daily attending upon her, both
heard by report, and perceived before her eyes, the
matter how it framed against her (good lady), although
she showed nor to Mistress Anne, nor unto the king, any
spark or kind of grudge or displeasure; but took and
accepted all things in good part, and with wisdom and
great patience dissimuled the same, having Mistress
Anne in more estimation for the king's sake than she
had before, declaring herself thereby to be a perfect
Griselda, as her patient acts shall hereafter more
evidently to all men be declared.

The king waxed so far in amours with this gentlewoman that he knew not how much he might advance
her.   This perceiving, the great lords of the council,

bearing a secret grudge against the cardinal, because that they could not rule in the scene well for him as they would, who kept them low, and ruled them as well as other mean subjects, whereat they caught an occasion to invent a mean to bring him out of the king's high favour, and them into more authority of rule and civil governance. After long and secret consultation amongst themselves, how to bring their malice to effect against the cardinal, they knew right well that it was very difficile for them to do anything directly of themselves. Wherefore, they perceiving the great affection that the king bare lovingly unto Mistress Anne Boleyn, fantasying in their heads that she should be for them a sufficient and an apt instrument to bring their malicious purpose to pass, with her they often consulted in this matter. And she having both a very good wit, and also an inward desire to be revenged of the cardinal, was as agreeable to their requests as they were themselves. Wherefore there was no more to do but only to imagine some presented circumstances to induce their malicious accusations. Insomuch that there was imagined and invented among them diverse imaginations and subtle devices, how this matter should be brought about. The enterprise thereof was so dangerous, that though they would fain have often attempted the matter with the king, yet they durst not; for they knew the great loving affection and especial favour that the king bare to the cardinal, and also they feared the wonderous wit of the cardinal. For this they understood very well, that if their matter that

they should propone against him were not grounded
upon a just and an urgent cause, the king's favour
being such towards him, and his wit such, that he
would with policy vanquish all their purpose and
travail, and then lie in wait to work them an utter
destruction and subversion. Wherefore they were
compelled, all things considered, to forbear their enterprise until they might espy a more convenient time
and occasion.

And yet the cardinal, espying the great zeal that the
king had conceived in this gentlewoman, ordered himself to please as well the king as her, dissimuling the
matter that lay hid in his breast, and prepared great
banquets and solemn feasts to entertain them both at
his own house. And thus the world began to grow
into wonderful inventions, not heard of before in this
realm. The love between the king and this gorgeous
lady grew to such a perfection, that divers imaginations
were imagined, whereof I leave to speak until I come
to the place where I may have more occasion.

Then began a certain grudge to arise between the
French king and the Duke of Bourbon, insomuch as
the duke, being vassal to the house of France, was constrained for the safeguard of his person to flee his
dominions, and to forsake his territory and country,
doubting the king's great malice and indignation. The
cardinal, having thereof intelligence, compassed in his
head, that if the king our sovereign lord (having an
occasion of wars with the realm of France), might
retain the duke to be his general in the wars there : in-

asmuch as the duke was fled unto the emperor, to invite him also, to stir wars against the French king. The cardinal having all this imagination in his head thought it good to move the king in this matter. And after the king was once advertised hereof, and conceived the cardinal's imagination and invention, he dreamed of this matter more and more, until at the last it came in question among the council in consultation, so that it was there finally concluded that an embassy should be sent to the emperor about this matter; with whom it was concluded that the king and the emperor should join in these wars against the French king, and that the Duke of Bourbon should be our sovereign lord's champion and general in the field; who had appointed him a great number of good soldiers over and besides the emperor's army, which was not small, and led by one of his own noblemen; and also that the king should pay the duke his wages and his retinue monthly. Insomuch as Sir John Russel (who was after Earl of Bedford) lay continually beyond the seas in a secret place, assigned both for to receive the king's money and to pay the same monthly to the duke. So that the duke began fierce war with the French king in his own territory and dukedom, which the French king had confiscated and seized into his hands; yet not known to the duke's enemies that he had any aid of the king our sovereign lord. And thus he wrought the French king much trouble and displeasure; insomuch as the French king was compelled of fine force to put harness on his back, and to prepare a puissant army royal, and in his own person to advance to defend and resist the duke's power and malice. The duke having understanding of the king's advancing was compelled of force to take Pavia, a strong town in Italy, with his host, for their security ; where as the king besieged him, and encamped him wondrous strongly, intending to enclose the duke within this town, that he should not issue. Yet notwithstanding the duke would and did many times issue and skirmish with the king's army.

Now let us leave the king in his camp before Pavia, and return again to the Lord Cardinal, who seemed to be more French than Imperial. But how it came to pass I cannot declare unto you : but the French king lying in his camp, sent secretly into England a privy person, a very witty man, to entreat of a peace between him and the king our sovereign lord, whose name was John Joachin ; he was kept as secret as might be, that no man had intelligence of his repair ; for he was no Frenchman, but an Italian born, a man before of no estimation in France, or known to be in favour with his master, but to be a merchant, and for his subtle wit elected to entreat of such affairs as the king had commanded him by embassy. This Joachin after his arrival here in England was secretly conveyed unto the king's manor of Richmond, and there remained until Whitsuntide, at which time the cardinal resorted thither, and kept there the said feast very solemnly. In which season my lord caused this Joachin divers times to dine with him, whose talk and behaviour seemed to be witty, sober, and wondrous discreet. He continued in England long after, until he had (as it seemed) brought his purposed embassy to pass which he had in commission. For after this there was sent out immediately a restraint unto Sir John Russel, into those parts where he made his abiding beyond the seas, that we should retain and keep back that month's wages still in his hands, which should have been paid unto the Duke of Bourbon, until the king's pleasure were to him further known ; for want of which money at the day appointed of payment, the duke and his retinue were greatly dismayed and sore disappointed ; and when they saw that their money was not brought unto them as it was wont to be. And being in so dangerous a case for want of victuals, which were wondrous scant and dear, there were many imaginations what should be the cause of the let thereof. Some said this, and some said they wist never what ; so that they mistrusted no thing less than the very cause thereof. Insomuch at the last, what for want of victuals and other necessaries which could not be gotten within the town, the captains and soldiers began to grudge and mutter ; and at the last, for lack of victuals, were like all to perish. They being in this extremity came before the Duke of Bourbon their captain, and said, " Sir, we must be of very force and necessity compelled to yield us into the danger of our enemies ; and better it was for us so to do than here to starve like dogs." When the duke heard the lamentations, and understood the extremities that they were brought unto for lack of money, he said again unto them, " Sirs," quoth he, " ye are both valiant men and

of noble courage, who have served here under me right
worthily ; and for your necessity, whereof I am parti-
cipant, I do not a little lament. Howbeit I shall
desire you, as ye are noble in hearts and courage, so to
take patience for a day or twain : and if succour come
not then from the King of England, as I doubt nothing
that he will deceive us, I will well agree that we shall
all put ourselves and all our lives unto the mercy of
our enemies ; " wherewith they were all agreeable.
And expecting the coming of the king's money the
space of three days (the which days passed), the duke
seeing no remedy called his noblemen, and captains,
and soldiers before him, and all weeping said, " O ye
noble captains and valiant men, my gentle companions,
I see no remedy in this necessity but either we must
yield us unto our enemies, or else famish. And to
yield the town and ourselves, I know not the mercy of
our enemies. As for my part I pass not of their
cruelties, for I know very well I shall suffer most cruel
death if I come once into their hands. It is not for
myself therefore that I do lament, but it is for your
sakes ; it is for your lives ; it is also for the safeguard
of your persons. For so that ye might escape the
danger of your enemies' hands, I would most gladly
suffer death. Therefore, good companions and noble
soldiers, I shall require you all, considering the dangerous misery and calamity that we stand in at this
present, to sell our lives most dearly rather than to be
murdered like beasts. If ye will follow my counsel
we will take upon us this night to give our enemies an

assault in their camp, and by that means we may either escape, or else give them an overthrow. And thus it were better to die in the field like men, than to live in captivity and misery as prisoners." To the which they all agreed. " Then," quoth the duke, " ye perceive that our enemy hath encamped us with a strong camp, and that there is no way to enter but one, which is so planted with great ordnance, and force of men, that it is not possible to enter that way to fight with our enemies without great danger. And also, ye see that now of late they have had small doubt of us, insomuch as they have kept but slender watch. Therefore my policy and advice shall be this : That about the dead time of the night, when our enemies be most quiet at rest, there shall issue from us a number of the most deliverest soldiers to assault their camp ; who shall give the assault right secretly, even directly against the entry of the camp, which is almost invincible. Your fierce and sharp assault shall be to them in the camp so doubtful, that they shall be compelled to turn the strength of their entry that lieth over against your assault, to beat you from the assault. Then will I issue out at the postern, and come to the place of their strength newly turned, and there, or they be ware, will I enter and fight with them at the same place where their guns and strength lay before, and so come to the rescue of you of the assault, and winning their ordnance which they have turned, beat them with their own pieces. And then we joining together in the field, I trust we shall have a fair hand of them." This device pleased them wondrous well. Then prepared they all that day for the purposed device, and kept them secret and close, without any noise or shot of piece within the town, which gave their enemies the less fear of any trouble that night, but every man went to their rest within their tents and lodgings quietly, nothing mistrusting that after ensued.

Then when all the king's host was at rest, the assailants issued out of the town without any noise, according to the former appointment, and gave a fierce and cruel assault at the place appointed; that they within the camp had as much to do to defend it as was possible : and even as the duke had before declared to his soldiers, they within were compelled to turn their shot that lay at the entry against the assailants. With that issued the duke, and with him about fifteen or sixteen thousand men or more, and secretly in the night, his enemies being not privy of his coming until he was entered the field. And at his first entry he was master of all the ordnance that lay there, and slew the gunners; and charged the said pieces and bent them against his enemies, of whom he slew wondrously a great number. He cut down tents and pavilions, and murdered them within them, or they wist of his coming, suspecting nothing less than the duke's entry ; so that he won the field or ever the king could arise to the rescue : who was taken in his lodging or ever he was armed. And when the duke had obtained the field, and the French king taken prisoner, his men slain, and his tents robbed and spoiled, which were wondrous rich. And in the spoil, searching of the king's treasure in his coffers there was found among them the league newly concluded between the King of England and the French king, under the great seal of England; which once by the duke perceived, he began to smell the impediment of his money which should have come to him from the king. Having upon due search of this matter further intelligence that all this matter and his utter undoing was concluded and devised by the Cardinal of England, the duke conceived such an indignation hereupon against the cardinal, that after he had established all things there in good order and security, he went incontinent unto Rome, intending there to sack the town, and to have taken the pope prisoner : where, at his first assault of the walls, he was the first man that was there slain. Yet, notwithstanding, his captains continued there the assault, and in conclusion won the town, and the pope fled unto Castle Angell, where he continued long after in great calamity.

I have written thus this history at large because it was thought that the cardinal gave the chief occasion of all this mischief. Ye may perceive what thing soever a man purposeth, be he prince or prelate, yet notwithstanding God disposeth all things at his will and pleasure. Wherefore it is great folly for any wise man to take any weighty enterprise of himself, trusting altogether to his own wit, not calling for grace to assist him in all his proceedings.

I have known and seen in my days that princes and

great men who would either assemble at any parliament, or in any other great business, first would most
reverently call to God for his gracious assistance
therein. And now I see the contrary. Wherefore me
seems that they trust more in their own wisdoms and
imaginations than they do to God's help and disposition; and therefore often they speed thereafter, and
their matters take no success. Therefore not only in
this history, but in divers others, ye may perceive right
evident examples. And yet I see no man almost in
authority or high estate regard or have any respect to
the same; the greater is the pity, and the more to be
lamented. Now will I desist from this matter and
proceed to other.

Upon the taking of the French king, many consultations and divers opinions were then in argument
among the council here in England. Whereof some
held opinion that if the king would invade the realm
of France in proper person, with a puissant army
royal, he might easily conquer the same; considering
that the French king, and the most part of the noble
peers of France, were then prisoners with the emperor.
Some again said how that were no honour for the
king our sovereign lord (the king being in capitivity).
But some said that the French king ought by the law
of arms to be the king's prisoner, forasmuch as he was
taken by the king's champion and general captain, the
Duke of Bourbon, and not by the emperor. So that
some moved the king to take war thereupon with the
emperor, unless he would deliver the French king out

C

of his hands and possession; with divers many other imaginations and inventions, even as men's fantasies served them, too long here to be rehearsed: the which I leave to the writers of chronicles.

Thus continuing long in debating upon the matter, and every man in the court had their talk, as will without wit led their fantasies; at the last it was devised by means of divers embassies sent into England out of the realm of France, desiring the king our sovereign lord to take order with the emperor for the French king's deliverance, as his royal wisdom should seem good, wherein the cardinal bare the stroke; so that after long deliberation and advice taken in this matter, it was thought good by the cardinal that the emperor should redeliver out of his ward the French king, upon sufficient pledges. And that the king's two sons, that is to say, the Dauphin and the Duke of Orleans should be delivered in hostage for the king their father; which was in conclusion brought to pass.

After the king's deliverance out of the emperor's bondage, and his two sons received in hostage to the emperor's use, and the king our sovereign lord's security for the recompense of all such demands and restitutions as should be demanded of the French king, the cardinal, lamenting the French king's calamity, and the pope's great adversity, who yet remained in Castle Angell, either as a prisoner, or else for his defence and safeguard (I cannot tell whether), travailed all that he could with the king and his council to take order as well for the delivery of the one as for the quietness of the other.

At last, as ye have heard here before, how divers of
the great estates and lords of the council lay in wait
with my Lady Anne Boleyn, to espy a convenient
time and occasion to take the cardinal in a brake;
they thought then, now is the time come that we
have expected, supposing it best to cause him to
take upon him the king's commission, and to travel
beyond the seas in this matter, saying, to encourage
him thereto, that it were more meet for his high discretion, wit, and authority, to compass and bring to
pass a perfect peace among these great and most mighty
princes of the world than any other within this realm
or elsewhere. Their intent and purpose was only but
to get him out of the king's daily presence, and to
convey him out of the realm, that they might have
convenient leisure and opportunity to adventure their
long desired enterprise, and by the aid of their chief
mistress, my Lady Anne, to deprave him so unto the
king in his absence, that he should be rather in his
high displeasure than in his accustomed favour, or at the
least to be in less estimation with his majesty. Well!
what will you have more? This matter was so handled
that the cardinal was commanded to prepare himself
to this journey; the which he was fain to take upon
him; but whether it was with his good will or no, I
am not well able to tell you. But this I know, that
he made a short abode after the determined resolution
thereof, but caused all things to be prepared onward
toward his journey. And every one of his servants
were appointed that should attend upon him in the same.

When all things were fully concluded, and for this noble embassy provided and furnished, then was no let, but advance forwards in the name of God. My Lord Cardinal had with him such of the lords and bishops and other worthy persons as were not privy of the conspiracy.

Then marched he forward out of his own house at Westminster, passing through all London, over London Bridge, having before him of gentlemen a great number, three in a rank, in black velvet livery coats, and the most part of them with great chains of gold about their necks. And all his yeomen, with noblemen's and gentlemen's servants following him in French tawny livery coats; having embroidered upon the backs and breasts of the said coats these letters: T. and C., under the cardinal's hat. His sumpter mules, which were twenty in number and more, with his carts and other carriages of his train, were passed on before, conducted and guarded with a great number of bows and spears. He rode like a cardinal, very sumptuously, on a mule trapped with crimson velvet upon velvet, and his stirrups of copper and gilt; and his spare mule following him with like apparel. And before him he had his two great crosses of silver, two great pillars of silver, the great seal of England, his cardinal's hat, and a gentleman that carried his valaunce, otherwise called a cloakbag; which was made altogether of fine scarlet cloth, embroidered over and over with cloth of gold very richly, having in it a cloak of fine scarlet. . Thus passed he through London, and all the way of his journey, having his harbingers passing before to provide lodging for his train.

The first journey he made to Dartford in Kent, unto Sir Richard Wiltshire's house, which is two miles beyond Dartford; where all his train were lodged that night, and in the country thereabouts. The next day he rode to Rochester, and lodged in the bishop's palace there; and the rest of his train in the city, and in Stroud on this side the bridge. The third day he rode from thence to Feversham, and there was lodged in the abbey, and his train in the town, and some in the country thereabouts. The fourth day he rode to Canterbury, where he was encountered with the worshipfullest of the town and country, and lodged in the abbey of Christchurch, in the prior's lodging. And all his train in the city, where he continued three or four days; in which time there was the great jubilee, and a fair in honour of the feast of St. Thomas their patron. In which day of the said feast, within the abbey there was made a solemn procession; and my Lord Cardinal went presently in the same, apparelled in his legantine ornaments, with his cardinal's hat on his head; who commanded the monks and all their quire to sing the litany after this sort, *Sancta Maria ora pro papa nostro Clemente;* and so perused the litany through, my Lord Cardinal kneeling at the quire door, at a form covered with carpets and cushions. The monks and all the quire standing all that while in the midst of the body of the church. At which time I saw the Lord Cardinal weep very tenderly; which was, as we supposed, for heaviness that the pope was at that present in such calamity and great danger of the Lance Knights.

The next day I was sent with letters from my Lord Cardinal unto Calais, by empost, insomuch as I was that same night at Calais. And at my landing I found standing upon the pier, without the Lantern Gate, all the council of the town, to whom I delivered and despatched my message and letters or ever I entered the town; where I lay two days or my lord came thither; who arrived in the haven the second day after my coming, about eight of the clock in the morning: where he was received in procession with all the worshipfullest persons of the town in most solemn wise. And in the Lantern Gate was set for him a form, with carpets and cushions, whereat he kneeled and made his prayers before his entry any further in the town; and there he was censed with two great censers of silver, and sprinkled with holy water. That done he arose up and passed on, with all that assembly before him, singing, unto St. Mary's church, where he standing at the high altar, turning himself to the people, gave them his benediction and clean remission. And then they conducted him from thence unto a house called the Checker, where he lay and kept his house as long as he abode in the town; going immediately to his naked bed, because he was somewhat troubled with sickness in his passage upon the seas.

That night, unto this place of the Checker, resorted

to him Mons. du Biez, Captain of Boulogne, with a
number of gallant gentlemen, who dined with him ;
and after some consultation with the cardinal, he with
the rest of the gentlemen departed again to Boulogne.
Thus the cardinal was daily visited with one or other
of the French nobility.

Then when all his train and his carriages were
landed at Calais, and everything prepared in a readiness
for his journey, he called before him all his noblemen
and gentlemen into his privy chamber ; where they
being assembled, he said unto them in this wise in
effect : " I have called you hither to this intent, to
declare unto you, that I considering the diligence that
ye minister unto me, and the good will that I bear you
again for the same, intending to remember your diligent
service hereafter, in place where ye shall receive condign thanks and rewards. And also I would show you
further what authority I have received directly from
the king's highness ; and to instruct you somewhat of
the nature of the Frenchmen ; and then to inform you
what reverence ye shall use unto me for the high
honour of the king's majesty, and also how ye shall
entertain the Frenchmen, whensoever ye shall meet
at any time. First, ye shall understand that the king's
majesty, upon certain weighty considerations, hath for
the more advancement of his royal dignity, assigned
me in this journey to be his lieutenant-general ; and
what reverence belongeth to the same I will tell you.
That for my part I must, by virtue of my commission
of lieutenantship, assume and take upon me, in all

honours and degrees, to have all such service and reverence as to his highness' presence is meet and due: and nothing thereof to be neglected or omitted by me that to his royal estate is appurtenant. And for my part ye shall see me that I will not omit one jot thereof. Therefore, because ye shall not be ignorant in that behalf, is one of the special causes of this your assembly, willing and commanding you as ye intend my favour not to forget the same in time and place, but every of you do observe this information and instruction as ye will at my return avoid the king's indignation, but to obtain his highness' thanks, the which I will further for you as ye shall deserve.

"Now to the point of the Frenchmen's nature, ye shall understand that their disposition is such, that they will be at the first meeting as familiar with you as they had been acquainted with you long before, and commune with you in the French tongue as though ye understood every word they spake: therefore in like manner, be ye as familiar with them again as they be with you. If they speak to you in the French tongue, speak you to them in the English tongue; for if you understand not them, they shall no more understand you." And my lord speaking merrily to one of the gentlemen there, being a Welshman, "Rice," quoth he, "speak thou Welsh to him, and I am well assured that thy Welsh shall be more diffuse to him than his French shall be to thee." And then quoth he again to us all, "Let all your entertainment and behaviour be according to all gentleness and humanity, that it may

be reported, after your departure from thence, that ye
be gentlemen of right good behaviour, and of much
gentleness, and that ye be men that know your duty
to your sovereign lord, and to your master, allowing
much your great reverence. Thus shall ye not only
obtain to yourselves great commendation and praise
for the same, but also advance the honour of your
prince and country. Now go your ways admonished
of all these points, and prepare yourselves against to-
morrow, for then we intend, God willing, to set forward." And thus, we being by him instructed and
informed, departed to our lodgings, making all things
in a readiness against the next day to advance forth
with my lord.

The next morrow, being Mary Magdalen's day, all
things being furnished, my Lord Cardinal rode out
of Calais with such a number of black velvet coats
as hath not been seen with an ambassador. All the
spears of Calais, Guines, and Hammes, were there
attending upon him in that journey, in black velvet
coats, and many great and massy chains of gold were
worn there.

Thus passed he forth with three gentlemen in a
rank, which occupied the length of three-quarters of a
mile or more, having all his accustomed and glorious
furniture carried before him, as I before have rehearsed, except the broad seal, the which was left with
Doctor Taylor, in Calais, then Master of the Rolls,
until his return. Passing thus on his way, and being
scant a mile of his journey, it began to rain so vehe-

mently that I have not seen the like for the time ; that
endured until we came to Boulogne ; and or we came
to Sandyngfeld, the Cardinal of Lorraine, a goodly young
gentleman, encountered my lord, and received him with
great reverence and joy ; and so passed forth together,
until they came to Sandyngfeld, which is a place of
religion, standing between the French, English, and
the Emperor's dominions, being neuter, holding of
neither of them.   And being come thither, met with
him there Le Countie Brion, Captain of Picardy, with
a great number of men of arms, as Stradiots and
Arbenois with others standing in array, in a great
piece of oats, all in harness, upon light horses, passing
with my lord, as it were in a wing, all his journey
through Picardy ; for my lord somewhat doubted the
emperor, lest he would lay an ambush to betray him ;
for which cause the French king commanded them to
await upon my lord for the assurance of his person
out of the danger of his enemies.   Thus rode he accompanied until he came to the town of Boulogne,
where he was encountered within a mile thereof, with
the worshipfullest citizens of the town, having among
them a learned man, that made to him an oration in
Latin ; unto the which my lord made answer semblably
in Latin.   And that done, Mons. du Biez, Captain of
Boulogne, with the retinue there of gentlemen, met him
on horseback ; which conveyed him into the town with
all this assembly, until he came to the abbey gate,
where he lighted and went directly into the church,
and made his prayers before the image of our Lady,

to whom he made his offering. And that done, he gave there his blessing to the people, with certain days of pardon. Then went he into the abbey where he was lodged, and his train were lodged in the high and basse towns.

The next morning, after he heard mass, he rode unto *Montreuil sur la mer*, where he was encountered in like case as he was the day before, with the worship-fullest of the town, all in one livery, having one learned that made an oration before him in Latin, whom he answered in like manner in Latin; and as he entered into the town, there was a canopy of silk embroidered with the letters and hat that was on the servants' coats, borne over him by the persons of most estimation within the town. And when he was alighted his foot-men seized the same as a fee due to their office. Now was there made divers pageants for joy of his coming, who was called there, and in all other places within the realm of France as he travelled, *Le Cardinal Pacifique;* and in Latin *Cardinalis Pacificus.* He was accompanied all that night with divers worthy gentle-men of the country thereabout.

The next day he rode toward Abbeville, where he was encountered with divers gentlemen of the town and country, and so conveyed unto the town, where he was most honourably received with pageants of divers kinds, wittily and costly invented, standing in every corner of the streets as he rode through the town; having a like canopy borne over him, being of more richer sort than the other at Montreuil, or at

Boulogne was; they brought him to his lodging, which was, as it seemed, a very fair house newly built with brick.   At which house King Louis married my Lady Mary, King Henry the Eighth's sister; which was after married to the Duke of Suffolk, Charles Brandon.   And being within, it was in manner of a gallery, yet notwithstanding it was very necessary.   In this house my lord remained eight or ten days; to whom resorted, daily, divers of the council of France, feasting them, and other noblemen, and gentlemen that accompanied the council, both at dinners and suppers.

Then when the time came that he should depart from thence, he rode to a castle beyond the waters of Somme, called Pincquigny Castle, adjoining unto the said water, standing upon a great rock or hill, within the which was a goodly college of priests; the situation whereof was most like unto the Castle of Windsor in England; and there he was received with a solemn procession, conveying him first into the church, and after unto his lodging within the castle. At this castle King Edward the Fourth met with the French king, upon the bridge that goeth over the water of Somme, as ye may read in the chronicles of England.

When my lord was settled within his lodging, it was reported unto me that the French king should come that day into Amiens, which was within six English miles of Pincquigny Castle; and being desirous to see his first coming into the town, I axed license and took with me one or two gentlemen of my lord's, and rode

incontinent thither, as well to provide me of a necessary lodging as to see the king. And when we came
thither, being but strangers, we took up our inn (for
the time) at the sign of the Angel, directly against the
west door of the cathedral church *de notre Dame Sainte
Marie*. And after we had dined there, tarrying until
three or four of the clock, expecting the king's coming,
in came Madame Regent, the king's mother, riding in
a very rich chariot; and in the same with her was her
daughter, the Queen of Navarre, furnished with a
hundred ladies and gentlewomen or more following,
riding upon white palfreys; over and besides divers
other ladies and gentlewomen that rode some in rich
chariots, and some in horse litters; who lighted at the
west door with all this train, accompanied with many
other noblemen and gentlemen besides her guard, which
was not small in number. Then, within two hours
after, the king came into the town with a great shot
of guns and divers pageants, made for the nonce at the
king's *bien venue*; having about his person both before
him and behind him, besides the wonderful number of
noblemen and gentlemen, three great guards diversely
apparelled. The *first* was of Soutches and Burgonyons,
with guns and havresacks. The *second* was of Frenchmen, some with bows and arrows, and some with bills.
The *third* guard was *pour le corps*, which was of tall
Scots, much more comelier persons than all the rest.
The French guard and the Scots had all one livery,
which was rich coats of fine white cloth, with a guard
of silver bullion embroidered an handful broad. The

king came riding upon a goodly genet, and lighted at the west door of the said church, and so was conveyed into the church up to the high altar, where he made his prayers upon his knees, and was then conveyed into the bishop's palace, where he was lodged, and also his mother.

The next morning I rode again to Pincquigny to attend upon my lord, at which time my lord was ready to take his mule towards Amiens; and passing on his journey thitherward, he was encountered from place to place with divers noble and worthy personages, making to him divers orations in Latin, to which he made answer again *extempore;* at whose excellent learning and pregnant wit they wondered very much. Then was word brought my lord that the king was coming to encounter him; with that, he having none other shift, was compelled to alight in an old chapel that stood by the highway, and there newly apparelled him into more richer apparel; and then mounted upon a new mule very richly trapped, with a footcloth and traps of crimson velvet upon velvet, purled with gold, and fringed about with a deep fringe of gold very costly, his stirrups of silver and gilt, the bosses and cheeks of his bridle of the same. And by that time that he was mounted again after this most gorgeous sort, the king was come very near, within less than a quarter of a mile English, mustering upon an hill side, his guard standing in array along the same, expecting my lord's coming; to whom my lord made as much haste as conveniently it became him; until he came within a pair of butt lengths, and there he staid awhile. The king perceiving that stood still; and having two worthy gentlemen young and lusty with him, both brethren to the Duke of Lorraine, and to the Cardinal of Lorraine; whereof one of them was called Monsieur dé Guise, and the other Monsieur Vaudemont; they were both apparelled like the king, in purple velvet lined with cloth of silver, and their coats cut, the king caused Monsieur Vaudemont to issue from him, and to ride unto my lord to know the cause of his tracting. This monsieur rode upon a fair courser, taking his race in a full gallop, even until he came unto my lord; and there caused his horse to come aloft once or twice so nigh my lord's mule, that he was in doubt of his horse; and with that he lighted from his courser, and doing his message to my lord with humble reverence; which done, he mounted again, and caused his horse to do the same at his departing as he did before, and so repaired again to the king; and, after his answer made, the king advanced forward. That seeing my lord did the like, and in the midway they met, em-bracing each other on horseback, with most amiable countenance entertaining each other right nobly. Then drew into the place all noblemen and gentlemen on both sides, with wonderful cheer made one to another, as they had been of an old acquaintance. The prease was such and so thick, that divers had their legs hurt with horses. Then the king's officers cried " *Marche, marche, devant, allez devant.*" And the king, and my Lord Cardinal on his right hand, rode together to

Amiens, every English gentleman accompanied with another of France. The train of French and English endured two long miles, that is to say from the place of their encounter unto Amiens; where they were very nobly received with shot of guns and costly pageants, until the king had brought my lord to his lodging, and there departed asunder for that night, the king being lodged in the bishop's palace. The next day after dinner, my lord with a great train of noblemen and gentlemen of England, rode unto the king's court; at which time the king kept his bed, being somewhat diseased, yet notwithstanding my lord came into his bedchamber, where sat on the one side of his bed his mother, Madame Regent, and on the other side the Cardinal of Lorraine, with divers other noblemen of France. And after a short communication, and drinking of a cup of wine with the king's mother, my lord departed again to his lodging, accompanied with divers gentlemen and noblemen of France, who supped with him. Thus continued the king and my lord in Amiens the space of two weeks and more, consulting and feasting each other divers times. And in the feast of the Assumption of our Lady, my lord rose betimes and went to the cathedral church *de notre Dame*, and there before my Lady Regent and the Queen of Navarre, in our Lady Chapel, he said his service and mass ; and after mass, he himself ministered the sacrament unto my Lady Regent and to the Queen of Navarre. And that done, the king resorted unto the church, and was conveyed into a rich travers at the high altar; and directly against him, on the other side of the altar, sat my Lord Cardinal in another rich travers, three gressis higher than the king's. And at the altar, before them both, a bishop sang high mass, and at the fraction of the host, the same bishop divided the sacrament between the king and the cardinal, for the performance of the peace concluded between them ; which mass was sung solemnly by the king's chapel, having among them cornets and sackbuts. And after mass was done the trumpeters blew in the roodeloft until the king was past inward to his lodging out of the church. And at his coming into the bishop's palace, where he intended to dine with my Lord Cardinal, there sat, within a cloister, about two hundred persons diseased with the king's evil, upon their knees. And the king, or ever he went to dinner, provised every of them with rubbing and blessing them with his bare hands, being bare-headed all the while ; after whom followed his almoner distributing of money unto the persons diseased. And that done he said certain prayers over them, and then washed his hands, and so came up into his chamber to dinner, where as my lord dined with him.

Then it was determined that the king and my lord should remove out of Amiens, and so they did, to a town or city called Compeigne, which was more than twenty English miles from thence ; unto which town I was sent to prepare my lord's lodging. And as I rode on my journey, being upon a Friday, my horse chanced to cast a shoe in a little village, where stood a fair castle. And as it chanced there dwelt a smith, to

whom I commanded my servant to carry my horse to
shoe, and standing by him while my horse was a
shoeing, there came to me one of the servants of the
castle, perceiving me to be the cardinal's servant and
an Englishman, who required me to go with him into
the castle to my lord his master, whom he thought
would be very glad of my coming and company. Whose
request I granted, because that I was always desirous
to see and be acquainted with strangers, in especial
with men in honour and authority, so I went with
him; who conducted me unto the castle, and being
entered in the first ward, the watchmen of that ward,
being very honest tall men, came and saluted me most
reverently, and knowing the cause of my coming,
desired me to stay a little while until they had advertised my lord their master of my being there; and so
I did. And incontinent the lord of the castle came
out to me, who was called Monsieur Crequi, a nobleman born, and very nigh of blood to King Louis, the
last king that reigned before this King Francis. And
at his first coming he embraced me, saying that I was
right heartily welcome, and thanked me that I so
gently would visit him and his castle, saying furthermore that he was preparing to encounter the king and
my lord, to desire them most humbly the next day to
take his castle in their way, if he could so intreat them.
And true it is that he was ready to ride in a coat of
velvet with a pair of velvet arming shoes on his feet,
and a pair of gilt spurs on his heels. Then he took
me by the hand, and most gently led me into his

castle, through another ward. And being once entered into the base court of the castle, I saw all his family and household servants standing in goodly order, in black coats and gowns, like mourners, who led me into the hall, which was hanged with hand-guns, as thick as one could hang by another upon the walls ; and in the hall stood an hawk's perch, whereon stood three or four fair goshawks. Then went we into the parlour, which was hanged with fine old arras, and being there but a while, communing together of my Lord of Suffolk, how he was there to have besieged the same, his servants brought to him bread and wine of divers sorts, whereof he caused me to drink. And after, " I will," quoth he, " show you the strength of my house, how hard it would have been for my Lord of Suffolk to have won it." Then led he me upon the walls, which were very strong, more than fifteen foot thick, and well garnished with great battery pieces of ordnance ready charged to be shot off against the king and my lord's coming.

When he had showed me all the walls and bulwarks about the castle, he descended from the walls, and came down into a fair inner court, where his genet stood for to mount upon, with twelve other genets, the most fairest and best that I ever saw, and in especial his own, which was a mare genet, he showed me that he might have had for her four hundred crowns. But upon the other twelve genets were mounted twelve goodly young gentlemen, called pages of honour ; all bare-headed in coats of cloth of gold, and black velvet cloaks, and on their legs boots of red Spanish leather, and spurs parcel gilt.

Then he took his leave of me, commanding his steward and other his gentlemen to attend upon me, and conduct me unto my lady his wife to dinner. And that done he mounted upon his genet, and took his journey forth out of his castle. Then the steward, with the rest of the gentlemen, led me up into a tower in the gatehouse, where then my lady their mistress lay, for the time that the king and my lord should tarry there.

I being in a fair great dining chamber, where the table was covered for dinner, and there I attended my lady's coming ; and after she came thither out of her own chamber, she received me most gently, like one of noble estate, having a train of twelve gentlewomen. And when she with her train came all out, she said to me, " Forasmuch," quoth she, " as ye be an English-man, whose custom is in your country to kiss all ladies and gentlewomen without offence, and although it be not so here in this realm, yet will I be so bold to kiss you, and so shall all my maidens." By means whereof I kissed my lady and all her women. Then went she to her dinner, being as nobly served as I have seen any of her estate here in England, having all the dinner time with me pleasant communication, which was of the usage and behaviour of our gentlewomen and gentlemen of England, and commended much the behaviour of them, right excellently ; for she was with the king at Ardres, when the great encounter and

meeting was between the French king and the king
our sovereign lord : at which time she was, both for
her person and goodly haviour, appointed to company
with the ladies of England. To be short, after dinner,
pausing a little, I took my leave of her, and so departed
and rode on my journey.

By reason of my tracting of time in Chastel de
Crequi, I was constrained that night to lie in a town
by the way, called *Montdidier*, the suburbs whereof my
Lord of Suffolk had lately burned. And in the next
morning I took my journey and came to Compeigne
upon the Saturday, then being there the market day ;
and at my first coming I took my inn in the midst of
the market-place, and being there set at dinner in a
fair chamber, that had a window looking into the
street, I heard a great rumour and clattering of bills.
With that I looked out into the street, and there I
espied where the officers of the town brought a prisoner
to execution, whose head they strake off with a sword.
And when I demanded the cause of his offence, it was
answered me, that it was for killing of a red deer in
the forest thereby, the punishment whereof is but
death. Incontinent they had set up the poor man's
head upon a pole in the market-place, between the
stag's horns ; and his quarters in four parts of the
forest.

Thus went I about to prepare my lord's lodging,
and to see it furnished, which was there in the great
castle of the town, whereof to my lord was assigned
the one half, and the other half was reserved for the

king; and in like wise there was a long gallery divided between them, wherein was made in the midst thereof a strong wall with a door and window, and there the king and my lord would many times meet at the same window, and secretly talk together, and divers times they would go the one to the other, at the said door.

Now was there lodged also Madame Regent, the king's mother, and all her train of ladies and gentle-women. Unto which place the Chancellor of France came (a very witty man), with all the king's grave counsellors, who took great pains daily in consultation. Insomuch as I heard my Lord Cardinal fall out with the Chancellor, laying unto his charge, that he went about to hinder the league which my said Lord Cardinal had before his coming concluded between the king our sovereign lord and the French king his master; insomuch that my lord stomached the matter very stoutly, and told him, " That it should not lie in his power to dissolve the amicable fidelity between them. And if his master the king being there present forsook his promise and followed his counsel, he should not fail after his return into England to feel the smart, and what a thing it is to break promise with the King of England, whereof he should be well assured." And therewithal he arose and went into his own lodging, wondrously offended. So that his stout countenance, and bold words, made them all in doubt how to pacify his displeasure, and revoke him again to the council, who was then departed in a fury. There was sending, there was coming, there was also intreating, and there was great submission made to him, to reduce him to his former friendly communication ; who would in no wise relent until Madame Regent came herself, who handled the matter so discreetly and wittily, that she reconciled him to his former communication. And by that means he brought other matters to pass, that before he could not attain, nor cause the council to grant ; which was more for fear, than for any affection to the matter, he had the heads of all the council so under his girdle that he might rule them all there as well as he might the council of England.

The next morning after this conflict, he rose early, about four of the clock, sitting down to write letters into England unto the king, commanding one of his chaplains to prepare him to mass, insomuch that his said chaplain stood revested until four of the clock at afternoon ; all which season my lord never rose once to ――――, nor yet to eat any meat, but continually wrote his letters, with his own hands, having all that time his nightcap and keverchief on his head. And about the hour of four of the clock, at afternoon, he made an end of writing, commanding one Christopher Gunner, the king's servant, to prepare him without delay to ride empost into England with his letters, whom he dispatched away or ever he drank. And that done, he went to mass, and said his other divine service with his chaplain, as he was accustomed to do ; and then went straight into a garden ; and after he had walked the space of an hour or more, and said his evensong, he went to dinner and supper all at once ; and making a small repast, he went to his bed, to take his rest for that night.

The next night following he caused a great supper to be provided for Madame Regent, and the Queen of Navarre, and other great estates of ladies and noble women.

There was also Madame Renée, one of the daughters of King Louis, whose sister (lately dead) King Francis had married. These sisters were, by their mother, inheritrices of the Duchy of Britanny, and forasmuch as the king had married one of the sisters, by whom he had the moiety of the said duchy, and to attain the other moiety, and so to be lord of the whole, he kept the said Lady Renée without marriage, intending that, she having none issue, the whole duchy might descend to him, or to his succession, after her death, for want of issue of her body.

But now let us return again to the supper or rather a solemn banquet, where all these noble persons were highly feasted ; and in the midst of their triumph, the French king, with the King of Navarre, came suddenly in upon them unknown, who took their places at the nether end of the table. There was not only plenty of fine meats, but also much mirth and solace, as well in communication as in instruments of music set forth with my lord's minstrels, who played there so cunningly and dulce all that night, that the king took therein great pleasure, insomuch that he desired my lord to lend them unto him the next night. And after supper and banquet finished, the ladies and gentlewomen went to dancing; among whom one Madame Fountaine, a maid, had the prize. And thus passed they the night in pleasant mirth and joy.

The next day the king took my lord's minstrels and rode unto a nobleman's house, where was some goodly image that he had avowed a pilgrimage unto, to perform his devotion. When he came there, he danced, and others with him, the most part of that night; my lord's minstrels played there so excellently all that night, that the shalme (whether it were with extreme labour of blowing, or with poisoning, as some judged, because they were more commended and accepted with the king than his own, I cannot tell), but he that played upon the shalme, an excellent man in that art, died within a day or twain after.

Then the king returned again unto Compeigne, and caused a wild boar to be lodged for him in the forest there; whither my lord rode with the king to the hunting of the wild swine within a toil; where the Lady Regent stood in chariots or wagons, looking on the toil, on the outside thereof, accompanied with many ladies and damosels; among whom my lord stood by the Lady Regent, to regard and behold the pastime and manner of hunting. There was within the toil divers goodly gentlemen with the king, ready garnished to this high enterprise and dangerous hunting of the perilous wild swine. The king being in his doublet and hosen only, without any other garments, all of sheep's colour cloth; his hosen, from the knee upward, was altogether

thrummed with silk very thick of the same colour :
having in a slip a fair brace of great white greyhounds,
armed, as the manner is to arm their greyhounds from
the violence of the boar's tusks.   And all the rest of
the king's gentlemen, being appointed to hunt this boar,
were likewise in their doublets and hosen, holding each
of them in their hands a very sharp boar's spear.

The king being thus furnished, commanded the hunts
to uncouch the boar, and that every other person should
go to a standing, among whom were divers gentlemen
and yeomen of England : and incontinent the boar
issued out of his den, chased with an hound into the
plain, and being there, stalked a while gazing upon the
people, and incontinent being forced by the hound, he
espied a little bush standing upon a bank over a ditch,
under the which lay two lusty gentlemen of France, and
thither fled the boar, to defend him, thrusting his head
snuffing into the same bush where these two gentlemen
lay, who fled with such speed as men do from the danger
of death.   Then was the boar by violence and pursuit
of the hounds and the hunts driven from thence, and
ran straight to one of my lord's footmen, a very comely
person, and an hardy, who held in his hand an English
javelin, with the which he was fain to defend himself
from the fierce assault of the boar, who foined at him
continually with his great tusks, whereby he was compelled at the last to pitch his javelin in the ground
between him and the boar, the which the boar brake
with his force of foining.   And with that the yeoman
drew his sword, and stood at defence ; and with that

the hunts came to the rescue, and put him once again to flight. With that he fled and ran to another young gentleman of England, called Master Ratcliffe, son and heir to the Lord Fitzwalter, and after Earl of Sussex, who by chance had borrowed of a French gentleman a fine boar spear, very sharp, upon whom, the boar being sore chafed, began to assault very eagerly, and the young gentleman deliverly avoided his strokes, and in turning about he struck the boar with such violence (with the same spear that he had borrowed) upon the houghs, that he cut the sinews of both his legs at one stroke, that the boar was constrained to sit down upon his haunches and defend himself, for he could go no more; this gentleman perceiving then his most advantage, thrust his spear into the boar under the shoulder up to the heart, and thus he slew the great boar. Wherefore among the noblemen of France it was reputed to be one of the noblest enterprises that a man might do (as though he had slain a man of arms); and thus our Master Ratcliffe bare then away the prize of that feat of hunting, this dangerous and royal pastime, in killing of the wild boar, whose tusks the Frenchman doth most commonly doubt above all other dangers, as it seemed to us Englishmen then being present.

In this time of my lord's being in France, over and besides his noble entertainment with the king and nobles, he sustained diverse displeasures of the French slaves, that devised a certain book, which was set forth in diverse articles upon the causes of my lord's being there : which should be, as they surmised, that my lord was come thither to conclude two marriages; the one between the king our sovereign lord and Madame Renée, of whom I spake heretofore; and the other between the then princess of England (now being queen of this realm), my Lady Mary the king's daughter and the French king's second son, the Duke of Orleans, who is at this present king of France: with diverse other conclusions and agreements touching the same. Of this book many were imprinted and conveyed into England, unknown to my lord, he being then in France, to the great slander of the realm of England, and of my Lord Cardinal. But whether they were devised of policy to pacify the mutterings of the people, which had diverse communications and imaginations of my lord's being there; or whether they were devised of some malicious person, as the dispositions of the common people are accustomed to do, upon such secret consultations, I know not; but whatsoever the occasion or cause was, the author hath set forth such books. This I am well assured, that after my lord was thereof well advertised, and had perused one of the said books, he was not a little offended, and assembled all the privy council of France together, to whom he spake his mind thus; saying, that it was not only a suspicion in them, but also a great rebuke and a defamation to the king's honour to see and know any such seditious untruths openly divulged and set forth by any malicious and subtle traitor of this realm; saying furthermore, that if the like had been attempted within the realm of England, he doubted not but to see it punished according to the traitorous demeanour and deserts. Notwithstanding I saw but small redress.

So this was one of the displeasures that the Frenchmen showed him, for all his pains and travail that he took for qualifying of their king's ransom.

Also another displeasure was this. There was no place where he was lodged after he entered the territory of France, but that he was robbed in his privy chamber, either of one thing or other; and at Compeigne he lost his standish of silver, and gilt: and there it was espied, and the party taken, which was but a little boy of twelve or thirteen years of age, a ruffian's page of Paris, which haunted my lord's lodging without any suspicion, until he was taken lying under my lord's privy stairs; upon which occasion he was apprehended and examined, and incontinent confessed all things that were missed, which he stole, and brought to his master the ruffian, who received the same, and procured him so to do. After the spial of this boy, my lord revealed the same unto the council, by means whereof the ruffian was apprehended, and set on the pillory, in the midst of the market-place; a goodly recompense for such an heinous offence. Also another displeasure was; some lewd person, whosoever it was, had engraved in the great chamber window where my lord lay, upon the leaning stone there, a cardinal's hat with a pair of gallows over it, in derision of my lord; with divers other unkind demeanours, the which I leave here to write, they be matters so slanderous.

Thus passing divers days in consultation, expecting the return of Christopher Gunner, which was sent into England with letters unto the king, as it is rehearsed heretofore, by empost, who at last returned again with other letters; upon receipt whereof my lord made haste to return into England.

In the morning that my lord should depart and remove, being then at mass in his closet, he consecrated the Chancellor of France a cardinal, and put upon him the habit due to that order; and then took his journey into Englandward, making such necessary expedition that he came to Guisnes, where he was nobly received of my Lord Sands, then captain there, with all the retinue thereof. And from thence he rode to Calais, where he tarried the shipping of his stuff, horses, and train; and in the meantime he established there a mart, to be kept for all nations; but how long it endured, and in what sort it was used, I know not, for I never heard of any great good that it did, or of any worthy assembly there of merchants or merchandise, that was brought thither for the furniture of so weighty a matter.

These things finished, and others for the weal of the town, he took shipping and arrived at Dover, from whence he rode to the king, being then in his progress at Sir Harry Wyatt's house, in Kent, it was supposed among us that he should be joyfully received at his home coming, as well of the king as of all other noblemen: but we were deceived in our expectation. Notwithstanding he went, immediately after his coming to the king, with whom he had long talk, and continued there in the court two or three days; and then returned to his house at Westminster, where he remained until Michaelmas term, which was within a fortnight after, and using his room of Chancellorship, as he was wont to do.

At which time he caused an assembly to be made in the Star Chamber, of all the noblemen, judges, and justices of the peace of every shire that were at that present in Westminster Hall, and there made to them a long oration, declaring unto them the cause of his embassy into France, and of his proceeding there; among the which he said, "he had concluded such an amity and friendship as never was heard of in this realm in our time before, as well between the emperor and us, as between the French king and our sovereign lord, concluding a perpetual peace, which shall be confirmed in writing, alternately, sealed with the broad seals of both the realms graved in fine gold; affirming furthermore, that the king should receive yearly his tribute, by that name, for the Duchy of Normandy, with all other costs which he hath sustained in the wars. And where there was a restraint made in France of the French queen's dower, whom the Duke of Suffolk had married, for divers years during the wars, it is fully concluded, that she shall not only receive the same yearly again, but also the arrearages being unpaid during the restraint. All which things shall be perfected at the coming of the great embassy out of France: in the which shall be a great number of

noblemen and gentlemen for the conclusion of the
same, as hath not been seen repair hither out of one
realm in an embassy. This peace thus concluded, there
shall be such an amity between gentlemen of each
realm, and intercourse of merchants with merchandise,
that it shall seem to all men the territories to be but
one monarchy. Gentlemen may travel quietly from
one country to another for their recreation and pastime;
and merchants, being arrived in each country, shall be
assured to travel about their affairs in peace and tran-
quillity: so that this realm shall joy and prosper for
ever. Wherefore it shall be well done for all true
Englishmen to advance and set forth this perpetual
peace, both in countenance and gesture, with such
entertainment as it may be a just occasion unto the
Frenchmen to accept the same in good part, and also
to use you with the semblable, and make of the same
a noble report in their countries.

"Now, good my lords and gentlemen, I most entirely
require you in the king's behalf, that ye will show
yourselves herein very loving and obedient subjects,
wherein the king will much rejoice at your towardness,
and give to every man his princely thanks for such
liberality and gentleness, as ye or any of you shall
minister unto them." And here he ended his persuasion, and so departed into the dining chamber, and
dined among the lords of the council.

This great embassy, long looked for, was now come
over with a great retinue, which were in number above
fourscore persons, of the most noblest and worthiest

gentlemen in all the court of France, who were right honourably received from place to place after their arrival, and so conveyed through London unto the bishop's palace in Paul's Churchyard, where they were lodged. To whom divers noblemen resorted and gave them divers goodly presents; and in especial the Mayor and city of London, as wine, sugar, wax, capons, wild fowl, beefs, muttons, and other necessaries in great abundance, for the expenses of their house. Then the next Sunday after their resort to London, they repaired to the court at Greenwich, and there, by the king's majesty, most highly received and entertained. They had a special commission to create and stall the king's highness in the Royal order of France; for which purpose they brought with them a collar of fine gold of the order, with a Michael hanging thereat, and robes to the same appurtenant, the which was wondrous costly and comely, of purple velvet, richly embroidered; I saw the king in all this apparel and habit, passing through the chamber of presence unto his closet; and afterward in the same habit at mass beneath in the chapel. And to gratify the French king with like honour, he sent incontinent unto him the like order of England by a nobleman (the Earl of Wiltshire), purposely for that intent, to create him one of the same order of England, accompanied with Garter the Herald, with all robes, garter, and other habiliments to the same belonging; as costly in every degree as the other was of the French king's, the which was done before the return of the great embassy.

D

And for the performance of this noble and perpetual peace, it was concluded and determined that a solemn mass should be sung in the cathedral church of Paul's by the cardinal ; against which. time there was prepared a gallery made from the west door of the church of Paul's through the body of the same, unto the quire door, railed on every side, upon the which stood vessels full of perfumes burning.   Then the king and my Lord Cardinal, and all the Frenchmen, with all other noblemen and gentlemen, were conveyed upon this gallery unto the high altar into the traverses ; then my Lord· Cardinal prepared himself to mass, associated with twenty-four mitres of bishops and abbots, attending upon him, and to serve him, in such ceremonies as to him, by virtue of his legatine prerogative, were due.

And after the last agnus, the king rose out of his· travers and kneeled upon a cushion and carpet at the high altar ; and the Grand Master of France, the chief ambassador, that represented the king his master, kneeled by the king's majesty, between whom my lord divided the sacrament, as a firm oath and assurance of this perpetual peace.   That done, the king resorted again to his travers, and the Grand Master in likewise to his.   This mass finished, which was sung with the king's chapel and the quire of Paul's, my Lord Cardinal took the instrument of this perpetual peace and amity, and read the same openly before the king and the assembly, both of English and French, to the which the king subscribed with his own hand, and the Grand

Master, for the French king, in like wise, the which was sealed with the seals of fine gold, engraven, and delivered to each other as their firm deeds; and all this done and finished they departed.

The king rode home to the cardinal's house at West-minster, to dinner, with whom dined all the Frenchmen, passing all day after in consultation in weighty matters, touching the conclusion of this peace and amity. That done, the king went again by water to Greenwich; at whose departing it was determined by the king's device, that the French gentlemen should resort unto Rich-mond to hunt there, in every of the parks, and from thence to Hampton Court, and therein likewise to hunt, and there my Lord Cardinal to make for them a supper, and lodge them there that night; and from thence they should ride to Windsor, and there to hunt, and after their return to London they should resort to the court, whereas the king would banquet them. And this perfectly determined, the king and the Frenchmen all departed.

Then was there no more to do but to make provision at Hampton Court for this assembly against the day appointed. My Lord Cardinal called for his principal officers of his house, as his steward, comptroller, and the clerks of his kitchen, whom he commanded to prepare for this banquet at Hampton Court; and neither to spare for expenses or travail, to make them such triumphant cheer, as they may not only wonder at it here, but also make a glorious report in their country, to the king's honour and that of this realm. His pleasure once known, to accomplish his commandment they sent forth all the caterers, purveyors, and other persons, to prepare of the finest viands that they could get, other for money or friendship among my lord's friends. Also they sent for all the expertest cooks, besides my lord's, that they could get in all England, where they might be gotten, to serve to garnish this feast.

The purveyors brought and sent in such plenty of costly provision, as ye would wonder at the same. The cooks wrought both night and day in divers subtleties and many crafty devices; where lacked neither gold, silver, nor any other costly thing meet for the purpose.

The yeomen and grooms of the wardrobes were busied in hanging of the chambers with costly hangings, and furnishing the same with beds of silk, and other furniture apt for the same in every degree. Then my Lord Cardinal sent me, being gentleman usher, with two other of my fellows, to Hampton Court, to foresee all things touching our rooms, to be noblily garnished accordingly. Our pains were not small or light, but travelling daily from chamber to chamber. Then the carpenters, the joiners, the masons, the painters, and all other artificers necessary to glorify the house and feast were set at work. There was carriage and re-carriage of plate, stuff, and other rich implements; so that there was nothing lacking or to be imagined or devised for the purpose. There were also fourteen score beds provided and furnished with all manner of furniture to them belonging, too long particularly here to rehearse. But to all wise men it sufficeth to imagine, that knoweth

what belongeth to the furniture of such triumphant
feast or banquet.

The day was come that to the Frenchmen was
assigned, and they ready assembled at Hampton Court,
something before the hour of their appointment.
Wherefore the officers caused them to ride to Hanworth, a place and park of the king's, within two or
three miles, there to hunt and spend the time until
night. At which time they returned again to Hampton
Court, and every of them conveyed to his chamber
severally, having in them great fires and wine ready to
refresh them, remaining there until their supper was
ready, and the chambers where they should sup were
ordered in due form. The first waiting-chamber was
hanged with fine arras, and so was all the rest, one
better than another, furnished with tall yeomen.
There was set tables round about the chamber,
banquet-wise, all covered with fine cloths of diaper.
A cupboard of plate, parcel gilt, having also in the
same chamber, to give the more light, four plates of
silver, set with lights upon them, a great fire in the
chimney.

The next chamber, being the chamber of presence,
hanged with very rich arras, wherein was a gorgeous
and a precious cloth of estate hanged up, replenished
with many goodly gentlemen ready to serve. The
boards were set as the other boards were in the other
chamber before, save that the high table was set and
removed beneath the cloth of estate, towards the midst
of the chamber, covered with fine linen cloths of damask

work, sweetly perfumed.   There was a cupboard made, for the time, in length, of the breadth of the nether end of the same chamber, six desks high, full of gilt plate, very sumptuous, and of the newest fashions; and upon the nethermost desk garnished all with plate of clean gold, having two great candlesticks of silver and gilt, most curiously wrought, the workmanship whereof, with the silver, cost three hundred marks, and lights of wax as big as torches burning upon the same.   This cupboard was barred in round about that no man might come nigh it; for there was none of the same plate occupied or stirred during this feast, for there was sufficient besides.   The plates that hung on the walls to give light in the chamber were of silver and gilt, with lights burning in them, a great fire in the chimney, and all other things necessary for the furniture of so noble a feast.

Now was all things in a readiness and supper time at hand.   My lord's officers caused the trumpets to blow to warn to supper, and the said officers went right discreetly in due order and conducted these noble personages from their chambers unto the chamber of presence where they should sup.   And they, being there, caused them to sit down ; their service was brought up in such order and abundance, both costly and full of subtleties, with such a pleasant noise of divers instruments of music, that the Frenchmen, as it seemed, were rapt into a heavenly paradise.

Ye must understand that my lord was not there, nor yet come, but they being merry and pleasant with their

fare, devising and wondering upon the subtleties.
Before the second course, my Lord Cardinal came in
among them, booted and spurred, all suddenly, and
bade them *proface ;* at whose coming they would have
risen and given place with much joy. Whom my lord
commanded to sit still, and keep their rooms ; and
straightways, being not shifted of his riding apparel, called
for a chair, and sat himself down in the midst of the
table, laughing and being as merry as ever I saw him
in all my life. Anon came up the second course, with
so many dishes, subtleties, and curious devices, which
were above a hundred in number, of so goodly proportion and costly, that I suppose the Frenchmen never
saw the like. The wonder was no less than it was
worthy indeed. There were castles with images in the ∠
same ; Paul's church and steeple, in proportion for the
quantity as well counterfeited as the painter should
have painted it upon a cloth or wall. There were
beasts, birds, fowls of divers kinds, and personages,
most lively made and counterfeit in dishes; some
fighting, as it were, with swords, some with guns and
crossbows, some vaulting and leaping; some dancing
with ladies, some in complete harness, justing with
spears, and with many more devices than I am able
with my wit to describe. Among all, one I noted :
there was a chess-board subtilely made of spiced plate,
with men to the same ; and for the good proportion,
because that Frenchmen be very expert in that play, my
lord gave the same to a gentleman of France, commanding that a case should be made for the same in all haste,

to preserve it from perishing in the conveyance thereof into his country. Then my lord took a bowl of gold, which was esteemed of the value of five hundred marks, filled with hypocras, whereof there was plenty, putting off his cap, said, " I drink to the king my sovereign lord and master, and to the king your master," and therewith drank a good draught. And when he had done, he desired the Grand Master to pledge him cup and all, the which cup he gave him; and so caused all the other lords and gentlemen in other cups to pledge these two royal princes.

Then went cups merrily about, that many of the Frenchmen were fain to be led to their beds. Then went my lord, leaving them sitting still, into his privy chamber to shift him; and making there a very short supper, or rather a small repast, returned again among them into the chamber of presence, using them so nobly, with so loving and familiar countenance and entertainment, that they could not commend him too much.

And whilst they were in communication and other pastimes, all their liveries were served to their chambers. Every chamber had a bason and a ewer of silver, some gilt, and some parcel gilt; and some two great pots of silver, in like manner, and one pot at the least with wine and beer, a bowl or goblet, and a silver pot to drink beer in; a silver candlestick or two, with both white lights and yellow lights of three sizes of wax; and a staff torch; a fine manchet, and a cheat loaf of bread. Thus was every chamber furnished throughout the house, and yet the two cupboards in the two banqueting chambers not once touched. Then being past midnight, as time served they were conveyed to their lodgings, to take their rest for that night. In the morning of the next day (not early), they rose and heard mass, and dined with my lord, and so departed towards Windsor, and there hunted, delighting much of the castle and college, and in the Order of the Garter. They being departed from Hampton Court, my lord returned again to Westminster, because it was in the midst of the term.

It is not to be doubted, but that the king was privy of all this worthy feast, and intended far to exceed the same; (whom I leave until the return of the French-men), who gave a special commandment to all his officers to devise a far more sumptuous banquet for the strangers, otherwise than they had at Hampton Court; which was not neglected, but most speedily put in execution with great diligence.

After the return of these strangers from Windsor, which place with the goodly order thereof they much commended, the day approached that they were invited to the court at Greenwich; where first they dined, and after long consultation of the sagest with our coun-sellors, and dancing of the rest and other pastimes, the time of supper came on. Then was the banqueting chamber in the tiltyard furnished for the entertainment of these strangers, to the which place they were con-veyed by the noblest persons being then in the court, where they both supped and banqueted. But to describe the dishes, the subtleties, the many strange

devices and order in the same, I do both lack wit in
my gross old head, and cunning in my bowels to
declare the wonderful and curious imaginations in
the same invented and devised.   Yet this ye shall
understand : that although it was at Hampton Court
marvellous sumptuous, yet did this banquet far exceed
the same, as fine gold doth silver in weight and
value ; and for my part I must needs confess (which
saw them both), that I never saw the like, or read in
any story or chronicle of any such feast.   In the
midst of this banquet, there was tourneying at the
barriers (even in the chamber), with lusty gentlemen
in gorgeous complete harness, on foot ; then was there
the like on horseback ; and after all this there was the
most goodliest disguising or interlude, made in Latin
and French, whose apparel was of such exceeding
riches, that it passeth my capacity to expound.

    This done, then came in such a number of the fair
ladies and gentlewomen that bare any bruit or fame of
beauty in all this realm, in the most richest apparel,
and devised in divers goodly fashions that all the
cunningest tailors could devise to shape or cut, to set
forth their beauty, gesture, and the goodly proportion
of their bodies : who seemed to all men more angelic
than earthly creatures made of flesh and bone ;—surely
to me, simple soul, it seemed inestimable to be described,
and so I think it was to other of a more higher judgment,—with whom these gentlemen of France danced
until another mask came in of noble gentlemen, who
danced and masked with these fair ladies and gentle-

women, every man as his fantasy served him. This done, and the maskers departed, there came in another mask of ladies so gorgeously apparelled in costly garments, that I dare not presume to take upon me to make thereof any declaration, lest I should rather deface than beautify them, therefore I leave it untouched. These lady maskers took each of them a French gentleman to dance and mask with them. Ye shall understand that these lady maskers spake good French, which delighted much these gentlemen, to hear these ladies speak to them in their own tongue.

Thus was this night occupied and consumed from five of the clock until two or three after midnight; at which time it was convenient for all estates to draw to their rest. And thus every man departed whither they had most relief. Then as nothing either health, wealth, or pleasure, can always endure, so ended this triumphant banquet, the which in the morning seemed to all the beholders but as a fantastical dream.

After all this solemn cheer, at a day appointed they prepared them to return with bag and baggage. Then, as to the office of all honourable persons doth appertain, they resorted in good order to the court, to take their leave of the king, and other noblemen, then being there : to whom the king committed his princely commendations to the king their master, and thanked them of their pains and travel, and after long communication with the most honourable of the embassy, he bad them adieu.

They were assigned by the council to repair to my

Lord Cardinal for to receive the king's most noble reward, wherefore they repaired to my lord, and taking of their leave, they received every man the king's reward after this sort; every honourable person in estimation had most commonly plate, to the value of three or four hundred pounds, and some more, and some less, besides other great gifts received at the king's hands before; as rich gowns, horses, or goodly geldings of great value and goodness; and some had weighty chains of fine gold, with divers other gifts, which I cannot now call to my remembrance; but this I know, that the least of them all had a sum of crowns of gold: the worst page among them had twenty crowns for his part: and thus they (nobly rewarded) departed. And my lord, after humble commendations had to the French king, bad them adieu. And the next day they conveyed all their stuff and furniture unto the seaside, accompanied with lusty young gentlemen of England: but what praise or commendation they made in their country at their return, in good faith, I cannot tell you, for I never heard any thing thereof.

Then began other matters to brew and take place that occupied all men's heads with divers imaginations, whose stomachs were therewith full filled without any perfect digestion. The long hid and secret love between the king and Mistress Anne Boleyn began to break out into every man's ears. The matter was then by the king disclosed to my Lord Cardinal; whose persuasion to the contrary, made to the king upon his knees, could not effect: the king was so amorously affectionate, that will bare place, and high discretion banished for the time. My lord, provoked by the king to declare his wise opinion in this matter for the further-ance of his desired affects, who thought it not meet for him alone to wade too far, to give his hasty judg-ment or advice in so weighty a matter, desired of the king license to ask counsel of men of ancient study, and of famous learning, both in the laws divine and civil. That obtained, he by his legatine authority sent out his commission unto all the bishops of this realm, and for other that were either exactly learned in any of the said laws, or else had in any estimation for their prudent counsel and judgment in princely affairs of long experience.

Then assembled these prelates before my Lord Cardinal at his place in Westminster, with many other famous and notable clerks of both the Universities (Oxford and Cambridge), and also divers out of colleges and cathedral churches of this realm, renowned and allowed learned and of witty discretion in the deter-mination of doubtful questions. Then was the matter of the king's case debated, reasoned and argued; con-sulting from day to day, and time to time; that it was to men learned a goodly hearing ; but in conclusion, it seemed me, by the departing of the ancient fathers of the laws, that they departed with one judgment con-trary to the expectation of the principal parties. I heard the opinion of some of the most famous persons, among that sort, report, that the king's case was so obscure and doubtful for any learned man to discuss;

the points therein were so dark to be credited that it was very hard to have any true understanding or intelligence. And therefore they departed without any resolution or judgment. Then in this assembly of bishops it was thought most expedient that the king should first send out his commissioners into all the Universities of Christendom, as well here in England as in foreign countries and regions, to have among them his Grace's case argued substantially, and to bring with them from thence the very definition of their opinions in the same, under the seals of every several University. Thus was their determination for this time; and thereupon agreed, that commissioners were incontinent appointed and sent forth about this matter into several Universities, as some to Oxford, some to Cambridge, some to Louvain, some to Paris, some to Orleans, some to Bologna, and some to Padua, and some to other. Although these commissioners had the travail, yet was the charges the king's; the which was no small sums of money, and all went out of the king's coffers into foreign regions. For as I heard it reported of credible persons (as it seemed indeed), that besides the great charges of the commissioners, there was inestimable sums of money given to the famous clerks to choke them, and in especial to such as had the governance and custody of their Universities' seals. Insomuch as they agreed, not only in opinions, but also obtained of them the Universities, seals (the which obtained), they returned home again furnished for their purpose. At whose return there was no small joy made of the principal parties. Insomuch as the commissioners were not only ever after in great estimation, but also most liberally advanced and rewarded, far beyond their worthy deserts. Notwithstanding, they prospered, and the matter went still forward, having then (as they thought) a sure foundation to ground them upon.

These proceedings being once declared to my Lord Cardinal, he sent again for all the bishops, whom he made privy of the expedition of the commissioners; and for the very proof thereof he showed them the opinions of the several Universities in writing under the Universities' seals. These matters being thus brought to pass, they went again to consultation how these matters should be ordered to the purpose. It was then thought good and concluded, by the advice of them all, that the king should (to avoid all ambiguities), send unto the pope a legation with the instruments, declaring the opinions of the Universities under their seals; to the which it was thought good that all these prelates in this assembly should join with the king in this legation, making intercession and suit to the pope for advice and judgment in this great and weighty matter; and if the pope would not directly consent to the same request, that then the ambassadors should farther require of him a commission to be directed (under lead), to establish a court judicial in England, (** *** ******) directed to my Lord Cardinal, and unto the Cardinal Campeggio (who was then Bishop of Bath), although he was a stranger,

which bishopric the king gave him at such time as he
was the pope's ambassador here in England, to hear
and determine according to the just judgment of their
conscience.   The which after long and great suit,
they obtained of the pope his commission.   This done
and achieved, they made return into England, making
report unto the king of their expedition, trusting
that his Grace's pleasure and purpose should now
be presently brought to pass, considering the estate
of the judges, who were the Cardinal of England and
Campeggio, being both his highness's subjects in
effect.

Long was the desire, and greater was the hope on
all sides, expecting the coming of the legation and
commission from Rome, yet at length it came.   And
after the arrival of the Legate Campeggio with his
solemn commission in England, he being sore vexed
with the gout, was constrained by force thereof to
make a long journey or ever he came to London ; who
should have been most solemnly received at Blackheath, and so with great triumph conveyed to London ;
but his glory was such, that he would in nowise be
entertained with any such pomp or vainglory, who
suddenly came by water in a wherry to his own house
without Temple Bar, called then Bath Place, which
was furnished for him with all manner of stuff and
implements of my lord's provision ; where he continued
and lodged during his abode here in England.

Then after some deliberation, his commission understood, read, and perceived, it was by the council deter-

mined, that the king, and the queen his wife, should
be lodged at Bridewell. And that in the Black Friars
a certain place should be appointed where as the king
and the queen might most conveniently repair to the
court, there to be erected and kept for the disputation
and determination of the king's case, where as these
two legates sat in judgment as notable judges; before
whom the king and the queen were duly cited and
summoned to appear. Which was the strangest and
newest sight and device that ever was read or heard
in any history or chronicle in any region; that a king
and a queen should be convented and constrained by
process compellatory to appear in any court as common
persons, within their own realm or dominion, to abide
the judgment and decrees of their own subjects, having
the royal diadem and prerogative thereof. Is it not
a world to consider the desire of wilful princes, when
they fully be bent and inclined to fulfil their volup-
tuous appetites, against the which no reasonable persuasions will suffice; little or nothing weighing or
regarding the dangerous sequel that doth ensue as well
to themselves as to their realm and subjects. And
above all things, there is no one thing that causeth
them to be more wilful than carnal desire and volup-
tuous affection of foolish love. The experience is
plain, in this case both manifest and evident, for what
surmised inventions have been invented, what laws
have been enacted, what noble and ancient monasteries
overthrown and defaced, what diversities of religious
opinions have risen, what executions have been com-

mitted, how many famous and notable clerks have
suffered death, what charitable foundations were per-
verted from the relief of the poor, unto profane uses,
and what alterations of good and wholesome ancient
laws and customs hath been caused by will and wilful
desire of the prince, almost to the subversion and dissolution of this noble realm.   All men may understand
what hath chanced to this region ; the proof thereof
hath taught all us Englishmen a common experience,
the more is the pity, and is to all good men very
lamentable to be considered.   If eyes be not blind
men may see, if ears be not stopped they may hear,
and if pity be not exiled they may lament the sequel
of this pernicious and inordinate carnal love.   The
plague whereof is not ceased (although this love lasted
but a while), which our Lord quench ; and take from
us his indignation !   *Quia peccavimus cum patribus
nostris, et injuste egimus, &c.*

Ye shall understand, as I said before, that there was
a court erected in the Black Friars in London, where
these two cardinals sat for judges.   Now will I set you
out the manner and order of the court there.   First,
there was a court placed with tables, benches, and
bars, like a consistory, a place judicial (for the judges
to sit on).   There was also a cloth of estate under the
which sat the king ; and the queen sat some distance
beneath the king : under the judges' feet sat the officers
of the court.   The chief scribe there was Dr. Stephens
(who was after Bishop of Winchester) ; the apparitor
was one Cooke, most commonly called Cooke of Win-

chester. Then sat there within the said court, directly before the king and the judges, the Archbishop of Canterbury, Doctor Warham, and all the other bishops. Then at both the ends, with a bar made for them, the counsellors on both sides. The doctors for the king were Doctor Sampson, that was after Bishop of Chichester, and Doctor Bell, who after was Bishop of Worcester, with divers other. The proctors on the king's part were Doctor Peter, who was after made the king's chief secretary, and Doctor Tregonell, and divers other.

Now on the other side stood the counsel for the queen, Doctor Fisher, Bishop of Rochester, and Doctor Standish, some time a Grey Friar, and then Bishop of St. Asaph in Wales, two notable clerks in divinity, and in especial the Bishop of Rochester, a very godly man and a devout person, who after suffered death at Tower Hill; the which was greatly lamented through all the foreign Universities of Christendom. There was also another ancient doctor, called, as I remember, Doctor Ridley, a very small person in stature, but surely a great and an excellent clerk in divinity.

The court being thus furnished and ordered, the judges commanded the crier to proclaim silence; then was the judges' commission, which they had of the pope, published and read openly before all the audience there assembled. That done, the crier called the king, by the name of "King Henry of England, come into the court, &c." With that the king answered and said, "Here, my lords!" Then he called also the queen, by

the name of "Katherine Queen of England, come into
the court, &c.;" who made no answer to the same, but
rose up incontinent out of her chair, where as she sat,
and because she could not come directly to the king
for the distance which severed them, she took pain to
go about unto the king, kneeling down at his feet in
the sight of all the court and assembly, to whom she
said in effect, in broken English, as followeth:

"Sir," quoth she, "I beseech you for all the loves
that hath been between us, and for the love of God, let
me have justice and right, take of me some pity and
compassion, for I am a poor woman and a stranger
born out of your dominion, I have here no assured
friend, and much less indifferent counsel; I flee to you
as to the head of justice within this realm. Alas! Sir,
wherein have I offended you, or what occasion of displeasure? Have I designed against your will and
pleasure; intending (as I perceive) to put me from you?
I take God and all the world to witness, that I have
been to you a true humble and obedient wife, ever
conformable to your will and pleasure, that never said
or did any thing to the contrary thereof, being always
well pleased and contented with all things wherein you
had any delight or dalliance, whether it were in little
or much, I never grudged in word or countenance, or
showed a visage or spark of discontentation. I loved
all those whom ye loved only for your sake, whether I
had cause or no; and whether they were my friends or
my enemies. This twenty years I have been your
true wife or more, and by me ye have had divers

children, although it hath pleased God to call them out of this world, which hath been no default in me.

"And when ye had me at the first, I take God to be my judge, I was a true maid without touch of man; and whether it be true or no, I put it to your conscience· If there be any just cause by the law that ye can allege against me, either of dishonesty or any other impediment to banish and put me from you, I am well content to depart to my great shame and dishonour; and if there be none, then here I most lowly beseech you let me remain in my former estate, and receive justice at your hands. The king your father was in the time of his reign of such estimation thorough the world for his excellent wisdom, that he was accounted and called of all men the second Solomon; and my father Ferdinand, King of Spain, who was esteemed to be one of the wittiest princes that reigned in Spain, many years before, were both wise and excellent kings in wisdom and princely behaviour. It is not therefore to be doubted, but that they elected and gathered as wise counsellors about them as to their high discretions was thought meet. Also, as me seemeth there was in those days as wise, as well learned men, and men of as good judgment as be at this present in both realms, who thought then the marriage between you and me good and lawful. Therefore it is a wonder to hear what new inventions are now invented against me, that never intended but honesty. And cause me to stand to the order and judgment of this new court, wherein ye may do me much wrong, if ye intend any cruelty ; for ye may condemn me for lack of sufficient answer, having no indifferent counsel, but such as be assigned me, with whose wisdom and learning I am not acquainted. Ye must consider that they cannot be indifferent counsellors for my part which be your subjects, and taken out of your own council before, wherein they be made privy, and dare not, for your displeasure, disobey your will and intent, being once made privy thereto. Therefore I most humbly require you, in the way of charity, and for the love of God, who is the just judge, to spare me the extremity of this new court, until I may be advertised what way and order my friends in Spain will advise me to take. And if ye will not extend to me so much indifferent favour, your pleasure then be fulfilled, and to God I commit my cause !"

And with that she rose up, making a low courtesy to the king, and so departed from thence. Many supposed that she would have resorted again to her former place ; but she took her way straight out of the house, leaning (as she was wont always to do) upon the arm of her General Receiver, called Master Griffith. And the king being advertised of her departure, commanded the crier to call her again, who called her by the name of " Katherine Queen of England, come into the court, &c." With that quoth Master Griffith, " *Madam, ye be called again.*" " On, on," quoth she, " it maketh no matter, for it is no indifferent court for me, therefore I will not tarry. Go on your ways." And thus she departed out of that court, without any farther answer at that time, or at any other, nor would never appear at any other court after.

The king perceiving that she was departed in such sort, calling to his Grace's memory all her lament words that she had pronounced before him and all the audience, said thus in effect: "Forasmuch," quoth he, "as the queen is gone, I will, in her absence, declare unto you all my lords here presently assembled, she hath been to me as true, as obedient, and as conformable a wife as I could in my fantasy wish or desire. She hath all the virtuous qualities that ought to be in a woman of her dignity, or in any other of baser estate. Surely she is also a noble woman born, if nothing were in her, but only her conditions will well declare the same." With that quoth my Lord Cardinal, "Sir, I most humbly beseech your highness to declare me before all this audience, whether I have been the chief inventor or first mover of this matter unto your majesty; for I am greatly suspected of all men herein." "My Lord Cardinal," quoth the king, "I can well excuse you herein. Marry (quoth he), ye have been rather against me in attempting or setting forth thereof. And to put you all out of doubt, I will declare unto you the special cause that moved me hereunto; it was a certain scrupulosity that pricked my conscience upon divers words that were spoken at a certain time by the Bishop of Bayonne, the French king's ambassador, who had been here long upon the debating for the conclusion of a marriage to be concluded between the princess our daughter Mary, and the Duke of Orleans, the French king's second son.

" And upon the resolution and determination thereof, he desired respite to advertise the king his master thereof, whether our daughter Mary should be legitimate, in respect of the marriage which was sometime between the queen here, and my brother the late Prince Arthur. These words were so conceived within my scrupulous conscience, that it bred a doubt within my breast, which doubt pricked, vexed, and troubled so my mind, and so disquieted me, that I was in great doubt of God's indignation; which (as seemed me), appeared right well; much the rather for that he hath not sent me any issue male; for all such issue male as I have received of the queen died incontinent after they were born; so that I doubt the punishment of God in that behalf. Thus being troubled in waves of a scrupulous conscience, and partly in despair of any issue male by her, it drave me at last to consider the estate of this realm, and the danger it stood in for lack of issue male to succeed me in this imperial dignity. I thought it good therefore in relief of the weighty burden of scrupulous conscience, and the quiet estate of this noble realm, to attempt the law therein, and whether I might take another wife in case that my first copulation with this gentlewoman were not lawful; which I intend not for any carnal concupiscence, nor for any displeasure or mislike of the queen's person or age, with whom I could be as well content to continue during my life, if our marriage may stand with God's laws, as with any woman alive; in which point consisteth all this doubt that we go now about to try by the learned wisdom and judgment of you our prelates and pastors of this realm here assembled for that purpose ; to whose conscience and judgment I have committed the charge according to the which (God willing) we will be right well contented to submit ourself, to obey the same for our part. Wherein after I once perceived my conscience wounded with the doubtful case herein, I moved first this matter in confession to you, my Lord of Lincoln, my ghostly father. And forasmuch as then yourself were in some doubt to give me counsel, moved me to ask farther counsel of all you my lords ; wherein I moved you first my Lord of Canterbury, axing your license, (forasmuch as you were our metropolitan) to put this matter in question; and so I did of all you my lords, to the which ye have all granted by writing under all your seals, the which I have here to be showed." " That is truth if it please your highness," quoth the Bishop of Canterbury, " I doubt not but all my brethren here present will affirm the same." " No, Sir, not I," quoth the Bishop of Rochester, " ye have not my consent thereto." " No ! ha' the !" quoth the king, " look here upon this, is not this your hand and seal ? " and showed him the instrument with seals. " No forsooth, Sire," quoth the Bishop of Rochester, "it is not my hand nor seal !" To that quoth the king to my Lord of Canterbury, " Sir, how say *ye*, is it not his hand and seal ? " " Yes, Sir," quoth my Lord of Canterbury. " That is not so," quoth the Bishop of Rochester, " for indeed you were in hand with me to have both my hand and seal, as other of my lords had already done; but then I said to you, that I would never consent to no such act, for it were much against my conscience; nor my hand and seal should never be seen at any such instrument, God willing, with much more matter touching the same communication between us." "You say truth," quoth the Bishop of Canterbury, "such words ye said unto me; but at the last ye were fully persuaded that I should for you subscribe your name, and put to a seal myself, and ye would allow the same." "All which words and matter," quoth the Bishop of Rochester, "under your correction, my lord, and supportation of this noble audience, there is no thing more untrue." "Well, well," quoth the king, "it shall make no matter; we will not stand with you in argument herein, for you are but one man." And with that the court was adjourned until the next day of this session.

The next court-day the cardinals sat there again, at which time the counsel on both sides were there present. The king's counsel alleged the marriage not good from the beginning, because of the carnal knowledge committed between Prince Arthur her first husband, the king's brother, and her. This matter being very sore touched and maintained by the king's counsel; and the contrary defended by such as took upon them to be on that other part with the good queen: and to prove the same carnal copulation they alleged many coloured reasons and similitudes of truth. It was answered again negatively on the other side, by which it seemed that all their former allegations were very doubtful to be tried, so that it was said that no man could know the truth. " Yes," quoth the Bishop of Rochester, "*Ego nosco veritatem*, I know the truth." " How know you the truth ?" quoth my Lord Cardinal. " Forsooth, my lord," quoth he, " *Ego sum professor veritatis*, I know that God is truth itself, nor he never spake but truth ; who saith, *quos Deus conjunxit, homo non separet.* And forasmuch as this marriage was made and joined by God to a good intent, I say that I know the truth ; the which cannot be broken or loosed by the power of man upon no feigned occasion." " So much doth all faithful men know," quoth my Lord Cardinal, " as well as you. Yet this reason is not sufficient in this case ; for the king's counsel doth allege divers presumptions, to prove the marriage not good at the beginning, *ergo*, say they, it was not joined by God at the beginning, and therefore it is not lawful ; for God ordaineth nor joineth nothing without a just order. Therefore it is not to be doubted but that these presumptions must be true, as it plainly appeareth ; and nothing can be more true in case these allegations cannot be avoided ; therefore to say that the matrimony was joined of God, ye must prove it farther than by that text which ye have alleged for your matter : for ye must first avoid the presumptions." " Then," quoth one Doctor Ridley, " it is a shame and a great dishonour to this honourable presence, that any such presumptions should be alleged in this open court, which be to all good and honest men most detestable to be rehearsed." " What," quoth my Lord Cardinal, "*Domine Doctor, magis reverenter.*" " No, no, my lord," quoth he, " there belongeth no reverence to be given to these abominable presumptions; for an unreverent tale would be unreverently answered." And there they left, and proceeded no farther at that time.

Thus this court passed from session to session, and day to day, insomuch that a certain day the king sent for my lord at the breaking up one day of the court to come to him into Bridewell. And to accomplish his commandment he went unto him, and being there with him in communication in his Grace's privy chamber from eleven until twelve of the clock and past at noon, my lord came out and departed from the king and took his barge at the Black Friars, and so went to his house at Westminster. The Bishop of Carlisle being with him in his barge said unto him, (wiping the sweat from his face), " Sir," quoth he, " it is a very hot day." " Yea," quoth my Lord Cardinal, " if ye had been as well chafed as I have been within this hour, ye would say it were very hot." And as soon as he came home to his house at Westminster, he went incontinent to his naked bed, where he had not lain fully the space of two hours, but that my Lord of Wiltshire came to speak with him of a message from the king. My lord, having understanding of his coming, caused him to be brought unto his bedside; and he being there, showed him the king's pleasure was, that he should incontinent (accompanied with the other cardinal) repair unto the queen at Bridewell, into her chamber, to persuade her by their wisdoms, advising her to surrender the whole matter unto the king's hands by her own will and consent; which should be much better to her honour than to stand to the trial of law and to be condemned, which would seem much to her slander and defamation. To fulfil the king's pleasure, my lord said he was ready, and would prepare him to go thither out of hand, saying farther to my Lord of Wiltshire, " Ye and other my lords of the council, which be near unto the king, are not a little to blame and misadvised to put any such fantasies into his head, whereby ye are the causes of great trouble to all the realm ; and at length get you but small thanks either of God or of the world," with many other vehement words and sentences that were like to ensue of this matter, which words caused my Lord of Wiltshire to water his eyes, kneeling all this while by my lord's bedside, and in conclusion departed. And then my lord rose up, and made him ready, taking his barge, and went straight to Bath Place to the other cardinal ; and so went together unto Bridewell, directly to the queen's lodging : and they, being in her chamber of presence, showed to the gentleman usher that they came to speak with the queen's grace. The gentleman usher advertised the queen thereof incontinent. With that she came out of her privy chamber with a skein of white thread about her neck, into the chamber of presence, where the cardinals were giving of attendance upon her coming. At whose coming quoth she, " Alack, my lords, I am very sorry to cause you to attend upon me ; what is your pleasure with me ?" " If it please you," quoth my Lord Cardinal, " to go into your privy chamber, we will show you the cause of our coming." " My lord," quoth she, " if you have any thing to say, speak it openly before all these folks ; for I fear nothing that ye can say or allege against me, but that I would all the world should both hear and see it ; therefore I pray you speak your minds openly." Then began my lord to speak to her in Latin. " Nay, good my lord," quoth she, " speak to me in English I beseech you ; although I understand Latin." " Forsooth then," quoth my lord, " Madam, if it please your grace, we come both to know your mind, how ye be disposed to do in this matter between the king and you, and also to declare secretly our opinions and our counsel unto you, which we have intended of very zeal and obedience that we bear to your grace." " My lords, I thank you then," quoth she, " of your good wills ; but to make answer to your request I cannot so suddenly, for I was set among my maidens at work, thinking full little of any such matter, wherein there needeth a longer delibera- tion, and a better head than mine, to make answer to so noble wise men as ye be ; I had need of good counsel in this case, which toucheth me so near ; and for any counsel or friendship that I can find in England, they are nothing to my purpose or profit. Think you, I pray you, my lords, will any Englishmen counsel or be friendly unto me against the king's pleasure, they being his subjects ? Nay forsooth, my lords ! and for my counsel in whom I do intend to put my trust be not here ; they be in Spain, in my native country. Alas, my lords ! I am a poor woman, lacking both wit and understanding sufficiently to answer such approved wise men as ye be both, in so weighty a matter. I pray you to extend your good and indifferent minds in your authority unto me, for I am a simple woman, destitute and barren of friendship and counsel here in a foreign region : and as for your counsel I will not refuse but be glad to hear."

And with that she took my lord by the hand and led him into her privy chamber, with the other cardinal ; where they were in long communication : we, in the other chamber, might sometimes hear the queen speak very loud, but what it was we could not understand. The communication ended, the cardinals departed and went directly to the king, making to him relation of their talk with the queen ; and after resorted home to their houses to supper.

Thus went this strange case forward from court-day to court-day, until it came to the judgment, so that every man expected the judgment to be given upon the next court-day. At which day the king came thither, and sat within a gallery against the door of the same that looked unto the judges where they sat, whom he might both see and hear speak, to hear what judgment they would give in his suit; at which time all their proceedings were first openly read in Latin. And that done, the king's learned counsel at the bar called fast for judgment. With that, quoth Cardinal

Campeggio, " I will give no judgment herein until I have made relation unto the pope of all our proceedings, whose counsel and commandment in this high case I will observe. The case is too high and notable, known throughout the world, for us to give any hasty judgment, considering the highness of the persons and the doubtful allegations; and also whose commissioners we be, under whose authority we sit here. It were therefore reason, that we should make our chief head of counsel in the same, before we proceed to judgment definitive. I come not so far to please any man, for fear, meed, or favour, be he king or any other potentate. I have no such respect to the persons that I will offend my conscience. I will not for favour or displeasure of any high estate or mighty prince do that thing that should be against the law of God. I am an old man, both sick and impotent, looking daily for death. What should it then avail me to put my soul in the danger of God's displeasure, to my utter damnation, for the favour of any prince or high estate in this world ? My coming and being here is only to see justice ministered according to my conscience, as I thought thereby the matter either good or bad] And forasmuch as I do understand, and having perceivance by the allegations and negations in this matter laid for both the parties, that the truth in this case is very doubtful to be known, and also that the party defendant will make no answer thereunto, but doth rather appeal from us, supposing that we be not indifferent, considering the king's high dignity and authority within this his own realm which

he hath over his own subjects; and we being his subjects, and having our livings and dignities in the same,
she thinketh that we cannot minister true and indifferent justice for fear of his displeasure.] Therefore,
to avoid all these ambiguities and obscure doubts, I
intend not to damn my soul for no prince or potentate
alive. I will therefore, God willing, wade no farther
in this matter, unless I have the just opinion and
judgment, with the assent of the pope, and such other
of his counsel as hath more experience and learning in
such doubtful laws than I have. Wherefore I will
adjourn this court for this time, according to the order
of the court in Rome, from whence this court and
jurisdiction is derived.][And if we should go further
than our commission doth warrant us, it were folly and
vain, and much to our slander and blame; and we
might be accounted for the same breakers of the order
of the higher court from whence we have (as I said)
our original authorities." With that the court was
dissolved, and no more pleas holden.

With that stepped forth the Duke of Suffolk from
the king, and by his commandment spake these words,
with a stout and an hault countenance, "It was never
merry in England," quoth he, "whilst we had cardinals
among us :" which words were set forth both with such
a vehement countenance, that all men marvelled what
he intended; to whom no man made answer. Then
the duke spake again in great despight. To the which
words my Lord Cardinal, perceiving his vehemency,
soberly made answer and said, "Sir, of all men within

E

this realm, ye have least cause to dispraise or be offended with cardinals ; for if I, simple cardinal, had not been, you should have had at this present no head upon your shoulders, wherein you should have a tongue to make any such report in despight of us, who intend you no manner of displeasure ; nor have we given you any occasion with such despight to be revenged with your hault words.   I would ye knew it, my lord, that I and my brother here intendeth the king and his realm as much honour, wealth, and quietness, as you or any other, of what estate or degree soever he be, within this realm ; and would as gladly accomplish his lawful desire as the poorest subject he hath.   But, my lord, I pray you, show me what ye would do if ye were the king's commissioner in a foreign region, having a weighty matter to treat upon : and the conclusion being doubtful thereof, would ye not advertise the king's majesty or ever ye went through with the same ?   Yes, yes, my lord, I doubt not.   Therefore I would ye should banish your hasty malice and despight out of your heart, and consider that we be but commissioners for a time, and can, nor may not, by virtue of our com- mission proceed to judgment, without the knowledge and consent of the chief head of our authority, and having his consent to the same ; which is the pope. Therefore we do no less nor otherwise than our warrant will bear us ; and if any man will be offended with us therefore, he is an unwise man.   Wherefore, my lord, hold your peace, and pacify yourself, and frame your tongue like a man of honour and of wisdom, and not to speak so quickly or reproachfully by your friends ; for ye know best what friendship ye have received at my hands, the which I yet never revealed to no person alive before now, neither to my glory, nor to your dishonour." And therewith the duke gave over the matter without any words to reply, and so departed and followed after the king, who was gone into Bridewell at the beginning of the duke's first words.

This matter continued long thus, and my Lord Cardinal was in displeasure with the king, for that the matter in his suit took no better success, the fault whereof was ascribed much to my lord, notwithstanding my lord excused him always by his commission, which gave him no farther authority to proceed in judgment, without knowledge of the pope, who reserved the same to himself.

At the last they were advertised by their post that the pope would take deliberation in respect of judgment until his courts were opened, which should not be before Bartholomew-tide next. The king considering the time to be very long or the matter should be determined, thought it good to send a new embassy to the pope, to persuade him to show such honourable favour unto his Grace, that the matter might be sooner ended than it was likely to be, or else at the next court in Rome, to rule the matter over, according to the king's request.

To this embassy was appointed Doctor Stephens, then secretary, that after was made Bishop of Winchester. Who went thither, and there tarried until the latter end of summer, as ye shall hear after.

The king commanded the queen to be removed out of the court, and sent to another place ; and his highness rode in his progress, with Mistress Anne Boleyn in his company, all the grece season.

It was so that the Cardinal Campeggio made suit to be discharged, that he might return again to Rome. And it chanced that the secretary, who was the king's ambassador to the pope, was returned home from Rome ; whereupon it was determined that the Cardinal Campeggio should resort to the king at Grafton in Northamptonshire, and that my Lord Cardinal should accompany him thither, where Campeggio should take his leave of the king.   And so they took their journey thitherward from the Moor, and came to Grafton upon the Sunday in the morning, before whose coming there rose in the court divers opinions, that the king would not speak with my Lord Cardinal ; and thereupon were laid many great wagers.

These two prelates being come to the gates of the court, where they alighted from their horses, supposing that they should have been received by the head officers of the house as they were wont to be ; yet forasmuch as Cardinal Campeggio was but a stranger in effect, the said officers received them, and conveyed him to his lodging within the court, which was prepared for him only.   And after my lord had brought him thus to his lodging, he left him there and departed, supposing to have gone directly likewise to his chamber, as he was accustomed to do.   And by the way as he was going, it was told him that he had no lodging

appointed for him in the court. And being therewith
astonied, Sir Henry Norris, Groom of the Stole to the
king, came unto him (but whether it was by the king's
commandment or no I know not), and most humbly
offered him his chamber for the time, until another
might somewhere be provided for him : " For, Sir, I
assure you," quoth he, " here is very little room in this
house, scantly sufficient for the king; therefore I
beseech your Grace to accept mine for the season."
Whom my lord thanked for his gentle offer, and went
straight to his chamber, where as my lord shifted his
riding apparel, and being thus in his chamber, divers
noble persons and gentlemen, being his loving friends,
came to visit him and to welcome him to the court, by
whom my lord was advertised of all things touching
the king's displeasure towards him ; which did him no
small pleasure ; and caused him to be the more readily
provided of sufficient excuses for his defence.

Then was my lord advertised by Master Norris, that
he should prepare himself to give attendance in the
chamber of presence against the king's coming thither,
who was disposed there to talk with him, and with the
other cardinal, who came into my lord's chamber, and
they together went into the said chamber of presence,
where the lords of the council stood in a row in order
along the chamber. My lord putting off his cap to
every of them most gently, and so did they no less to
him : at which time the chamber was so furnished
with noblemen, gentlemen, and other worthy persons,
that only expected the meeting, and the countenance

of the king and him, and what entertainment the king made him.

Then immediately after came the king into the chamber, and standing there under the cloth of estate, my lord kneeled down before him, who took my lord by the hand, and so he did the other cardinal. Then he took my lord up by both arms and caused him to stand up, whom the king, with as amiable a cheer as ever he did, called him aside, and led him by the hand to a great window, where he talked with him, and caused him to be covered.

Then, to behold the countenance of those that had made their wagers to the contrary, it would have made you to smile ; and thus were they all deceived, as well worthy for their presumption. The king was in long and earnest communication with him, insomuch as I heard the king say : " How can that be : is not this your own hand ? " and plucked out from his bosom a letter or writing, and showed him the same ; and as I perceived that it was answered so by my lord that the king had no more to say in that matter ; but said to him : " My lord, go to your dinner, and all my lords here will keep you company ; and after dinner I will resort to you again, and then we will commune further with you in this matter ; " and so departed the king, and dined that same day with Mistress Anne Boleyn, in her chamber, who kept there an estate more like a queen than a simple maid.

Then was a table set up in the chamber of presence for my lord, and other lords of the council, where they all dined together; and sitting thus at dinner communing of divers matters. Quoth my lord, " It were well done if the king would send his chaplains and bishops to their cures and benefices." " Yea marry," quoth my Lord of Norfolk, " and so it were for you too." " I could be contented therewith, very well," quoth my lord, " if it were the king's pleasure to grant me license, with his favour, to go to my benefice of Winchester." " Nay," quoth my Lord of Norfolk, " to your benefice of York, where consisteth your greatest honour and charge." " Even as it shall please the king," quoth my lord, and so fell into other communications. For the lords were very loth to have him planted so near the king as to be at Winchester. Immediately after dinner they fell in secret talk until the waiters had dined.

And as I heard it reported by them that waited upon the king at dinner, that Mistress Anne Boleyn was much offended with the king, as far as she durst, that he so gently entertained my lord, saying, as she sat with the king at dinner, in communication of him, " Sir," quoth she, " is it not a marvellous thing to consider what debt and danger the cardinal hath brought you in with all your subjects ? " " How so, sweetheart ? " quoth the king. " Forsooth," quoth she, "there is not a man within all your realm, worth five pounds, but he hath indebted you unto him;" (meaning by a loan that the king had but late of his subjects). " Well, well," quoth the king, " as for that there is in him no blame ; for I know that matter better than you, or any other." "Nay, Sir," quoth she, "besides all that, what things hath he wrought within this realm to your great slander and dishonour ? There is never a nobleman within this realm that if he had done but half so much as he hath done, but he were well worthy to lose his head. If my Lord of Norfolk, my Lord of Suffolk, my lord my father, or any other noble person within your realm had done much less than he, but they should have lost their heads or this." "Why, then I perceive," quoth the king, "ye are not the cardinal's friend ?" "Forsooth, Sir," then quoth she, "I have no cause, nor any other that loveth your grace, no more have your grace, if ye consider well his doings." At this time the waiters had taken up the table, and so they ended their communication. Now ye may perceive the old malice beginning to break out, and newly to kindle the brand that after proved to a great fire, which was as much procured by his secret enemies, of whom I touched something before, as of herself.

After all this communication, the dinner thus ended, the king rose up and went incontinent into the chamber of presence, where as my lord, and other of the lords were attending his coming, he called my lord into the great window, and talked with him there a while very secretly. And at the last, the king took my lord by the hand and led him into his privy chamber, sitting there in consultation with him all alone without any other of the lords of the council, until it was night; the which blanked his enemies very sore, and made them to stir the coals; being in doubt what this matter would grow unto, having now none other refuge to trust to but Mistress Anne, in whom was all their whole and firm trust and affiance, without whom they doubted all their enterprise but frustrate and void.

Now was I fain, being warned that my lord had no lodging in the court, to ride into the country to provide for my lord a lodging; so that I provided a lodging for him at a house of Master Empson's, called Euston, three miles from Grafton, whither my lord came by torch light, it was so late or the king and he departed. At whose departing the king commanded him to resort again early in the morning to the intent they might finish their talk which they had then begun and not concluded.

After their departing my lord came to the said house at Euston to his lodging, where he had to supper with him divers of his friends of the court; and sitting at supper, in came to him Doctor Stephens, the secretary, late ambassador unto Rome; but to what intent he came I know not; howbeit my lord took it, that he came to dissemble a certain obedience and love towards him, or else to espy his behaviour and to hear his communication at supper. Notwithstanding my lord bade him welcome, and commanded him to sit down at the table to supper; with whom my lord had this communication, under this manner. "Master Secretary," quoth my lord, "ye be welcome home out of Italy; when came ye from Rome?" "Forsooth," quoth he,

" I came home almost a month ago." " And where," quoth my lord, " have you been ever since ? " " Forsooth," quoth he, " following the court this progress." " Then have ye hunted, and had good game and pastime," quoth my lord. " Forsooth, sir," quoth he, " and so I have, I thank the king's majesty." " What good greyhounds have ye ? " quoth my lord. " I have some, sir," quoth he. And thus in hunting, and like disports, passed they all their communication at supper ; and after supper my lord and he talked secretly together, till it was midnight or they departed.

The next morning my lord rose early and rode straight to the court; at whose coming the king was ready to ride, willing my lord to resort to the council with the lords in his absence, and said he could not tarry with him, commanding him to return with Cardinal Campeggio, who had taken his leave of the king. Whereupon my lord was constrained to take his leave also of the king, with whom the king departed amiably in the sight of all men. The king's sudden departing in the morning was by the special labour of Mistress Anne, who rode with him, only to lead him about, because he should not return until the cardinals were gone, the which departed after dinner, returning again towards the Moor.

The king rode that morning to view a ground for a new park, which is called at this day Hartwell Park, where Mistress Anne had made provision for the king's dinner, fearing his return or the cardinals were gone.

Then rode my lord and the other cardinal after

dinner on their way homeward, and so came to the monastery of St. Alban's (whereof he himself was commendatory), and there lay one whole day; and the next day they rode to the Moor; and from thence the Cardinal Campeggio took his journey towards Rome, with the king's reward; what it was I am un-certain. Nevertheless, after his departure, the king was informed that he carried with him great treasures of my lord's (conveyed in great tuns), notable sums of gold and silver to Rome, whither they surmised my lord would secretly convey himself out of this realm. Insomuch that a post was sent speedily after the cardinal to search him; whom they overtook at Calais, where he was stayed until search was made; there was not so much money found as he received of the king's reward, and so he was dismissed and went his way.

After Cardinal Campeggio was thus departed and gone, Michaelmas Term drew near, against the which my lord returned unto his house at Westminster; and when the term began, he went to the hall in such like sort and gesture as he was wont most commonly to do, and sat in the chancery, being Chancellor. After which day he never sat there more. The next day he tarried at home, expecting the coming of the Dukes of Suffolk and Norfolk, who came not that day; but the next day they came thither unto him; to whom they declared how the king's pleasure was that he should surrender and deliver up the great seal into their hands, and to depart simplily unto Asher, a house

situate nigh Hampton Court, belonging to the Bishoprick of Winchester. My lord understanding their
message, demanded of them what commission they had
to give him any such commandment ? Who answered
him again, that they were sufficient commissioners in
that behalf, having the king's commandment by his
mouth so to do. " Yet," quoth he, " that is not sufficient for me, without farther commandment of the
king's pleasure; for the great seal of England was
delivered me by the king's own person, to enjoy during
my life, with the ministration of the office and high
room of chancellorship of England : for my surety
whereof, I have the king's letters patent to show."
Which matter was greatly debated between the dukes
and him with many stout words between them ; whose
words and checks he took in patience for the time :
insomuch that the dukes were fain to depart again
without their purpose at that present ; and returned
again unto Windsor to the king : and what report they
made I cannot tell; howbeit, the next day they came
again from the king, bringing with them the king's
letters. After the receipt and reading of the same
by my lord, which was done with much reverence, he
delivered unto them the great seal, contented to obey
the king's high commandment; and seeing that the
king's pleasure was to take his house, with the contents,
was well pleased simply to depart to Asher, taking
nothing but only some provision for his house.

And after long talk between the dukes and him, they
departed, with the great seal of England, to Windsor,

unto the king. Then went my Lord Cardinal and called all officers in every office in his house before him, to take account of all such stuff as they had in charge. And in his gallery there was set divers tables, whereupon a great number of rich stuffs of silk, in whole pieces, of all colours, as velvet, satin, damask, caffa, taffeta, grograine, sarcenet, and of other not in my remembrance ; also there lay a thousand pieces of fine holland cloth, whereof as I heard him say afterward, there was five hundred pieces thereof, conveyed both from the king and him.

Furthermore there was also all the walls of the gallery hanged with cloth of gold, and tissue of divers makings, and cloth of silver likewise on both the sides ; and rich cloth of baudkin, of divers colours. There also hung the richest suits of copes of his own provision (which he caused to be made for his colleges of Oxford and Ipswich), that ever I saw in England. Then had he two chambers adjoining to the gallery, the one called the *gilt .chamber*, and the other called, most commonly, the *council chamber*, wherein were set in each two broad and long tables, upon tressels, whereupon was set such a number of plate of all sorts, as were almost incredible. In the *gilt chamber* was set out upon the tables nothing but all gilt plate ; and a cupboard standing under a window, was garnished all wholly with plate of clean gold, whereof some was set with pearl and rich stones. And in the *council chamber* was set all white plate and parcel gilt ; and under the tables, in both the chambers, were set baskets with old plate, which was not esteemed but for broken plate and old, not worthy to be occupied, and books containing the value and weight of every parcel laid by them ready to be seen ; and so was also books set by all manner of stuff, containing the contents of every thing. Thus every thing being brought into good order and furnished, he gave the charge of the delivery thereof unto the king, to every officer within his office, of such stuff as they had before in charge, by indenture of every parcel ; for the order of his house was such, as that every officer was charged by indenture with all such parcels as belonged to their office.

Then all things being ordered as it is before re-hearsed, my lord prepared him to depart by water. And before his departing, he commanded Sir William Gascoigne, his treasurer, to see these things before remembered delivered safely to the king at his repair thither. That done, the said Sir William said unto my lord, " Sir, I am sorry for your grace, for I under-stand ye shall go straightway to the Tower." " Is this the good comfort and counsel," quoth my lord, "that ye can give your master in adversity ? It hath been always your natural inclination to be very light of credit; and much more lighter in reporting of false news. I would ye should know, Sir William, and all other such blasphemers, that it is nothing more false than that, for I never (thanks be to God) deserved by no ways to come there under any arrest, although it has pleased the king to take my house ready furnished for his pleasure at this time.. I would all the world knew, and so I confess, to have nothing, either riches, honour, or dignity, that hath not grown of him and by him ; therefore it is my very duty to surrender the same to him again as his very own, with all my heart, or else I were an unkind servant. Therefore go your ways, and give good attendance unto your charge, that nothing be embezzled." And therewithal he made him ready to depart, with all his gentlemen and yeomen, which was no small number, and took his barge at his privy stairs, and so went by water unto Putney, where all his horses waited his coming. And at the taking of his barge there was no less than a thousand boats full of men and women of the city of London, *waffeting* up and down in Thames, expecting my lord's departing, supposing that he should have gone directly from thence to the Tower, whereat they rejoiced, and I dare be bold to say that the most part never received damage at his hands.

O wavering and new-fangled multitude ! Is it not a wonder to consider the inconstant mutability of this uncertain world ! The common people always desiring alterations and novelties of things for the strangeness of the case ; which after turneth them to small profit and commodity. For if the sequel of this matter be well considered and digested, ye shall understand that they had small cause to triumph at his fall. What hath succeeded all wise men doth know, and the common sort of them hath felt. Therefore to grudge or wonder at it, surely were but folly ; to study a

redress, I see not how it can be holpen, for the inclination and natural disposition of Englishmen is, and
hath always been, to desire alteration of officers, which
hath been thoroughly fed with long continuance in
their rooms with sufficient riches and possessions; and
they being put out, then cometh another hungry and a
lean officer in his place, that biteth nearer the bone
than the old. So the people be ever pilled and polled
with hungry dogs, through their own desire of change
of new officers, nature hath so wrought in the people,
that it will not be redressed. Wherefore I cannot see
but always men in authority be disdained with the
common sort of men ; and such most of all, that justly
ministereth equity to all men indifferently. For
where they please some one which receiveth the
benefit of the law at their hands according to
justice, there doth they in likewise displease the
contrary party, who supposeth to sustain great wrong,
where they have equity and right. Thus all good
justices be always in contempt with some for execut-
ing of indifferency. And yet such ministers must be,
for if there should be no ministers of justice the
world should run full of error and abomination, and
no good order kept, no quietness among the people.
There is no good man but he will commend such justices as dealeth uprightly in their rooms, and rejoice at
their continuance and not at their fall; and whether
this be true or no, I put it to the judgment of all discreet persons. Now let us leave, and begin again
where we left.

When he was with all his train arrived and landed at Putney, he took his mule, and every man his horse. And setting forth, not past the length of a pair of garden butts, he espied a man coming riding empost down the hill, in Putney town, demanding of his footmen who they thought it should be? And they answered again and said, that they supposed it should be Sir Harry Norris. And by-and-bye he came to my lord and saluted him, and said " that the king's majesty had him commended to his Grace, and willed him in any wise to be of good cheer, for he was as much in his highness's favour as ever he was, and so shall be." And in token thereof, he delivered him a ring of gold, with a rich stone, which ring he knew very well, for it was always the privy token between the king and him whensoever the king would have any special matter dispatched at his hands. And said furthermore, " that the king commanded him to be of good cheer, and take no thought, for he should not lack. And although the king hath dealt with you unkindly as ye suppose, he saith that it is for no dis-pleasure that he beareth you, but only to satisfy more the minds of some (which he knoweth be not your friends), than for any indignation : and also ye know right well, that he is able to recompense you with twice as much as your goods amounteth unto ; and all this he bade me, that I should show you ; therefore, Sir, take patience. And for my part, I trust to see you in better estate than ever ye were." But when he heard Master Norris rehearse all the good and comfortable words of the king, he quickly lighted from off his mule, all alone, as though he had been the youngest person amongst us, and incontinent kneeled down in the dirt upon both his knees, holding up his hands for joy.   Master Norris perceiving him so quickly· from his mule upon the ground, mused, and was astonied.   And therewith he alighted also, and kneeled by him, embracing him in his arms, and asked him how he did, calling upon him to credit his message. "Master Norris," quoth he, "when I consider your comfortable and joyful news, I can do no less than to rejoice, for the sudden joy surmounted my memory, having no respect neither to the place or time, but thought it my very bounden duty to render thanks to God my maker, and to the king my sovereign lord and master, who hath sent me such comfort in the very place where I received the same."

And talking with Master Norris upon his knees in the mire, he would have pulled off his under cap of velvet, but he could not undo the knot under his chin; wherefore with violence he rent the laces and pulled it from his head, and so kneeled bare-headed.   And that done, he covered again his head, and arose, and would have mounted his mule, but he could not mount again with such agility as he lighted before, where his foot-men had as much ado to set him in his saddle as they could have.   Then rode he forth up the hill into the town, talking with Master Norris.   And when he came upon Putney Heath, Master Norris took his leave and would have departed.   Then quoth my lord unto him, "Gentle Norris, if I were lord of a realm, the one half thereof were insufficient a reward to give you for your pains, and good comfortable news. But, good Master Norris, consider with me, that I have nothing left me but my clothes on my back. Therefore I desire you to take this small reward of my hands;" the which was a little chain of gold, made like a bottle chain, with a cross of gold hanging thereat, wherein was a piece of the *Holy Cross*, which he wore continually about his neck, next his skin ; and said furthermore, "I assure you, Master Norris, that when I was in prosperity, although it seem but small in value, yet I would not gladly have departed with it for the value of a thousand pounds. Therefore I beseech you to take it in gree, and wear it about your neck for my sake, and as often as ye shall happen to look upon it, have me in remembrance to the king's majesty, as opportunity shall serve you, unto whose highness and clemency, I desire you to have me most lowly commended ; for whose charitable disposition towards me, I can do nothing but only minister my prayer unto God for the preservation of his royal estate, long to reign in honour, health, and quiet life. I am his obedient subject, vassal, and poor chaplain, and do so intend, God willing, to be during my life, accounting that of myself I am of no estimation nor of no substance, but only by him and of him, whom I love better than myself, and have justly and truly served, to the best of my gross wit." And with that he took Master Norris by the hand and bade him

farewell. And being gone but a small distance, he
returned, and called Master Norris again, and when
he was returned, he said unto him : " I am sorry,"
quoth he, " that I have no condign token to send to
the king. But if ye would at this my request present
the king with this poor fool, I trust his highness
would accept him well, for surely for a nobleman's
pleasure he is worth a thousand pounds." So Master
Norris took the fool with him; with whom my lord
was fain to send six of his tall yeomen, to conduct
and convey the fool to the court ; for the poor fool
took on and fired so in such a rage when he saw that
he must needs depart from my lord. Yet notwithstanding they conveyed him with Master Norris to
the court, where the king received him most gladly.

After the departure of Master Norris with his
token to the king, my lord rode straight to Asher, a
house appertaining to the Bishoprick of Winchester,
situate within the county of Surrey, not far from
Hampton Court, where my lord and his family continued the space of three or four weeks, without beds,
sheets, table-cloths, cups and dishes to eat our meat, or
to lie in. Howbeit, there was good provision of all
kind of victuals, and of drink, both beer and wine,
whereof there was sufficient and plenty. My lord was
of necessity compelled to borrow of the Bishop of
Carlisle, and of Sir Thomas Arundell, both dishes to eat
his meat in, and plate to drink in, and also linen cloths
to occupy. And thus continued he in this strange
estate until the feast of All-hallown-tide was past.

It chanced me upon All-hallown day to come there into the *Great Chamber* at Asher, in the morning, to give mine attendance, where I found Master Cromwell leaning in the great window, with a Primer in his hand, saying of our Lady mattins; which had been since a very strange sight. He prayed not more earnestly than the tears distilled from his eyes. Whom I bade good morrow. And with that I perceived the tears upon his cheeks. To whom I said, " Why, Master Cromwell, what meaneth all this your sorrow ? Is my lord in any danger, for whom ye lament thus ? or is it for any loss that ye have sustained by any misadventure ? "

" Nay, nay," quoth he, " it is my unhappy adventure, which am like to lose all that I have travailed for all the days of my life, for doing of my master true and diligent service." " Why, Sir," quoth I, " I trust ye be too wise, to commit any thing by my lord's commandment, otherwise than ye might do of right, whereof ye have any cause to doubt of loss of your goods." " Well, well," quoth he, " I cannot tell ; but all things I see before mine eyes, is as it is taken ; and this I understand right well, that I am in disdain with most men for my master's sake ; and surely without just cause. Howbeit, an ill name once gotten will not lightly be put away. I never had any promotion by my lord to the increase of my living. And thus much will I say to you, that I intend, God willing, this afternoon, when my lord hath dined, to ride to London, and so to the court, where I will either make or mar, or I come again. I will put myself in prease, to see what any man is able to lay to my charge of untruth or misdemeanour. " Marry, Sir," quoth I, " in so doing, in my conceit, ye shall do very well and wisely, beseeching God to be your guide, and send you good luck, even as I would myself." And with that I was called into the closet, to see and prepare all things ready for my lord, who intended that day to say mass there himself ; and so I did.

And then my lord came thither with his chaplain, one Doctor Marshall, saying first his mattins, and heard two masses on his knees. And then after he was confessed, he himself said mass. And when he had finished mass, and all his divine service, returned into his chamber, where he dined among divers of his doctors, where as Master Cromwell dined also ; and sitting at dinner, it chanced that my lord commended the true and faithful service of his gentlemen and yeomen. Whereupon Master Cromwell took an occasion to say to my lord, that in conscience he ought to consider their truth and loyal service that they did him, in this his present necessity, which never forsaketh him in all his trouble.

" It shall be well done, therefore," said he, " for your Grace to call before you all these your most worthy gentlemen and right honest yeomen, and let them understand, that ye right well consider their patience, truth, and faithfulness ; and then give them your commendation, with good words and thanks, the which shall be to them great courage to sustain. your mishap in patient misery, and to spend their life and substance in your service."

"Alas, Thomas," quoth my lord unto him, "ye know I have nothing to give them, and words without deeds be not often well taken. For if I had but as I have had of late, I would depart with them so frankly as they should be well content: but nothing hath no savour; and I am ashamed, and also sorry that I am not able to requite their faithful service. And although I have cause to rejoice, considering the fidelity I perceive in the number of my servants, who will not depart from me in my miserable estate, but be as diligent, obedient, and serviceable about me as they were in my great triumphant glory, yet do I lament again the want of substance to distribute among them." "Why, Sir," quoth Master Cromwell, "have ye not here a number of chaplains, to whom ye have departed very liberally with spiritual promotions, insomuch as some may dispend, by your Grace's preferment, a thousand marks by the year, and some five hundred marks, and some more, and some less; ye have no one chaplain within all your house, or belonging unto you, but he may dispend at the least well (by your procurement and preferment) three hundred marks yearly, who had all the profit and advantage at your hands, and other your servants none at all; and yet hath your poor servants taken much more pains for you in one day than all your idle chaplains hath done in a year. Therefore if they will not freely and frankly consider your liberality, and depart with you of the same goods gotten in your service, now in your great indigence and necessity, it is pity that they live; and all the world will have them in indignation and hatred, for their abominable ingratitude to their master and lord."

"I think no less, Thomas," quoth my lord, " wherefore, I pray you, cause all my servants be called and to assemble without, in my great chamber, after dinner, and see them stand in order, and I will declare unto them my mind, according to your advice." After that the board's end was taken up, Master Cromwell came to me and said, "Heard you not, what my lord said even now ?" " Yes, Sir," quoth I, " that I did." " Well, then," quoth he, " assemble all my lord's servants up into the great chamber;" and so I did, and when they were all there assembled, I assigned all the gentlemen to stand on the right side of the chamber, and the yeomen on the left side. And at the last my lord came thither, apparelled in a white rochet upon a violet gown of cloth like a bishop's, who went straight into the great window. Standing there a while, and his chaplains about him, beholding the number of his servants divided in two parts, he could not speak unto them for tenderness of his heart ; the flood of tears that distilled from his eyes declared no less : the which perceived by his servants, caused the fountains of water to gush out of their faithful hearts down their cheeks, in such abundance as it would cause a cruel heart to lament. At the last, after he had turned his face to the wall, and wiped his eyes

with his handkerchief, he spake to them after this sort
in effect : " Most faithful gentlemen and true-hearted
yeomen, I do not only lament to see your persons
present about me, but I do lament my negligent ingratitude towards you all on my behalf, in whom hath
been a great default, that in my prosperity I have
not done for you so much as I might have done, either
in word or deed, which was then in my power to do :
but then I knew not my jewels and special treasures
that I had of you my faithful servants in my house ;
but now approved experience hath taught me, and
with the eyes of my discretion, which before were hid,
I do perceive well the same.   There was never thing
that repented me more that ever I did than doth the
remembrance of my oblivious negligence and ungentle-
ness, that I have not promoted or preferred you to
condign rooms and preferments, according to your
demerits.   Howbeit, it is not unknown to you all, that
I was not so well furnished of temporal advancements,
as I was of spiritual preferments.   And if I should
have promoted you to any of the king's offices and
rooms, then should I have incurred the indignation of
the king's servants, who would not much let to report
in every place behind my back, that there could no
office or room in the king's gift escape the cardinal and
his servants, and thus should I incur the obloquy and
slander before the whole world.   But now it is come
to this pass, that it hath pleased the king to take all
that ever I have into his possession, so that I have
nothing left me but my bare clothes upon my back, the

which be but simple in comparison to those that ye
have seen me have or this : howbeit, if they may do
you any good or pleasure, I would not stick to divide
them among you, yea, and the skin of my back, if it
might countervail any thing in value among you.
But, good gentlemen and yeomen, my trusty and
faithful servants, of whom no prince hath the like, in
my opinion, I most heartily require you to take with
me some patience a little while, for I doubt not but
that the king, considering the offence suggested against
me by my mortal enemies, to be of small effect, will
shortly, I doubt not, restore me again to my living,
so that I shall be more able to divide some part thereof
yearly among you, whereof ye shall be well assured.
For the surplusage of my revenues, whatsoever shall
remain at the determination of my accompts, shall be,
God willing, distributed among you.   For I will never
hereafter esteem the goods and riches of this uncertain
world but as a vain thing, more than shall be sufficient
for the maintenance of mine estate and dignity, that
God hath or shall call me unto in this world during
my life.   And if the king do not thus shortly restore
me, then will I see you bestowed according to your
own requests, and write for you, either to the king, or
to any other noble person within this realm, to retain
you into service ; for I doubt not but the king, or any
nobleman, or worthy gentleman of this realm, will
credit my letter in your commendation.   Therefore,
in the mean time, mine advice is, that ye repair home
to your wives, such as have any : and such among you

as hath none, to take this time to visit your parents
and friends in the country. There is none of you all,
but once in a year would require license to visit your
wives and other of your friends : take this time, I
pray you, in respect thereof, and at your return I will
not refuse you, if I should beg with you. I consider
that the service of my house hath been such, and of
such sort, that ye be not meet or apt to serve any
man under the degree of a king; therefore I would
wish you to serve no man but the king, who I am sure
will not reject you. Therefore I desire you to take
your pleasures for a month, and then ye may come
again unto me, and I trust by that time the king's
majesty will extend his clemency upon me." " Sir,"
quoth Master Cromwell, " there is divers of these your
yeomen, that would be glad to see their friends, but
they lack money : therefore here is divers of your chaplains who have received at your hands great benefices
and high dignities ; let them therefore now show themselves unto you as they are bound by all humanity to
do. I think their honesty and charity is not so
slender and void of grace that they would not see you
lack where they may help to refresh you. And for
my part, although I have not received of your Grace's
gift one penny towards the increase of my yearly
living, yet will I depart with you this towards the
dispatch of your servants," and therewith delivered
him five pounds in gold. " And now let us see what
your chaplains will do. I think they will depart with
you much more than I have done, who be more able

to give you a pound than I one penny." "Go to, masters," quoth he to the chaplains : insomuch as some gave to him ten pounds, some ten marks, some a hundred shillings, and so some more and some less, as at that time their powers did extend ; whereby my lord received among them as much money of their liberality as he gave to each of his yeomen a quarter's wages, and board wages for a month; and they departed down into the hall, where some determined to go to their friends, and some said that they would not depart from my lord until they might see him in better estate.   My lord returned into his chamber lamenting the departure from his servants, making his moan unto Master Cromwell, who comforted him the best he could, and desired my lord to give him leave to go to London, where he would either make or mar or he came again, which was always his common saying. Then after long communication with my lord in secret, he departed and took his horse, and rode to London, at whose departing I was by, whom he bade farewell ; and said, " Ye shall hear shortly of me, and if I speed well, I will not fail to be here again within these two days."   And so I took my leave of him, and he rode forth on his journey.   Sir Rafe Sadler (now knight) was then his clerk, and rode with him.

After that my lord had supped that night, and all men gone to bed (being All-hallown day) it chanced so, about midnight, that one of the porters came unto my chamber door, and there knocked, and waking me, I perceived who it was ; and asked him,

" what he would have that time of the night ? " " Sir,"
quoth the porter, " there is a great number of horsemen at the gate, that would come in, saying to me,
that it is Sir John Russell, and so it appears to me by
his voice ; what is your pleasure that I should do ? "
" Marry," quoth I, " go down again, and make a great
fire in your lodge, against I come to dry them ; "
for it rained all that night the sorest that it did all
that year before. Then I rose and put on my night-
gown, and came to the gates, and asked who was
there. With that Master Russell spake, whom I
knew by his voice, and then I caused the porter to
open the gates and let them all in, who were wet
to the skin ; desiring Master Russell to go into the
lodge to the fire ; and he showed me that he was
come from the king unto my lord in message, with
whom he required me to speak. " Sir," quoth I,
" I trust your news be good ? " " Yea, I promise you
on my fidelity," quoth he, " and so, I pray you, show
him, I have brought him such news that will please
him right well." " Then I will go," quoth I, " and
wake him, and cause him to rise." I went incontinent to my lord's chamber door, and waked my lord,
who asked me " what I would have ? " " Sir," said
I, " to show you that Sir John Russell is come from
the king, who is desirous to speak with you ; " and
then he called up one of his grooms to let me in ; and
being within I told him " what a journey Sir John
Russell had that night." " I pray God," quoth he,
" all be for the best." " Yes, Sir," quoth I, " he

showed me, and so bade me tell you, that he had brought you such news as ye would greatly rejoice thereat." "Well, then," quoth he, "God be praised, and welcome be his grace! Go ye and fetch him unto me, and by that time I will be ready to talk with him."

Then I returned from him to the lodge, and brought Master Russell from thence to my lord, who had cast on his night-gown. And when Master Russell was come into his presence, he most humbly reverenced him, upon his knee, to whom my lord bowed down, and took him up, and bade him welcome. "Sir," quoth he, "the king commendeth him unto you;" and delivered him a great ring of gold with a Turkis, for a token; "and willeth you to be of good cheer; who loveth you as well as ever he did, and is not a little disquieted for your troubles, whose mind is full of your remembrance. Insomuch as his Grace, before he sat to supper, called me unto him, and commanded me to take this journey secretly to visit you, to your comfort the best of my power. And, Sir, if it please your Grace, I have had this night the sorest journey, for so little a way, that ever I had to my remembrance."

My lord thanked him for his pains and good news, and demanded of him if he had supped; and he said "Nay." "Well, then," quoth my lord to me, "cause the cooks to provide some meat for him; and cause a chamber with a good fire to be made ready for him, that he may take his rest a while upon a bed." All which commandment I fulfilled ; and in the meantime my lord and Master Russell were in very secret communication ; and in fine, Master Russell went to his chamber, taking his leave of my lord for all night, and said, " he would not tarry but a while, for he would, God willing, be at the court at Greenwich again before day, for he would not for any thing that it were known, his being with my lord that night." And so being in his chamber, having a small repast, rested him a while upon a bed, whilst his servants supped and dried themselves by the fire ; and then incontinent he rode away with speed to the court. And shortly after his being there, my lord was restored again unto plenty of household stuff, vessels, and plate, and of all things necessary some part, so that he was indifferently furnished much better than he was of late, and yet not so abundantly as the king's pleasure was, the default whereof was in the officers, and in such as had the oversight of the delivery thereof ; and yet my lord rejoiced in that little in comparison to that he had before.

Now let us return again to Master Cromwell, to see how he hath sped, since his departure last from my lord. The case stood so, that there should begin, shortly after All-hallown-tide, the Parliament, and he, being within London, devised with himself to be one of the burgesses of the Parliament, and chanced to meet with one Sir Thomas Rush, knight, a special friend of his, whose son was appointed to be one of the burgesses of that Parliament, of whom he

obtained his room, and by that means put his foot into
the Parliament House : then within two or three days
after his entry into the Parliament, he came unto my
lord, to Asher, with a much pleasanter countenance
than he had at his departure, and meeting with me
before he came to my lord, said unto me, " that he had
once adventured to put in his foot, where he trusted
shortly to be better regarded, or all were done." And
when he was come to my lord, they talked together in
secret manner ; and that done, he rode out of hand
again that night to London, because he would not be
absent from the Parliament the next morning.   There
could nothing be spoken against my lord in the
Parliament House but he would answer it incontinent,
or else take until the next day, against which time he
would resort to my lord to know what answer he
should make in his behalf ; insomuch that there was
no matter alleged against my lord but that he was ever
ready furnished with a sufficient answer ; so that at
length, for his honest behaviour in his master's cause,
he grew into such estimation in every man's opinion,
that he was esteemed to be the most faithfullest servant
to his master of all other, wherein he was of all men
greatly commended.

Then was there brought in a Bill of Articles into
the Parliament House to have my lord condemned of
treason ; against which bill Master Cromwell inveighed
so discreetly, with such witty persuasions and deep
reasons, that the same bill could take there no effect.
Then were his enemies compelled to indict him in a

premunire, and all was done only to the intent to entitle the king to all his goods and possessions, the which he had gathered together, and purchased for his colleges in Oxford and Ipswich, and for the maintenance of the same, which was then abuilding in most sumptuous wise. Wherein when he was demanded by the judges, which were sent to him purposely to examine him what answer he would make to the same, he said : "The king's highness knoweth right well whether I have offended his majesty and his laws or no, in using of my prerogative legatine, for the which ye have me indicted. Notwithstanding I have the king's license in my coffers, under his hand and broad seal, for exercising and using the authority thereof, in the largest wise, within his highness's dominions, the which remaineth now in the hands of my enemies. Therefore, because I will not stand in question or trial with the king in his own cause, I am content here of mine own frank will and mind, in your presence, to confess the offence in the indictment, and put me wholly in the mercy and grace of the king, having no doubt in his godly disposition and charitable conscience, whom I know hath an high discretion to consider the truth, and my humble submission and obedience. And although I might justly stand on the trial with him therein, yet I am content to submit myself to his clemency, and thus much ye may say to him in my behalf, that I am entirely in his obedience, and do intend, God willing, to obey and fulfil all his princely pleasure in every thing that he will command me to

F

do ; whose will and pleasure I never yet disobeyed or repugned, but was always contented and glad to accomplish his desire and commandment before God, whom I ought most rathest to have obeyed; the which negligence now greatly repenteth me. Notwithstanding, I most heartily require you, to have me most humbly to his royal majesty commended, for whom I do and will pray for the preservation of his royal person, long to reign in honour, prosperity, and quietness, and to have the victory over his mortal and cankered enemies." And they took their leave of him and departed.

Shortly after the king sent the Duke of Norfolk unto him in message; but what it was I am not certain. But my lord being advertised that the duke was coming even at hand, he caused all his gentlemen to wait upon him down through the hall into the base court, to receive the duke at the entry of the gates; and commanded all his yeomen to stand still in the hall in order. And he and his gentlemen went to the gates, where he encountered with my Lord of Norfolk, whom he received bare-headed; who embraced each other: and so led him by the arm through the hall into his chamber. And as the duke passed through the hall, at the upper end thereof he turned again his visage down the hall, regarding the number of the tall yeomen that stood in order there, and said : " Sirs," quoth he, " your diligent and faithful service unto my lord here your master, in this time of his calamity, hath purchased for yourselves of all noble men much honesty; insomuch as the king commanded me to say to you in his Grace's name, that for your true and loving service that ye have done to your master, his highness will see you all furnished at all times with services according to your demerits." With that my Lord Cardinal put off his cap, and said to my Lord of Norfolk : " Sir," quoth he, " these men be all approved men : wherefore it were pity they should want other service or living ; and being sorry that I am not able to do for them as my heart doth wish, do therefore require you, my good lord, to be good lord unto them, and extend your good word for them, when ye shall see opportunity at any time hereafter ; and that ye will prefer their diligent and faithful service to the king." " Doubt ye not thereof," quoth my Lord of Norfolk, " but I will do for them the best of my power : and when I shall see cause, I will be an earnest suitor for them to the king ; and some of you I will retain myself in service for your honesty's sake. And as ye have begun, so continue and remain here still with my lord until ye hear more of the king's pleasure : God's blessing and mine be with you !" And so went up into the great chamber to dinner, whom my Lord Cardinal thanked, and said unto him, " Yet, my lord, of all other noblemen, I have most cause to thank you for your noble heart and gentle nature, which ye have showed me behind my back, as my servant, Thomas Cromwell, hath made report unto me. But even as ye are a nobleman indeed, so have ye showed yourself no less to all men in calamity, and in especial to me, and even as ye have abated my glory and high estate, and brought it full low, so have ye extended your honourable favour most charitably unto me, being prostrate before you. Forsooth, Sir, ye do right well deserve to bear in your arms the noble and gentle lion, whose natural inclination is, that when he hath vanquished any beast, and seeth him yielded, lying prostrate before him at his feet, then will he show most clemency unto his vanquished, and do him no more harm, nor suffer any other devouring beast to damage him : whose nature and quality ye do ensue ; therefore these verses may be applied to your lordship :

Parcere prostratis scit nobilis ira leonis :
Tu quoque fac simile, quisquis regnabis in orbem."

With that the water was brought them to wash before dinner, to the which my lord called my Lord of Norfolk to wash with him: but he refused of courtesy, and desired to have him excused, and said "that it became him not to presume to wash with him any more now, than it did before in his glory." " Yes, forsooth," quoth my Lord Cardinal, " for my authority and dignity legatine is gone, wherein consisted all my high honour." " A straw," quoth my Lord of Norfolk, " for your legacy. I never esteemed your honour the more or higher for that. But I regarded your honour, for that ye were Archbishop of York, and a cardinal, whose estate of honour surmounteth any duke now being within this realm ; and so will I honour you, and acknowledge the same, and bear you reverence accordingly. Therefore, I beseech you, content yourself, for

I will not presume to wash with you; and therefore
I pray you, hold me excused." Then was my Lord
Cardinal constrained to wash alone; and my Lord of
Norfolk all alone also. When he had done, my Lord
Cardinal would fain have had him to sit down on the
chair, in the inner side of the table, but surely he refused the same also with much humbleness. Then
was there set another chair for my Lord of Norfolk,
over against my Lord Cardinal, on the outside of the
table, the which was by my Lord of Norfolk based
something beneath my lord, and during the dinner all
their communication was of the diligent service of the
gentlemen which remained with my lord there attending upon him at dinner, and how much the king and
all other noblemen doth esteem them with worthy
commendations for so doing; and at this time how
little they be esteemed in the court that are come to
the king's service, and have forsaken their master in
his necessity; whereof some he blamed by name. And
with this communication, the dinner being ended, they
rose from the table, and went together into my lord's
bedchamber, where they continued in consultation a
certain season. And being there, it chanced Master
Shelley, the judge, to come thither, sent from the king;
whereof relation was made to my lord, which caused
the duke and him to break up their communication;
and the duke desired to go into some chamber to
repose him for a season. And as he was coming out
of my lord's chamber, he met with Master Shelley, to
whom Master Shelley made relation of the cause of

his coming, and desired the duke to tarry and to assist
him in doing of his message; whom he denied and
said, " I have nothing to do with your message, wherein
I will not meddle ;" and so departed into a chamber,
where he took his rest for an hour or two. And in
the mean time my lord issued out of his chamber, and
came to Master Shelley to know his message. Who
declared unto him, after due salutation, "that the king's
pleasure was to have his house at Westminster, (then
called York Place, belonging to the Bishoprick of
York,) intending to make of that house a palace royal;
and to possess the same according to the laws of this
his Grace's realm. His highness hath therefore sent
for all the judges, and for all his learned counsel, to
know their opinions in the assurance thereof; in whose
determinations it was fully resolved, that your Grace
should recognise, before a judge, the right thereof to be
in the king and his successors ; and so his highness
shall be assured thereof. Wherefore it hath pleased
his majesty to appoint me by his commandment to
come hither, to take of you this recognisance, who hath
in you such affiance, that ye will not refuse so to do
accordingly. Therefore I shall desire your Grace to
know your good will therein." " Master Shelley,"
quoth my lord, " I know that the king of his own
nature is of a royal stomach, and yet not willing more
than justice shall lead him unto by the law. And
therefore, I counsel you, and all other fathers of the
law and learned men of his counsel, to put no more
into his head than the law may stand with good

conscience ; for when ye tell him, this is the law, it were well done ye should tell him also that, although *this* be the law, yet *this* is conscience ; for law without conscience is not good to be given unto a king in counsel to use for a lawful right, but always to have a respect to conscience, before the rigour of the common law, for *laus est facere quod decet, non quod licet.* The king ought of his royal dignity and prerogative to mitigate the rigour of the law, where conscience hath the most force ; therefore, in his royal place of equal justice, he hath constitute a chancellor, an officer to execute justice with clemency, where conscience is opposed by the rigour of the law. And therefore the Court of Chancery hath been heretofore commonly called the Court of Conscience ; because it hath juris-diction to command the high ministers of the common law to spare execution and judgment, where conscience hath most effect. Therefore I say to you in this case, although you, and other of your profession, perceive by your learning that the king may, by an order of your laws, lawfully do that thing which ye demand of me ; how say you, Master Shelley, may I do it with justice and conscience, to give that thing away from me and my successors which is none of mine ? If this be law, with conscience, show me your opinion, I pray you." "Forsooth, my lord," quoth he, "there is some con-science in this case ; but having regard to the king's high power, and to be employed to a better use and purpose, it may the better be suffered with conscience ; who is sufficient to make recompense to the church of

York with double the value." " That I know well,"
quoth my lord, " but here is no such condition neither
promised nor agreed, but only a bare and simple departure with another's right for ever.   And if every
bishop may do the like, then might every prelate give
away the patrimony of their churches which is none of
theirs ; and so in process of time leave nothing for
their successors to maintain their dignities, which, all
things considered, should be but small to the king's
honour.   Sir, I do not intend to stand in terms with
you in this matter, but let me see your commission."
To whom Master Shelley showed the same, and that .
seen, and perceived by him, said again thus : " Master
Shelley," quoth he, " ye shall make report to the king's
highness, that I am his obedient subject, and faithful
chaplain and beadman, whose royal commandment and
request I will in no wise disobey, but most gladly
fulfil and accomplish his princely will and pleasure in
all things, and in especial in this matter, inasmuch
as ye, the fathers of the laws, say that I may lawfully
do it.   Therefore I charge your conscience and discharge mine.   Howbeit, I pray you, show his majesty
from me, that I most humbly desire his highness to
call to his most gracious remembrance, that there is
both heaven and hell."   And therewith the clerk was
called, who wrote my lord's recognisance, and after
some secret talk Master Shelley departed.   Then rose
my Lord of Norfolk from his repose, and after some
communication with my lord he departed.

Thus continued my lord at Asher, who received

daily messages from the court, whereof some were not so good as some were bad, but yet much more evil than good. For his enemies, perceiving the great affection that the king bare always towards him, devised a mean to disquiet and disturb his patience ; thinking thereby to give him an occasion to fret and chafe, that death should rather ensue than increase of health or life, the which they most desired. They feared him more after his fall than they did before in his prosperity, doubting much his readoption into authority, by reason that the king's favour remained still towards him in such force, whereby they might rather be in danger of their estates, than in any assurance, for their cruelty ministered, by their malicious inventions, surmised and brought to pass against him.

Therefore they took this order among them in their matters, that daily they would send him something, or do something against him, wherein they thought that they might give him a cause of heaviness or lamentation. As some day they would cause the king to send for four or five of his gentlemen from him to serve the king : and some other day they would lay matters newly invented against him. Another day they would take from him some of his promotions ; or of their promotions whom he had preferred before. Then would they fetch from him some of his yeomen ; insomuch as the king took into service sixteen of them at once, and at one time put them into his guard. This order of life he led continually ; that there was no one day but, or ever he went to bed, he had an occasion greatly to chafe or fret the heart out of his belly, but that he was a wise man, and bare all their malice in patience.

At Christmas he fell sore sick, that he was likely to die. Whereof the king being advertised, was very sorry therefore, and sent Doctor Buttes, his Grace's physician, unto him, to see in what estate he was. Doctor Buttes came unto him, and finding him very sick lying in his bed ; and perceiving the danger he was in repaired again unto the king. Of whom the king demanded, saying, " How doth yonder man, have you seen him ? " " Yea, Sir," quoth he. " How do you like him ? " quoth the king. " Forsooth, Sir," quoth he, " if you will have him dead, I warrant your Grace he will be dead within these four days, if he receives no comfort from you shortly, and Mistress Anne." " Marry," quoth the king, " God forbid that he should die. I pray you, good Master Buttes, go again unto him, and do your cure upon him; for I would not lose him for twenty thousand pounds." " Then must your Grace," quoth Master Buttes, " send him first some comfortable message, as shortly as is possible." " Even so will I," quoth the king, " by you. And therefore make speed to him again, and ye shall deliver him from me this ring for a token of our good will and favour towards him (in the which ring was engraved the king's visage within a ruby, as lively counterfeit as was possible to be devised). This ring he knoweth very well ; for he gave me the same ; and

tell him, that I am not offended with him in my heart
nothing at all, and that shall he perceive, and God send
him life, very shortly. Therefore bid him be of good
cheer, and pluck up his heart, and take no despair.
And I charge you come not from him, until ye have
brought him out of all danger of death." And then
spake he to Mistress Anne, saying, " Good sweetheart,
I pray you at this my instance, as ye love us, to send
the cardinal a token with comfortable words ; and in
so doing ye shall do us a loving pleasure." She being
not minded to disobey the king's earnest request, whatsoever she intended in her heart towards the cardinal ;
took incontinent her tablet of gold hanging at her
girdle, and delivered it to Master Buttes, with very
gentle and comfortable words and commendations to
the cardinal. And thus Master Buttes departed, and
made speedy return to Asher, to my Lord Cardinal ;
after whom the king sent Doctor Clement, Doctor
Wotton, and Doctor Cromer the Scot, to consult and
assist Master Buttes for my lord's health.

After that Master Buttes had been with my lord,
and delivered the king's and Mistress Anne's tokens
unto him, with the most comfortable words he could
devise on their behalf, whereat he rejoiced not a little,
advancing him a little in his bed, and received their
tokens most joyfully, thanking Master Buttes for his
comfortable news and pains. Master Buttes showed
him furthermore, that the king's pleasure was, that he
should minister unto him for his health ; and to join
with him for the better and most assured and brief

ways, to be had for the same, hath sent Doctor Wotton,
Doctor Clement, and Doctor Cromer, to join with him
in counsel and ministration. " Therefore, my lord,"
quoth he, " it were well done that they should be
called in to visit your person and estate, wherein I
would be glad to hear their opinions, trusting in
Almighty God that, through his grace and assistance,
we shall ease you of your pains, and rid you clean
from your disease and infirmity." Wherewith my lord
was well pleased and contented to hear their judgments ; for indeed he trusted more to the Scottish
doctor than he did to any of the other, because he
was the very occasion that he inhabited here in
England, and before he gave him partly his exhibition
in Paris. Then when they were come into his chamber, and had talked with him, he took upon him to
debate his disease learnedly among them, so that they
might understand that he was seen in that art. After
they had taken order for ministration, it was not long
or they brought him out of all danger and fear of
death ; and within four days they set him on his feet,
and got him a good stomach to his meat. This done,
and he in a good estate of amendment, they took their
leave to depart, to whom my lord offered his reward ;
the which they refused, saying that the king gave
them in special commandment, to take nothing of him
for their pains and ministration ; for at their return
his highness said that he would reward them of his own
costs : and thus with great thanks they departed from
my lord, whom they left in good estate of recovery.

After this time my lord daily amended, and so continued still at Asher until Candlemas; against which feast, the king caused to be sent him three or four cart-loads of stuff, and most part thereof was locked in great standards, (except beds and kitchen-stuff,) wherein was both plate and rich hangings, and chapel-stuff. Then my lord, being thus furnished, was therewith well contented; although they whom the king assigned did not deliver him so good nor so rich stuff, as the king's pleasure was, yet was he joyous thereof, and rendered most humble thanks to the king, and to them that appointed the said stuff for him, saying to us his servants, at the opening of the same stuff in the standards, the which we thought, and said, might have been better appointed, if it had pleased them that appointed it: " Nay, Sirs," quoth my lord to us, " he that hath nothing is glad of somewhat, though it be never so little, and although it be not in com-parison half so much and good as we had before, yet we rejoice more of this little than we did of the great abundance that we then had; and thank the king very much for the same, trusting after this to have much more. Therefore let us all rejoice, and be glad, that God and the king hath so graciously remembered to restore us to some things to maintain our estate like a noble person."

Then commanded he Master Cromwell, being with him, to make suit to the king's majesty, that he might remove thence to some other place, for he was weary of that house of Asher: for with continual use thereof the house waxed unsavoury; supposing that if he might remove from thence he should much sooner recover his health. And also the council had put into the king's head, that the new gallery at Asher, which my lord had late before his fall newly set up, should be very necessary for the king, to take down and set it up again at Westminster; which was done accordingly, and stands at this present day there. The taking away thereof before my lord's face was to him a corrosive, which was invented by his enemies only to torment him, the which indeed discouraged him very sore to tarry any longer there. Now Master Cromwell thought it but vain and much folly to move any of the king's council to assist and prefer his suit to the king, among whom rested the number of his mortal enemies, for they would rather hinder his removing, or else remove him farther from the king, than to have holpen him to any place nigh the king's common trade; wherefore he refused any suit to them, and made only suit to the king's own person; whose suit the king graciously heard, and thought it very convenient to be granted; and through the special motion of Master Cromwell, the king was well contented that he should remove to Richmond, which place my lord had a little before repaired to his great cost and charge; for the king had made an exchange thereof with him for Hampton Court. All this his removing was done without the knowledge of the king's council, for if they might have had any intelligence thereof before, then would they have persuaded the king to the contrary: but when they were advertised of the king's grant and pleasure, they dissimuled their countenances in the king's presence, for they were greatly afraid of him, lest his nigh being, the king might at length some one time resort to him, and so call him home again, considering the great affection and love that the king daily showed towards him ; wherefore they doubted his rising again, if they found not a mean to remove him shortly from the king. Insomuch that they thought it convenient for their purpose to inform the king upon certain considerations which they invented, that it were very necessary that my lord should go down into the North unto his benefice of York, where he should be a good stay for the country ; to the which the king, supposing that they had meant no less than good faith, granted and condescended to their suggestions ; which were forced so with wonderful imagined considerations, that the king, understanding nothing of their intent, was lightly persuaded to the same. Whereupon the Duke of Norfolk commanded Master Cromwell, who had daily access unto him, to say to my lord, that it is the king's pleasure that he should with speed go to his benefice, where lieth his cure, and look to that according to his duty. Master Cromwell at his next repair to my lord, who lay then at Richmond, declared unto him what my Lord of Norfolk said, how it was determined that he should go to his benefice. " Well then, Thomas," quoth my lord, " seeing there is no other remedy, I do intend to go to my benefice of Winchester, and I pray you, Thomas, so show my Lord of Norfolk." " Contented, Sir," quoth Master Cromwell, and accord-

ing to his commandment did so.   To the which my
Lord of Norfolk answered and said, "What will he
do there?   Nay," quoth he, "let him go into his
province of York, whereof he hath received his honour,
and there lieth the spiritual burden and charge of his
conscience, as he ought to do, and so show him."   The
lords, who were not all his friends, having intelligence
of his intent, thought to withdraw his appetite from
Winchester, and would in no wise permit him to plant
himself so nigh the king: they moved therefore the
king to give my lord but a pension out of Winchester,
and to distribute all the rest among the nobility and
other of his worthy servants; and in likewise to do the
same with the revenues of St. Albans; and of the
revenues of his colleges in Oxford and Ipswich, the
which the king took into his own hands; whereof
Master Cromwell had the receipt and government
before by my lord's assignment.   In consideration
thereof it was thought most convenient that he should
have so still.   Notwithstanding, out of the revenues of
Winchester and St. Albans the king gave to some one
nobleman three hundred marks, and to some a hundred
pounds, and to some more and to some less, according
to the king's royal pleasure.   Now Master Cromwell
executed his office, the which he had over the lands of
the college, so justly and exactly that he was had in
great estimation for his witty behaviour therein, and
also for the true, faithful, and diligent service extended
towards my lord his master.

It came at length so to pass that those to whom the

king's majesty had given any annuities or fees for term of life by patent out of the fore-named revenues could not be good, but only during my lord's life, forasmuch as the king had no longer estate or title therein, which came to him by reason of my lord's attainder in the premumire; and to make their estates good and sufficient according to their patents, it was thought necessary to have my lord's confirmation unto their grants. And this to be brought about, there was no other mean but to make suit to Master Cromwell to obtain their confirmation at my lord's hands, whom they thought might best obtain the same.

Then began both noblemen and other who had any patents of the king, out either of Winchester or St. Albans, to make earnest suit to Master Cromwell for to solicit their causes to my lord, to get of him his confirmations; and for his pains therein sustained, they promised every man, not only worthily to reward him, but also to show him such pleasures as should at all times lie in their several powers, whereof they assured him. Wherein Master Cromwell perceiving an occasion and a time given him to work for himself, and to bring the thing to pass which he long wished for; intended to work so in this matter, to serve their desires, that he might the sooner bring his own enterprise to purpose.

Then at his next resort to my lord, he moved him privily in this matter to have his counsel and his advice, and so by their witty heads it was devised that they should work together by one line, to bring by their policies Master Cromwell in place and estate, where he might do himself good and my lord much profit. Now began matters to work to bring Master Cromwell into estimation in such sort as was afterwards much to his increase of dignity ; and thus every man, having an occasion to sue for my lord's confirmation, made now earnest travail to Master Cromwell for these purposes, who refused none to make promise that he would do his best in that case.   And having a great occasion of access to the king for the disposition of divers lands, whereof he had the order and governance ; by means whereof, and by his witty demeanour, he grew continually into the king's favour, as ye shall hear after in this history.   But first let us resort to the great business about the assurance of all these patents which the king hath given to divers noblemen and other of his servants, wherein Master Cromwell made a continuance of great suit to my lord for the same, that in process of time he served all their turns so that they had their purposes, and he their good wills.   Thus rose his name and friendly acceptance with all men.   The fame of his honesty and wisdom sounded so in the king's ears that, by reason of his access to the king, he perceived to be in him no less wisdom than fame had made of him report, forasmuch as he had the government and receipts of those lands which I showed you before ; and the conference that he had with the king therein enforced the king to repute him a very wise man, and a meet instrument to serve his Grace, as it after came to pass.

Sir, now the lords thought long to remove my lord farther from the king, and out of his common trade; wherefore among other of the lords, my Lord of Norfolk said to Master Cromwell, " Sir," quoth he, " me thinketh that the cardinal your master maketh no haste northward; show him, that if he go not away shortly, I will, rather than he should tarry still, tear him with my teeth. Therefore I would advise him to prepare him away as shortly as he can, or else he shall be sent forward." These words Master Cromwell reported to my lord at his next repair unto him, who then had a just occasion to resort to him for the dispatch of the noblemen's and others' patents. And here I will leave of this matter, and show you of my lord's being at Richmond.

My lord, having license of the king to repair and remove to Richmond, made haste to prepare him thitherward; and so he came and lodged within the great park there, which was a very pretty house and a neat, lacking no necessary rooms that to so small a house was convenient and necessary; where was to the same a very proper garden garnished with divers pleasant walks and alleys; my lord continued in this lodge from the time that he came thither, shortly after Candlemas, until it was Lent, with a privy number of servants, because of the smallness of the house, and the rest of his family went to board wages.

I will tell you a certain tale by the way of communication. Sir, as my lord was accustomed towards night to walk in the garden there, to say his service,

it was my chance then to wait upon him there ; and
standing still in an alley, whilst he in another walked
with his chaplain, saying of his service ; as I stood, 1
espied certain images of beasts counterfeit in timber,
standing in a corner under the lodge wall, to the
which I repaired to behold.   Among whom I saw
there a dun cow, whereon I mused most, because it
seemed me to be the most lively entaylled among
all the rest.   My lord being, as I said, walking on
the other side of the garden, perceived me, came suddenly upon me at my back, unawares, and said:
" What have you espied here, that you so attentively
look upon ? "   " Forsooth, if it please your Grace,"
quoth I, " here I do behold these entaylled images ;
the which I suppose were ordained for to be set up
within some place about the king's palace : howbeit,
Sir, among them all, I have most considered the dun
cow, in the which (as it seemeth me) the workman
has most apertly showed his cunning."   " Yea, marry,
Sir," quoth my lord, " upon this dun cow dependeth
a certain prophecy, the which I will show you, for
peradventure ye never heard of it before.   There is a
saying," quoth he, " that

> " When this cow rideth the bull,
>   Then priest, beware thy skull."

Of which prophecy neither my lord that declared it,
nor I that heard it, understood the effect ; although
that even then it was a-working to be brought to pass.
For this cow the king gave as one of his beasts appertaining of antiquity unto his earldom of Richmond.

which was his ancient inheritance ; this prophecy was
after expounded in this wise. This dun cow, because
it was the king's beast, betokened the king; and the
bull betokened Mistress Anne Boleyn, which was after
queen, because that her father, Sir Thomas Boleyn,
gave the same beast in his cognisance. So that when
the king had married her, the which was then unknown
to my lord, or to any other at that time, then was this
prophecy thought of all men to be fulfilled. For what
a number of priests, both religious and secular, lost
their heads for offending of such laws as were then
made to bring this marriage to effect, is not unknown
to all the world. Therefore it was judged of all men
that this prophecy was then fulfilled when the king
and she were joined in marriage. Now, how dark and
obscure riddles and prophecies be, you may behold in
this same : for before it was brought to pass there
was not the wisest prophesier could perfectly discuss
it, as it is now come to effect and purpose. Trust
therefore, by mine advice, to no kind of dark riddles
and prophecies, wherein ye may, as many have been,
be deceived, and brought to destruction. And many
times the imaginations and travailous business to avoid
such dark and strange prophecies, hath been the very
occasion to bring the same the sooner to effect and
perfection. Therefore let men beware to divine or
assure themselves to expound any such prophecies,
for whoso doeth shall first deceive themselves, and
secondly, bring many into error ; the experience hath
been lately experienced, the more pity. But if men

will needs think themselves so wise, to be assured of
such blind prophecies, and will work their wills therein,
either in avoiding or in fulfilling the same, God send
him well to speed, for he may as well, and much more
sooner, take damage than avoid the danger thereof!
Let prophecies alone, in God's name, apply your vo-
cation, and commit the exposition of such dark riddles
and obscure prophecies to God, that disposeth them as
his divine pleasure shall see cause to alter and change
all your enterprises and imaginations to nothing, and
deceive all your expectations, and cause you to repent
your great folly, the which when ye feel the smart,
will yourself confess the same to be both great folly
and much more madness to trust in any such fantasies.
Let God therefore dispose them, who governeth and
punisheth according to man's deserts, and not to all
men's judgments.

You have heard herebefore what words the Duke of
Norfolk had to Master Cromwell touching my lord's
going to the North to his benefice of York, at such
time as Master Cromwell declared the same to my
lord, to whom my lord answered in this wise : " Marry,
Thomas," quoth he, " then it is time to be going, if my
Lord of Norfolk take it so.   Therefore I pray you go
to the king and move his highness in my behalf, and
say that I would, with all my heart, go to my benefice
at York, but for want of money ; desiring his Grace to
assist me with some money towards my journey.   For
ye may say that the last money that I received of his
majesty hath been too little to pay my debts, com-

pelled by his counsel so to do ; therefore to constrain
me to the payment thereof, and his highness having
all my goods, hath been too much extremity ; wherein
I trust his Grace will have a charitable respect. Ye
may say also to my Lord of Norfolk, and other of the
council, that I would depart if I had money." " Sir,"
quoth Master Cromwell, " I will do my best." And
after other communication he departed again, and went
to London.

My lord then in the beginning of Lent removed out
of the lodge into the Charterhouse of Richmond, where
he lay in a lodging, which Doctor Collet, sometime
Dean of Paul's, had made for himself until he removed
northward, which was in the Passion Week after ; and
he had to the same house a secret gallery, which went
out of his chamber into the Charterhouse church,
whither he resorted every day to their service ; and at
afternoons he would sit in contemplation with one or
other of the most ancient fathers of that house in his
cell, who among them by their counsel persuaded him
from the vain-glory of this world, and gave him divers
shirts of hair, the which he often wore afterward,
whereof I am certain. And thus he continued for the
time of his abode there in godly contemplation.

Now when Master Cromwell came to the court, he
chanced to move my Lord of Norfolk that my lord
would gladly depart northward but for lack of money,
wherein he desired his assistance to the king. Then
went they both jointly to the king, to whom my Lord
of Norfolk declared how my lord would gladly depart

northward, if he wanted not money to bring him thither; the king thereupon referred the assignment thereof to the council, whereupon they were in divers opinions. Some said he should have none, for he had sufficient of late delivered him; some would he should have sufficient and enough; and some contrariwise would he should have but a small sum; and some thought it much against the council's honour, and much more against the king's high dignity, to see him want the maintenance of his estate which the king had given him in this realm; and who also hath been in such estimation with the king, and in great authority under him; it should be rather a great slander in foreign realms to the king and his whole council, to see him want that lately had so much, and now so little. "Therefore, rather than he should lack," quoth one among them, " (although he never did me good or any pleasure), yet would I lay my plate to gage for him for a thousand pounds, rather than he should depart so simply as some would have him for to do. Let us do to him as we would be done unto; considering his small offence, and his inestimable substance that he only hath departed withal the same, for satisfying of the king's pleasure, rather than he would stand in defence with the king in defending of his case, as he might justly have done, as ye all know. Let not malice cloak this matter whereby that justice and mercy may take no place; ye have all your pleasures fulfilled which ye have long desired, and now suffer conscience to minister unto him some liberality; the day may come that some of us may be in the same case, ye have such alterations in persons, as well assured as ye suppose yourselves to be, and to stand upon as sure a ground, and what hangeth over our heads we know not ; I can say no more : now do as ye list." Then after all this they began again to consult in this matter, and after long debating and reasoning about the same, it was concluded, that he should have by the way of prest, a thousand marks out of Winchester bishoprick, beforehand of his pension, which the king had granted him out of the same, for the king had resumed the whole revenues of the bishoprick of Winchester, into his own hands ; yet the king out of the same had granted divers great pensions unto divers noblemen and unto other of his council ; so that I do suppose, all things accompted, his part was the least. So that, when this determination was fully concluded, they declared the same to the king, who straightway commanded the said thousand marks to be delivered out of hand to Master Cromwell ; and so it was. The king, calling Master Cromwell to him secretly, bade him to resort to him again when he had received the said sum of money. And according to the same commandment he repaired again to the king ; to whom the king said : " Show my lord your master, although our council hath not assigned any sufficient sum of money to bear his charges, yet ye shall show him in my behalf, that I will send him a thousand pound, of my benevolence ; and tell him that he shall not lack, and bid him be of good cheer." Master

Cromwell upon his knees most humbly thanked the king on my lord's behalf, for his great benevolence and noble heart towards my lord : " Those comfortable words of your Grace," quoth he, " shall rejoice him more than three times the value of your noble reward." And therewith departed from the king and came to my lord directly to Richmond ; to whom he delivered the money, and showed him all the arguments in the council, which ye have heard before, with the progress of the same ; and of what money it was, and whereof it was levied, which the council sent him ; and of the money which the king sent him, and of his comfortable words ; whereof my lord rejoiced not a little, and was greatly comforted. And after the receipt of this money my lord consulted with Master Cromwell about his departure, and of his journey, with the order thereof.

Then my lord prepared all things with speed for his journey into the North, and sent to London for livery clothes for his servants that should ride with him thither. Some he refused, such as he thought were not meet to serve ; and some again of their own mind desired him of his favour to tarry still here in the south, being very loth to abandon their native country, their parents, wives, and children, whom he most gladly licensed with good will and favour, and rendered unto them his hearty thanks for their painful service and long tarriance with him in his troublesome decay and overthrow. So that now all things being furnished towards this journey, he took the same in the beginning of the Passion Week, before Easter ; and so rode

to a place, then the abbot's of Westminster, called
Hendon; and the next day he removed to a place
called the Rye; where my Lady Parrey lay; the next
day he rode to Royston, and lodged in the monastery
there; and the next he removed to Huntingdon, and
there lodged in the Abbey; and from thence he removed to Peterborough, and there lodged also within
the Abbey, being then Palm Sunday, where he made
his abode until the Thursday in Easter week, with all
his train; whereof the most part went to board wages
in the town, having twelve carts to carry his stuff of
his own, which came from his college in Oxford, where
he had three score carts to carry such necessaries as
belonged to his buildings there. Upon Palm Sunday
he went in procession, with the monks, bearing his
palm; setting forth God's service right honourably,
with such singing men as he then had remaining with
him. And upon Maundy Thursday he made his
Maundy in our Lady's Chapel, having fifty-nine poor
men, whose feet he washed, wiped, and kissed; each
of these poor men had twelve pence in money, three
ells of canvas to make them shirts, a pair of new
shoes, a cast of bread, three red herrings, and three
white herrings, and the odd person had two shillings.
Upon Easter Day in the morning he rode to the
resurrection, and that day he went in procession in his
cardinal's vesture, with his hat and hood on his head,
and he himself sang there the high mass very devoutly;
and granted clean remission to all the hearers; and
there continued he all the holidays.

My lord continuing at Peterborough after this manner, intending to remove from thence, sent me to Sir William Fitzwilliams, a knight, which dwelt within three or four miles of Peterborough, to provide him there a lodging until Monday next following, on his journey northward.   And being with him, to whom I declared my lord's request, and he being thereof very glad, rejoiced not a little that it would please my lord to visit his house in his way ; saying, that he should be most heartiliest welcome of any man alive, the king's majesty excepted ; and that he should not need to discharge the carriage of any of his stuff for his own use during the time of his being there ; but have all things furnished ready against his coming to occupy, his own bed excepted.   Thus upon my report made to my lord at my return, he rejoiced of my message, commanding me therein to give warning to all his officers and servants to prepare themselves to remove from Peterborough upon Thursday next.   Then every man made all things in such readiness as was convenient, paying in the town for all things as they had taken of any person for their own use, for which `cause my lord caused a proclamation to be made in the town, that if any person or persons in the town or country there were offended or grieved against any of my lord's servants, that they should resort to my lord's officers of whom they should have redress, and truly answered as the case justly required.   So that, all things being furnished, my lord took his journey from Peterborough upon the Thursday in Easter week, to Master Fitz-

williams, where he was joyously received, and had
right worthy and honourable entertainment at the only
charge and expense of the said Master Fitzwilliams,
all the time of his being there.

The occasion that moved Master Fitzwilliams thus
to rejoice of my lord's being in his house was, that he
sometime being a merchant of London and sheriff
there, fell in debate with the city of London upon a
grudge between the aldermen of the bench and him,
upon a new corporation that he would erect of a new
mystery called Merchant Taylors, contrary to the
opinion of divers of the bench of aldermen of the
city, which caused him to give and surrender his
cloak, and departed from London, and inhabited
within the country ; and against the malice of all the
said aldermen and other rulers in the commonweal of
the city, my lord defended him, and retained him into
service, whom he made first his treasurer of his house,
and then after his high chamberlain ; and in conclusion, for his wisdom, gravity, port, and eloquence,
being a gentleman of a comely stature, made him one
of the king's counsel : and he so continued all his life
afterward. Therefore in consideration of all these
gratitudes received at my lord's hands, as well in his
trouble as in his preferment, was most gladdest like a
faithful friend of good remembrance to requite him with
the semblable gratuity, and right joys that he had any
occasion to minister some pleasure, such as lay then in
his power to do.

Thus my lord continued there until the Monday

next ; where lacked no good cheer of costly viands, both of wine and other goodly entertainment; so that upon the said Monday my lord departed from thence unto Stamford; where he lay all that night. And the next day he removed from thence unto Grantham, and was lodged in a gentleman's house, called Master Hall. And the next day he rode to Newark, and lodged in the castle all that night; the next day he rode to Southwell, a place of my lord's within three or four miles of Newark, where he intended to continue all that summer, as he did after.

Here I must declare to you a notable tale of communication which was done at Master Fitzwilliams before his departure from thence, between my lord and me, the which was this : Sir, my lord being in the garden at Master Fitzwilliams, walking, saying of his evensong with his chaplain, I being there giving attendance upon him, his evensong finished, he commanded his chaplain that bare up the train of his gown whilst he walked, to deliver me the same, and to go aside when he had done ; and after the chaplain was gone a good distance, he said unto me in this wise : "Ye have been late at London," quoth he. "Forsooth, my lord," quoth I, "not since that I was there to buy your liveries for your servants." "And what news was there then," quoth he ; "heard you no communication there of me ? I pray you tell me." Then perceiving that I had a good occasion to talk my mind plainly unto him, I said, "Sir, if it please your Grace, it was my chance to be at a dinner in a certain place

within the city, where I, among divers other honest
and worshipful gentlemen happed to sit, which were
for the most part of my old familiar acquaintance,
wherefore they were the more bolder to enter in communication with me, understanding that I was still
your Grace's servant ; they asked me a question, which·
I could not well assoil them."   " What was that ? "
quoth my lord.   " Forsooth, Sir," quoth I, " first they
asked me how ye did, and how ye accepted your adversity, and trouble, and the loss of your goods ; to
the which I answered, that you were in health (thanks
be to God), and took all things in good part ; and so
it seemed me, that they were all your indifferent
friends lamenting your decay, and loss of your room
and goods, doubting much that the sequel thereof
could not be good in the commonwealth.   For often
changing of such officers which be fat fed, into the
hands of such as be lean and hungry for riches, they
will sure travail by all means to get abundance, and
so the poor commons be pillaged and extorted for
greedy lucre of riches and treasure : they said that ye
were full fed, and intended now much to the advancement of the king's honour and the commonwealth.
Also they marvelled much that ye, being of so excellent a wit and high discretion, would so simply confess
yourself guilty in the premunire, wherein ye might full
well have stood in the trial of your case.   For they
understood, by the report of some of the king's learned
counsel, that your case well considered, ye had great
wrong ; to the which I could make, as me thought, no

sufficient answer, but said, ‘That I doubt not your so
doing was upon some greater consideration than my
wit could understand.’ ”   “ Is this,” quoth he, “ the
opinion of wise men ? ”   “ Yea, forsooth, my lord,”
quoth I, “ and almost of all other men.”   “ Well,
then,” quoth he, “ I see that their wisdoms perceive
not the ground of the matter that moved me so to do.
For I considered, that my enemies had brought the
matter so to pass against me, and conveyed it so, that
they made it the king’s case, and caused the king to
take the matter into his own hands and quarrel, and
after that he had upon the occasion thereof seized all
my goods and possessions into his demayns, and then
the quarrel to be his, rather than yield, or take a foil
in the law, and thereby restore to me all my goods
again, he would sooner (by the procurement of my
enemies and evil-willers) imagine my utter undoing
and destruction ; whereof the most ease therein had
been for me perpetual imprisonment.   And rather than
I would jeopard so far, or put my life in any such
hazard, yet had I most liefest to yield and confess the
matter, committing the sole sum thereof, as I did, unto
the king’s clemency and mercy, and live at large, like
a poor vicar, than to lie in prison with all the goods
and honours that I had.   And therefore it was the
most best way for me, all things considered, to do as I
have done, than to stand in trial with the king, for he
would have been loth to have been noted a wrong-
doer, and in my submission, the king, I doubt not, had
a great remorse of conscience, wherein he would rather

pity me than malign me. And also there was a continual serpentine enemy about the king that would, I
am well assured, if I had been found stiff-necked, have
called continually upon the king in his ear (I mean the
night-crow) with such a vehemency that I should with
the help of her assistance have obtained sooner the
king's indignation than his lawful favour ; and his
favour once lost (which I trust at this present I have)
would never have been by me recovered. Therefore I
thought it better for me to keep still his loving favour,
with loss of my goods and dignities, than to win my
goods and substance with the loss of his love and
princely favour, which is but only death ; *Quia indig-
natio principis mors est.* And this was the special
ground and cause that I yielded myself guilty in the
premunire ; which I perceive all men knew not,
wherein since I understand the king hath conceived a
certain prick of conscience ; who took to himself the
matter more grievous in his secret stomach than all men
knew, for he knew whether I did offend him therein
so grievously as it was made or no, to whose conscience
I do commit my cause, truth, and equity." And thus
we left the substance of all this communication ;
although we had much more talk ; yet is this sufficient
to cause you to understand as well the cause of his
confession in his offence, as also the cause of the loss
of all his goods and treasure.

Now let us return where we left, my lord being in
the castle of Newark, intending to ride to Southwell,
which was four miles from thence, took now his

journey thitherward against supper. Where he was fain for lack of reparation of the bishop's place, which appertained to the see of York, to be lodged in a prebendary's house against the said place, and there kept house until Whitsuntide next, against which time he removed into the place, newly amended and repaired, and there continued the most part of the summer, surely not without great resort of the most worshipfullest gentlemen of the country, and divers other, of whom they were most gladly entertained, and had of him the best cheer he could devise for them, whose gentle and familiar behaviour with them caused him to be greatly beloved and esteemed through the whole country.

He kept a noble house, and plenty of both meat and drink for all comers, both for rich and poor, and much alms given at his gates. He used much charity and pity among his poor tenants and other ; although the fame thereof was no pleasant sound in the ears of his enemies, and of such as bare him no good will, howbeit the common people will report as they find cause ; for he was much more familiar among all persons than he was accustomed, and most gladdest when he had an occasion to do them good. He made many agreements and concords between gentleman and gentleman, and between some gentlemen and their wives that had been long asunder, and in great trouble, and divers other agreements between other persons ; making great assemblies for the same purpose, and feasting of them, not sparing for any costs, where he might make a peace and amity ; which purchased him much love and friendship in the country.

It chanced that upon Corpus Christi eve, after supper, my lord commanded me to prepare all things for him in a readiness against the next day, for he intended to sing high mass in the minster that day ; and I, not forgetting his commandments, gave like warning to all his officers of his house, and other of my fellows, to foresee that all things appertaining to their rooms were fully furnished to my lord's honour. This done I went to my bed, where I was scantly asleep and warm, but that one of the porters came to my chamber door, calling upon me, and said, there was two gentlemen at the gate that would gladly speak with my lord from the king. With that I arose up and went incontinent unto the gate with the porter, demanding what they were that so fain would come in. They said unto me, that there was Master Brereton, one of the gentlemen of the king's privy chamber, and Master Wrotherly, who were come from the king empost, to speak with my lord. Then having understanding what they were, I caused the porter to let them in. And after their entry they desired me to speak with my lord without delay, for they might not tarry ; at whose request I repaired to my lord's chamber, and waked him, who was asleep. But when he heard me speak, he demanded of me what I would have. " Sir," quoth I, " there be beneath in the porter's lodge, Master Brereton, gentleman of the king's privy chamber, and Master Wrotherly, come from the king to speak with you : they will not tarry ; therefore they beseech your Grace to speak with you out of hand." " Well then," quoth my lord, " bid them come up into my dining chamber, and I will prepare myself to come to them." Then I resorted to them again, and showed them that my lord desired them to come up unto him, and he would talk with them, with a right good will. · They thanked me, and went with me unto my lord, and as soon as they perceived him, being in his night apparel, did to him humble reverence ; whom he took by the hands, demanding of them, how the king his sovereign lord did. " Sir," said they, " right well in health and merry, thanks be unto our Lord. Sir," quoth they, " we must desire you to talk with you apart." " With a right good will," quoth my lord, who drew them aside into a great window, and there talked with them secretly ; and after long talk they took out of a male a certain coffer covered with green velvet, and bound with bars of silver and gilt, with a lock of the same, having a key which was gilt, with the which they opened the same chest ; out of the which they took a certain instrument or writing, containing more than one skin of parchment, having many great seals hanging at it, whereunto they put more wax for my lord's seal; the which my lord sealed with his own seal, and subscribed his name to the same ; and that done they would needs depart, and (forasmuch as it was after midnight) my lord desired them to tarry, and

take a bed.   They thanked him, and said they might
in no wise tarry, for they would with all speed to the
Earl of Shrewsbury's directly without let, because they
would be there or ever he stirred in the morning.   And
my lord, perceiving their hasty speed, caused them to
eat such cold meat as there was in store within the
house, and to drink a cup or two of wine.   And that
done, he gave each of them four old sovereigns of gold,
desiring them to take it *in gree*, saying, that if he had
been of greater ability, their reward should have been
better ; and so taking their leave they departed.   And
after they were departed, as I heard say, they were
not contented with their reward.   Indeed they were
not none of his indifferent friends, which caused them
to accept it so disdainously.   Howbeit, if they knew
what little store of money he had at that present, they
would I am sure, being but his indifferent friends,
have given him hearty thanks : but nothing is more
lost or cast away than is such things which be given
to such ingrate persons.   My lord went again to bed ;
and yet, all his watch and disturbance that he had
that night notwithstanding, he sang high mass the
next day as he appointed before.   There was none in
all his house besides myself and the porter that knew
of the coming or going of these two gentlemen ; and
yet there lay within the house many worshipful
strangers.

    After this sort and manner my lord continued at
Southwell, until the latter end of grease time ; at which
time he intended to remove to Scroby, which was

another house of the bishoprick of York. And against the day of his removing, he caused all his officers to prepare, as well for provision to be made for him there, as also for carriage of his stuff, and other matters concerning his estate. His removing and intent was not so secret, but that it was known abroad in the country; which was lamentable to all his neighbours about Southwell, and as it was lamentable unto them, so was it as much joy to his neighbours about Scroby.

Against the day of his removing divers knights and other gentlemen of worship in the country came to him to Southwell, intending to accompany and attend upon him in that journey the next day, and to conduct him through the forest unto Scroby. But he being of their purpose advertised, how they did intend to have lodged a great stag or twain for him by the way, purposely to show him all the pleasure and disport they could devise, and having, as I said, thereof intelligence, was very loth to receive any such honour and disport at their hands, not knowing how the king would take it; and being well assured that his enemies would rejoice much to understand that he would take upon him any such presumption, whereby they might find an occasion to inform the king how sumptuous and pleasant he was, notwithstanding his adversity and overthrow, and so to bring the king into a wrong opinion of him, and caused small hope of reconcilement, but rather that he sought a mean to obtain the favour of the country to withstand the king's proceedings, with divers such imaginations, wherein he might rather sooner catch displeasure than favour and honour. And also he was loth to make the worshipful gentlemen privy to this his imagination, lest peradventure they should conceive some toy or fantasy in their heads by means thereof, and so to eschew their accustomed access, and absent themselves from him, which should be as much to his grief as the other was to his comfort. Therefore he devised this mean way, as hereafter followeth, which should rather be taken for a laughing disport than otherwise: first he called me unto him secretly at night, going to his rest, and commanded me in anywise most secretly that night to cause six or seven horses, besides his mule for his own person, to be made ready by the break of the day for him and such persons as he appointed to ride with him to an Abbey called Welbeck, where he intended to lodge by the way to Scroby, willing me to be also in a readiness to ride with him, and to call him so early that he might be on horseback, after he had heard mass, by the breaking of the day. Sir, what will you more? All things being accomplished according to his commandment, and the same finished and done, he, with a small number before appointed, mounted upon his mule, setting forth by the breaking of the day towards Welbeck, which is about sixteen miles from thence; whither my lord and we came before six of the clock in the morning, and so went straight to his bed, leaving all the gentlemen strangers in their beds at Southwell, nothing privy of my lord's

secret departure, who expected his uprising until it was
eight of the clock.   But after it was known to them
and to all the rest there remaining behind him, then
every man went to horseback, galloping after, supposing to overtake him.   But he was at his rest in
Welbeck or ever they rose out of their beds in Southwell, and so their chief hunting and coursing of the
great stag was disappointed and dashed.   But at their
thither resort to my lord, sitting at dinner, the matter
was jested, and laughed out merrily, and all the matter
well taken.

My lord the next day removed from thence, to
whom resorted divers gentlemen of my lord the Earl
of Shrewsbury's servants, to desire my lord, in their
master's name, to hunt in a park of the earl's called
Worksop Park, the which was within a mile of
Welbeck, and the very best and next way for my lord
to travel through on his journey, where much plenty
of game was laid in a readiness to show him pleasure.
Howbeit he thanked my lord their master for his
gentleness, and them for their pains; saying that he
was no meet man for any such pastime, being a man
otherwise disposed, such pastimes and pleasures were
meet for such noblemen as delight therein.   Nevertheless he could do no less than to account my Lord of
Shrewsbury to be much his friend, in whom he found
such gentleness and nobleness in his honourable offer,
to whom he rendered his most lowly thanks.   But in
no wise they could entreat him to hunt.   Although the
worshipful gentlemen being in his company provoked

him all that they could do thereto, yet he would not
consent, desiring them to be contented; saying that he
came not into the country, to frequent or follow any
such pleasures or pastimes, but only to attend to a
greater care that he had in hand, which was his duty,
study, and pleasure. And with such reasons and
persuasions he pacified them for that time. Howbeit
yet as he rode through the park, both my Lord of
Shrewsbury's servants, and also the foresaid gentlemen
moved him once again, before whom the deer lay very
fair for all pleasant hunting and coursing. But it
would not be; but he made as much speed to ride
through the park as he could. And at the issue out
of the park he called the earl's gentlemen and the
keepers unto him, desiring them to have him commended to my lord their master, thanking him for his
most honourable offer and good will, trusting shortly to
visit him at his own house : and gave the keepers
forty shillings for their pains and diligence who conducted him through the park. And so rode to another
abbey called Rufford Abbey, to dinner ; and after he
rode to Blythe Abbey, where he lay all night. And
the next day he came to Scroby, where he continued
until after Michaelmas, ministering many deeds of
charity. Most commonly every Sunday (if the weather
did serve) he would travel unto some parish church
thereabout, and there would say his divine service, and
either hear or say mass himself, causing some one of
his chaplains to preach unto the people. And that
done, he would dine in some honest house of that

town, where should be distributed to the poor a great alms, as well of meat and drink as of money to supply the want of sufficient meat, if the number of the poor did so exceed of necessity.   And thus with other good deeds practising and exercising during his abode there at Scroby, as making of love-days and agreements between party and party, being then at variance, he daily frequented himself there about such business and deeds of honest charity.

Then about the feast of St. Michael next ensuing my lord took his journey towards Cawood Castle, the which is within seven miles of York; and passing thither he lay two nights and a day at St. Oswald's Abbey, where he himself confirmed children in the church, from eight of the clock in the morning until twelve of the clock at noon.   And making a short dinner, resorted again to the church at one of the clock, and there began again to confirm more children until four of the clock, where he was at the last constrained for weariness to sit down in a chair, the number of the children was such.   That done, he said his evensong, and then went to supper, and rested him there all that night.   And the next morning he applied himself to depart towards Cawood; and or ever he departed, he confirmed almost a hundred children more ; and then rode on his journey.   And by the way there were assembled at a stone cross standing upon a green, within a quarter of a mile of Ferrybridge, about the number of two hundred children, to confirm ; where he alighted, and never removed his foot until he had

confirmed them all ; and then took his mule again and
rode to Cawood, where he lay long after with much
honour and love of the country, both of the worshipful
and of the simple, exercising himself in good deeds of
charity, and kept there an honourable and plentiful
house for all comers ; and also built and repaired the
castle, which was then greatly decayed, having a great
multitude of artificers and labourers, above the number
of three hundred persons, daily in wages.

And lying there, he had intelligence by the gentlemen of the country, that used to repair unto him, that
there was sprung a great variance and deadly hate
between Sir Richard Tempest and Mr. Brian Hastings,
then being but a squire, but after made knight, between
whom was like to ensue great murder, unless some
good mean might be found to redress the inconvenience
that was most likeliest to ensue. My lord being
thereof advertised, lamenting the case, made such
means by his wisdom and letters, with other persuasions, that these two gentlemen were content to resort
to my lord to Cawood, and there to abide his order,
high and low. Then was there a day appointed of
their assembly before my lord, at which day they came
not without great number on each part. Wherefore
against that day, my lord had required many worshipful gentlemen to be there present, to assist him with
their wisdoms to appease these two worthy gentlemen,
being at deadly feud. And to see the king's peace kept,
commanding no more of their number to enter into the
castle with these two gentlemen than six persons of

each of their menial servants, and all the rest to remain
without in the town, or where they listed to repair. And
my lord himself issuing out of the gates, calling the
number of both parties before him, straightly charging
them most earnestly to observe and keep the king's
peace, in the king's name, upon their perils, without
either bragging or quarrelling either with other; and
caused them to have both beer and wine sent them
into the town; and then returned again into the
castle, being about nine of the clock. And because he
would have these gentlemen to dine with him at his
own table, thought it good in avoiding of further inconvenience to appease their rancour before. Whereupon he called them into his chapel; and there, with
the assistance of the other gentlemen, he fell into
communication with the matter, declaring unto them
the dangers and mischiefs that through their wilfulness
and folly were most likeliest to ensue; with divers
other good exhortations. Notwithstanding, the parties
laying and alleging many things for their defence,
sometime adding each to other stout and despiteful
words of defiance, the which my lord and the other
gentlemen had much ado to qualify, their malice was
so great. Howbeit, at length, with long continuance
and wise arguments, and deep persuasions made by my
lord, they were agreed, and finally accorded about four
of the clock at afternoon; and so made them friends.
And, as it seemed, they both rejoiced, and were right
well contented therewith, to the great comfort of all
the other worshipful gentlemen, causing them to shake

hands, and to go arm in arm to dinner; and so went to dinner, though it was very late to dine, yet notwithstanding they dined together with the other gentlemen at my lord's table, where they drank lovingly each to other, with countenance of great amity. After dinner my lord caused them to discharge their routs and assembly that remained in the town, and to retain with them no more servants than they were accustomed most commonly to ride with. And that done, these gentlemen, fulfilling his commandment, tarried at Cawood, and lay there all night; whom my lord entertained in such sort that they accepted his noble heart in great worthiness and friendship, trusting to have of him a special jewel in their country : having him in great estimation and favour, as it appeared afterward by their behaviour and demeanour towards him.

It is not to be doubted but that the worshipful persons, as doctors and prebendaries of the close of York, would and did resort unto him according to their duties, as unto their father and patron of their spiritual dignities being at his first coming into the country, their church of York being within seven miles. Wherefore ye shall understand that Doctor Hickden, dean of the church of York, with the treasurer, and divers other head officers of the same, repaired to my lord, welcoming him most joyously into the country ; saying, that it was to them no small comfort to see him among them, as their chief head, which hath been so long absent from them, being all that while like fatherless children comfortless, trusting shortly to see

him among them in his own church. "It is," quoth
he, "the especial cause of my travel into this country,
not only to be among you for a time, but also to spend
my life with you as a very father, and as a mutual
brother." "Sir, then," quoth they, "ye must understand that the ordinary rules of our church hath been
of an ancient custom, whereof although ye be head and
chief governor, yet be ye not so well acquainted with
them as we be. Therefore, we shall under the supportation of your Grace, declare some part thereof to you,
as well of our ancient customs as of the laws and usage
of the same. Therefore ye shall understand that where
ye do intend to repair unto us, the old law and custom
of our church hath been, that the archbishop being our
chief head and pastor, as your Grace now be, might nor
ought not to come above the choir door, nor have any
stall in the choir, until he by due order were there
stalled. For, if ye should happen to die before your
stallation, ye shall not be buried above in the choir,
but in the body of the same church beneath. Therefore we shall, *una voce*, require your Grace in the name
of all other our brethren, that ye would vouchsafe to
do herein as your noble predecessors and honourable
fathers hath done; and that ye will not infringe or
violate any of our laudable ordinances and constitutions
of our church, to the observance and preservation
whereof we be obliged, by virtue of an oath at our
first admittance, to see them observed and fulfilled to
the uttermost of our powers, with divers other matters
remaining of record in our treasury house among other

things." "Those records," quoth my lord, "would I gladly see; and these seen and digested, I shall then show you further of my mind." And thus of this matter they ceased communication, and passed forth in other matters; so that my lord assigned them a day to bring in their records. At which day they brought with them their register book of records, wherein was written their constitutions and ancient rules, whereunto all the fathers and ministers of the church of York were most chiefly bound, both to see it done and performed, and also to perform and observe the same themselves. And when my lord had seen, read and considered the effect of their records, and debated with them substantially therein, he determined to be stalled there in the minster the next Monday after All-hallown day. Against which day there was made necessary preparation for the furniture thereof, but not in so sumptuous a wise as his predecessors did before him; nor yet in such a sort as the common fame was blown abroad of him to his great slander, and to the reporters much more dishonesty, to forge such lies and blasphemous reports, wherein there is nothing more untrue. The truth whereof I perfectly know, for I was made privy to the same, and sent to York to foresee all things, and to prepare according for the same, which should have been much more mean and base than all other of his predecessors heretofore hath done.

It came so to pass, that upon All-hallown day, one of the head officers of the church, which should, by virtue of his office, have most doings in this stallation,

was to dine with my lord at Cawood; and sitting at
dinner they fell in communication of the order of his
stallation, who said to my lord that he ought to go
upon cloth from St. James's chapel (standing without
the gates of the city of York) unto the minster, the
which should be distributed among the poor. My
lord, hearing this, made answer to the same in this
wise. " Although," quoth he, " that our predecessors
went upon cloth right sumptuously, we do intend, God
willing, to go afoot from thence without any such glory,
in the vamps of our hosen. For I take God to be my
very judge that I 'presume not to go thither for any
triumph or vain-glory, but only to fulfil the observance and rules of the church, to the which, as ye say,
I am bound. And therefore I shall desire you all to
hold you contented with my simplicity, and also I
command all my servants to go as humbly without any
other sumptuous apparel than they be constantly used,
and that is comely and decent to wear. For I do
assure you, I do intend to come to York upon Sunday
at night, and lodge there in the dean's house, and upon
Monday to be stalled; and there to make a dinner for
you of the close, and for other worshipful gentlemen
that shall chance to come to me at that time; and the
next day to dine with the mayor, and so return home
again to Cawood that night, and thus to finish the
same, whereby I may at all times resort to York Minster
without other scrupulosity or offence to any of you."

This day could not be unknown to all the country,
but that some must needs have knowledge thereof,

whereby that notice was given unto the gentlemen of the country, and they being thereof as well advertised as abbots, priors, and others, of the day of this solemnization, sent in such provision of dainty victuals that it is almost incredible ; wherefore I omit to declare unto you the certainty thereof. As of great and fat beeves and muttons, wildfowl, and venison, both red and fallow, and divers other dainty meats, such as the time of the year did serve, sufficient to furnish a great and a sumptuous feast, all which things were unknown to my lord : forasmuch as he being prevented and disappointed of his reasonable purposed intent, because he was arrested, as ye shall hear hereafter ; so that the most part of this provision was sent to York that same day that he was arrested, and the next day following ; for his arrest was kept as close and secret from the country as it could be, because they doubted the people, which had him in great love and estimation for his accustomed charity and liberality used daily among them, with familiar gesture and countenance, which be the very means to allure the love and hearts of the people in the north parts.

Or ever I wade any further in this matter, I do intend to declare unto you what chanced him before this his last trouble at Cawood, as a sign or token given by God what should follow of his end, or of trouble which did shortly ensue, the sequel whereof was of no man then present either premeditate or imagined. Therefore, forasmuch as it is a notable thing to be considered, I will (God willing) declare~ it as truly as it chanced according to my simple remembrance, at the which I myself was present.

My lord's accustomed enemies in the court about the king had now my lord in more doubt than they had before his fall, considering the continual favour that the king bare him, thought that at length the king might call him home again; and if he so did, they supposed that he would rather imagine against them than to remit or forget their cruelty, which they most unjustly imagined against him. Wherefore they compassed in their heads that they would either by some means dispatch him by some sinister accusation of treason, or to bring him into the king's indignation by some other ways. This was their daily imagination and study, having as many spials, and as many eyes to attend upon his doings as the poets feigned Argus to have; so that he could neither work nor do any thing, but that his enemies had knowledge thereof shortly after. Now at the last, they espied a time wherein they caught an occasion to bring their purpose to pass, thinking thereby to have of him a great advantage; for the matter being once disclosed unto the king, in such a vehemency as they purposed, they thought the king would be moved against him with great displeasure. And that by them executed and done, the king, upon their information, thought it good that he should come up to stand to his trial; which they liked nothing at all; notwithstanding he was sent for after this sort. First, they devised that he should come up upon arrest in ward, which they knew right

well would so sore grieve him that he might be the
weaker to come into the king's presence to make answer.
Wherefore they sent Sir Walter Walshe, knight, one of
the gentlemen of the king's privy chamber, down into
the country unto the Earl of Northumberland (who
was brought up in my lord's house), and they twain
being in commission jointly to arrest my lord of hault
treason. This conclusion fully resolved, they caused
Master Walshe to prepare himself to this journey with
this commission, and certain instructions annexed to
the same ; who made him ready to ride, and took his
horse at the court gate about one of the clock at noon,
upon All-hallown day, towards the north. Now am I
come to the place where I will declare the thing that
I promised you before of a certain token of my lord's
trouble ; which was this.

My lord sitting at dinner upon All-hallown day, in
Cawood Castle, having at his board's end divers of his
most worthiest chaplains, sitting at dinner to keep him
company, for lack of strangers, ye shall understand,
that my lord's great cross of silver accustomably stood
in the corner, at the table's end, leaning against the
tappet or hanging of the chamber. And when the
table's end was taken up, and a convenient time for
them to arise ; in arising from the table, one Doctor
Augustine, physician, being a Venetian born, having a
boisterous‑gown of black velvet upon him, as he would
have come out at the table's end, his gown overthrew
the cross that stood there in the corner, and the cross
trailing down along the tappet, it chanced to fall upon

Doctor Bonner's head, who stood among others by the
tappet, making of curtsy to my lord, and with one of
the points of the cross razed his head a little, that the
blood ran down.   The company standing there were
greatly astonied with the chance.   My lord sitting in
his chair, looking upon them, perceiving the chance,
demanded of me being next him, what the matter
meant of their sudden abashment.   I showed him how
the cross fell upon Doctor Bonner's head.   "Hath it,"
quoth he, "drawn any blood?"   "Yea forsooth, my
lord," quoth I, "as it seemeth me."   With that he
cast down his head, looking very soberly upon me a
good while without any word speaking; at the last
quoth he (shaking of his head), "*malum omen;*" and
therewith said grace, and rose from the table, and went
into his bedchamber, there lamenting, making his
prayers.   Now mark the signification, how my lord
expounded this matter unto me afterward at Pomfret
Abbey.   First, ye shall understand, that the cross,
which belonged to the dignity of York, he understood
to be himself; and Augustine, that overthrew the
cross, he understood to be he that should accuse him,
by means whereof he should be overthrown.   The
falling upon Master Bonner's head, who was master of
my lord's faculties and spiritual jurisdictions, who was
damnified by the overthrowing of the cross by the
physician, and the drawing of blood betokened death,
which shortly after came to pass; about the very same
time of the day of this mischance, Master Walshe
took his horse at the court gate, as nigh as it could be

judged. And thus my lord took it for a very sign or token of that which after ensued, if the circumstance be equally considered and noted, although no man was there present at that time that had any knowledge of Master Walshe's coming down, or what should follow. Wherefore, as it was supposed, that God showed him more secret knowledge of his latter days and end of his trouble than all men supposed; which appeared right well by divers talks that he had with me at divers times of his last end. And now that I have declared unto you the effect of this prodigy and sign, I will return again to my matter.

The time drawing nigh of his stallation; sitting at dinner, upon the Friday next before Monday on the which he intended to be stalled at York, the Earl of Northumberland and Master Walshe, with a great company of gentlemen, as well of the earl's servants as of the country, which he had gathered together to accompany him in the king's name, not knowing to what purpose or what intent, came into the hall at Cawood, the officers sitting at dinner, and my lord not fully dined, but being at his fruits, nothing knowing of the earl's being in his hall. The first thing that the earl did, after he came into the castle, he commanded the porter to deliver him the keys of the gates, who would in no wise deliver him the keys, although he were very roughly commanded in the king's name, to deliver them to one of the earl's servants. Saying unto the earl, " Sir, ye do intend to deliver them to one of your servants to keep them

and the gates, and to plant another in my room; I
know no cause why ye should so do, and this I assure
you that you have no one servant, but that I am as
able to keep them as he, to what purpose soever it be.
And also, the keys were delivered me by my lord my
master, with a charge both by oath, and by other precepts and commandments. Therefore I beseech your
lordship to pardon me, though I refuse your commandment. For whatsoever ye shall command me to do
that belongeth to my office, I shall do it with a right
good will as justly as any other of your servants."
With that quoth the gentlemen there present unto the
earl, hearing him speak so stoutly like a man, and with
so good reason : " Sir," quoth they, " he is a good fellow,
and speaketh like a faithful servant to his master ; and
like an honest man : therefore give him your charge,
and let him keep still the gates ; who, we doubt not,
will be obedient to your lordship's commandment."
" Well then," quoth the earl, " hold him a book," and
commanded him to lay his hand upon the book,
whereat the porter made some doubt, but being persuaded by the gentlemen there present, was contented,
and laid his hand upon the book, to whom, quoth the
earl, "Thou shalt swear, to keep well and truly these
gates to the king our sovereign lord's use, and to do all
such things as we shall command thee in the king's
name, being his highness's commissioners, and as it shall
seem to us at all times good, as long as we shall be
here in this castle ; and that ye shall not let in nor
out at these gates, but such as ye shall be commanded

by us, from time to time," and upon this oath he received the keys at the earl's and Master Walshe's hands.

Of all these doings knew my lord nothing ; for they
stopped the stairs that went up to my lord's chamber
where he sat, so that no man could pass up again that
was come down. At the last one of my lord's servants
chanced to look down into the hall at a loop that was
upon the stairs, and returned to my lord, and showed
him that my Lord of Northumberland was in the hall ;
whereat my lord marvelled, and would not believe him
at the first ; but commanded a gentleman, being his
gentleman usher, to go down and bring him perfect
word. Who going down the stairs, looking down at
the loop, where he saw the earl, who then returned to
my lord, and showed him that it was very he. " Then,"
quoth my lord, " I am sorry that we have dined, for I
fear that our officers be not stored of any plenty of
good fish, to make him such honourable cheer as to his
estate is convenient, notwithstanding he shall have such
as we have, with a right good will and loving heart.
Let the table be standing still, and we will go down and
meet him, and bring him up ; and then he shall see
how far forth we be at our dinner." With that he
put the table from him, and rose up ; going down he
encountered the earl upon the midst of the stairs,
coming up, with all his men about him. And as soon
as my lord espied the earl, he put off his cap, and said
to him, " My lord, ye be most heartily welcome ; (and
therewith they embraced each other). Although, my
lord," quoth he, " that I have often desired, and wished

in my heart to see you in my house, yet if ye had loved
me as I do you, ye would have sent me word before of
your coming, to the intent that I might have received
you according to your honour and mine. Notwithstanding ye shall have such cheer as I am able to make
you, with a right good will ; trusting that ye will accept
the same of me as of your very old and loving friend,
hoping hereafter to see you oftener, when I shall be
more able and better provided to receive you with better
fare." And then my lord took the Earl of Northumberland by the hand, and led him up into the chamber ;
whom followed all the earl's servants ; where the table
stood in the state that my lord left it when he rose,
saying unto the earl, " Sir, now ye may perceive how far
forth we were at our dinner." Then my lord led the earl
to the fire, saying, " My lord, ye shall go into my bedchamber, where is a good fire made for you, and there
ye may shift your apparel until your chamber be made
ready. Therefore let your male be brought up : and
or ever I go, I pray you give me leave to take these
gentlemen, your servants, by the hands." And when
he had taken them all by the hands, he returned to
the earl, and said, " Ah, my lord, I perceive well that
ye have observed my old precepts and instructions
which I gave you, when you were abiding with me in
your youth, which was, to cherish your father's old
servants, whereof I see here present with you a great
number. Surely, my lord, ye do therein very well and
nobly, and like a wise gentleman. For these be they
that will not only serve and love you, but they will

also live and die with you, and be true and faithful
servants to you, and glad to see you prosper in honour ;
the which I beseech God to send you, with long life."
This said, he took the earl by the hand, and led him
into his bedchamber. And they being there all alone,
save only I, that kept the door, according to my duty,
being gentleman usher ; these two lords standing at a
window by the chimney, in my lord's bedchamber, the
earl trembling said, with a very faint and soft voice,
unto my lord (laying his hand upon his arm), "My
lord, I arrest you of high treason." With which
words my lord was marvellously astonied, standing
both still a long space without any further words. But
at the last, quoth my lord, "What moveth you, or by
what authority do you this ?" "Forsooth, my lord,"
quoth the earl, "I have a commission to warrant me
and my doing." "Where is your commission ?" quoth
my lord ; "let me see it." "Nay, Sir, that you may
not," quoth the earl. "Well, then," quoth my lord,
"I will not obey your arrest : for there hath been
between some of your predecessors and mine great
contentions and debate grown upon an ancient grudge,
which may succeed in you, with like inconvenience, as
it hath done heretofore. Therefore, unless I see your
authority and commission, I will not obey you." Even
as they were debating this matter between them in the
chamber, so busy was Master Walshe in arresting of
Doctor Augustine, the physician, at the door within
the portal, whom I heard say unto him, "Go in then,
traitor, or I shall make thee." And with that, I

opened the portal door, and the same being opened, Master Walshe thrust Doctor Augustine in before him with violence. These matters on both the sides astonished me very sore, musing what all this should mean ; until at the last, Master Walshe, being entered the chamber, began to pluck off his hood, the which he had made him with a coat of the same cloth, of cotton, to the intent he would not be known. And after he had plucked it off, he kneeled down to my lord, to whom my lord spake first, commanding him to stand up, saying thus, " Sir, here my Lord of Northumberland hath arrested me of treason, but by what authority or commission he showeth me not ; but saith he hath one. If ye be privy thereto, or be joined with him therein, I pray you show me." "Indeed, my lord," quoth Master Walshe, " if it please your Grace. it is true that he hath one." " Well, then," said my lord, " I pray you let me see it." " Sir, I beseech your Grace hold us excused," quoth Master Walshe, " there is annexed unto our commission a schedule with certain instructions which ye may in no wise be privy unto." " Why," quoth my lord, " be your instructions such that I may not see them ? Peradventure, if I might be privy to them, I could the better help you to perform them. It is not unknown unto you both I am assured, but I have been privy and of counsel in as weighty matters as this is, for I doubt not for my part, but I shall prove and clear myself to be a true man, against the expectation of all my cruel enemies. I have an understanding whereupon all this matter groweth. Well, there is no more to do. I trow, gentleman, ye be one of the king's privy chamber; your name, I suppose, is Walshe; I am content to yield unto you, but not to my Lord of Northumberland, without I see his commission. And also you are a sufficient commissioner yourself in that behalf, inasmuch as ye be one of the king's privy chamber; for the worst person there is a sufficient warrant to arrest the greatest peer of this realm, by the king's only commandment, without any commission. Therefore I am ready to be ordered and disposed at your will, put therefore the king's commission and your authority in execution, in God's name, and spare not, and I will obey the king's will and pleasure. For I fear more the cruelty of my unnatural enemies, than I do my truth and allegiance; wherein, I take God to witness, I never offended the king's majesty in word or deed; and therein I dare stand face to face with any man alive, having indifferency, without partiality."

Then came my Lord of Northumberland unto me, standing at the portal door, and commanded me to avoid the chamber: and being loth to depart from my master, I stood still, and would not remove; to whom he spake again, and said, "There is no remedy, ye must needs depart." With that I looked upon my lord (as who sayeth, shall I go?), upon whom my lord looked very heavily, and shook at me his head. Perceiving by his countenance it booted me not to abide, and so I departed the chamber, and went into the next chamber, where abode many gentlemen of

my fellows, and other, to learn of me some news of
the matter within ; to whom I made report what I saw
and heard; which was to them great heaviness to
hear.

Then the earl called divers gentlemen into the
chamber, which were for the most part his own
servants ; and after the earl and Master Walshe had
taken the keys of all my lord's coffers from him, they
gave the charge and custody of my lord's person unto
these gentlemen. And then they departed, and went .
about the house to set all things in order that night
against the next morning, intending then to depart
from thence (being Saturday) with my lord ; the which
they deferred until Sunday, because all things could
not be brought to pass as they would have it. They
went busily about to convey Doctor Augustine away to
Londonward, with as much speed as they could, sending with him divers honest persons to conduct him,
who was tied under the horse's belly. And this done,
when it was night, the commissioners assigned two
grooms of my lord's to attend upon him in his chamber
that night where they lay ; and the most part of the
rest of the earl's gentlemen and servants watched in
the next chamber and about the house continually until
the morrow, and the porter kept the gates, so that no
man could go in or out until the next morning. At
which time my lord rose up, supposing that he
should have departed that day, howbeit he was kept
close secretly in his chamber, expecting continually
his departure from thence. Then the earl sent for me

into his own chamber, and being there he commanded me to go in to my lord, and there to give attendance upon him, and charged me upon an oath that I should observe certain articles. And going away from him, toward my lord, I met with Master Walshe in the court, who called me unto him, and led me into his chamber, and there showed me that the king's highness bare towards me his princely favour, for my diligent and true service that I daily ministered towards my lord and master. "Wherefore," quoth he, "the king's pleasure is, that ye shall be about your master as most chiefest person, in whom his highness putteth great confidence and assured trust; whose pleasure is therefore, that ye shall be sworn unto his majesty to observe certain articles, in writing, the which I will deliver you." "Sir," quoth I, "my Lord of Northumberland hath already sworn me to divers articles." "Yea," quoth he, "but my lord could not deliver you the articles in writing, as I am commanded specially to do. Therefore, I deliver you this bill with these articles, the which ye shall be sworn to fulfil." "Sir," then quoth I, "I pray you to give me leave to peruse them, or ever I be sworn, to see if I be able to perform them." "With a right good will," quoth he. And when I had perused them, and understood that they were but reasonable and tolerable, I answered, that I was contented to obey the king's pleasure, and to be sworn to the performance of them. And so he gave me a new oath: and then I resorted to my lord, where he was in his chamber sitting in a chair, the tables being covered for him ready to go to dinner. But as soon as he perceived me coming in, he fell into such a woful lamentation, with such rueful terms and watery eyes, that it would have caused the flintiest heart to have relented and burst for sorrow. And as I and other could, we comforted him ; but it would not be. " For," quoth he, " now that I see this gentle- man (meaning me) how faithful, how diligent, and how painful since the beginning of my trouble he hath served me, abandoning his own country, his wife, and children ; his house and family, his rest and quiet- ness, only to serve me, and remembering with myself that I have nothing to reward him for his honest merits, grieveth me not a little. And also the sight of him putteth me in remembrance of the number of my faithful servants, that I have here remaining with me in this house ; whom I did intend to have preferred and advanced, to the best of my power, from time to time, as occasion should serve. But now, alas ! I am prevented, and have nothing left me here to reward them ; for all is deprived me, and I am left here their desolate and miserable master, bare and wretched, with- out help or succour, but of God alone. Howbeit," quoth he to me (calling me by my name), " I am a true man, and therefore ye shall never receive shame of me for your service." I, perceiving his heaviness and lamentable words, said thus unto him : " My lord, I nothing mistrust your truth : and for the same I dare and will be sworn before the king's person and his honourable council. Wherefore (kneeling upon my knees before him, I said), my lord, comfort yourself, and be of good cheer. The malice of your uncharitable enemies, nor their untruth, shall never prevail against your truth and faithfulness, for I doubt not but coming to your answer, my hope is such, that ye shall so acquit and clear yourself of all their surmised and feigned accusations, that it shall be to the king's contentation, and much to your advancement and restitution of your former dignity and estate." "Yea," quoth he, "if I may come to mine answer, I fear no man alive; for he liveth not upon the earth that shall look upon this face (pointing to his own face), shall be able to accuse me of any untruth; and that knoweth mine enemies full well, which will be an occasion that I shall not have indifferent justice, but they will rather seek some other sinister ways to destroy me." "Sir," quoth I, "ye need not therein doubt, the king being so much your good lord, as he hath always showed himself to be, in all your troubles." With that came up my lord's meat; and so we left our communication; I gave him water, and sat him down to dinner; with whom sat divers of the earl's gentlemen, notwithstanding my lord did eat very little meat, but would many times burst out suddenly in tears, with the most sorrowfullest words that hath been heard of any woful creature. And at the last he fetched a great sigh from the bottom of his heart, saying these words of Scripture, "*O constantia Martirum laudabilis! O charitas inextinguibilis! O paciencia invincibilis, quæ licet inter pressuras persequentium visa sit despicabilis, inve-*

nictur in laudem et gloriam ac honorem in tempore tribulationis." And thus passed he forth his dinner in great lamentation and heaviness, who was more fed and moistened with sorrow and tears than with either pleasant meats or delicate drinks. I suppose there was not a dry eye among all the gentlemen sitting at the table with him. And when the table was taken up, it was showed my lord, that he could not remove that night (who expected none other all that day), quoth he, " Even when it shall seem my Lord of Northumberland good."

The next day, being Sunday, my lord prepared himself to ride when he should be commanded; and after dinner, by that time that the earl had appointed all things in good order within the castle, it drew fast to night. There was assigned to attend upon him five of us, his own servants, and no more; that is to say I, one chaplain, his barber, and two grooms of his chamber, and when he should go down the stairs out of the great chamber, my lord demanded for the rest of his servants; the earl answered, that they were not far; the which he had inclosed within the chapel, because they should not disquiet his departure. " Sir, I pray you," quoth my lord, " let me see them or ever I depart, or else I will never go out of this house." " Alack, my lord," quoth the earl, " they should trouble you; therefore I beseech you to content yourself." " Well," quoth my lord, " then will I not depart out of this house, but I will see them, and take my leave of them in this chamber." And his servants being inclosed in the chapel, having understanding of my lord's departing away, and that they should not see him before his departure, began to grudge, and to make such a rueful noise, that the commissioners doubted some tumult or inconvenience to arise by reason thereof, thought it good to let them pass out to my lord, and that done they came to him into the great chamber where he was, and there they kneeled down before him; among whom was not one dry eye, but pitifully lamented their master's fall and trouble. To whom my lord gave comfortable words and worthy praises for their diligent faithfulness and honest truth towards him, assuring them, that what chance soever should happen unto him, that he was a true man and a just to his sovereign lord. And thus with a lamentable manner, shaking each of them by the hands, was fain to depart, the night drew so fast upon them.

My lord's mule and our horses were ready brought into the inner court; where we mounted, and coming to the gate which was shut, the porter opened the same to let us pass, where was ready attending a great number of gentlemen with their servants, such as the earl assigned to conduct and attend upon his person that night to Pomfret, and so forth, as ye shall hear hereafter. But to tell you of the number of people of the country that were assembled at the gates which lamented his departing was wondrous, which was about the number of three thousand persons; who at the opening of the gates, after they had a sight of his person, cried all with a loud voice, "God save your

II

Grace, God save your Grace! The foul evil take all them that hath thus taken you from us! we pray God that a very vengeance may light upon them!" Thus they ran crying after him through the town of Cawood, they loved him so well. For surely they had a great loss of him, both the poor and the rich: for the poor had of him great relief; and the rich lacked his counsel in any business that they had to do, which caused him to have such love among them in the country.

Then rode he with his conductors towards Pomfret; and by the way as he rode, he asked me if I had any familiar acquaintance among the gentlemen that rode with him. "Yea, Sir," said I, "what is your pleasure?" "Marry," quoth he, "I have left a thing behind me which I would fain have." "Sir," said I, "if I knew what it were, I would send for it out of hand." "Then," said he, "let the messenger go to my Lord of Northumberland, and desire him to send me the red buckram bag, lying in my almonry in my chamber, sealed with my seal." With that I departed from him, and went straight unto one Sir Roger Lassels, knight, who was then steward to the Earl of Northumberland (being among the rout of horsemen as one of the chiefest rulers), whom I desired to send some of his servants back unto the earl his master for that purpose; who granted most gently my request, and sent incontinent one of his servants unto my lord to Cawood for the said bag; who did so honestly his message, that he brought the same to my lord immediately after he was in his chamber within the Abbey of Pomfret; where he lay all night. In which bag was no other thing enclosed but three shirts of hair, which he delivered to the chaplain, his ghostly father, very secretly.

Furthermore, as we rode toward Pomfret, my lord demanded of me, whither they would lead him that night. " Forsooth, Sir," quoth I, " but to Pomfret." " Alas," quoth he, " shall I go to the castle, and lie there, and die like a beast ? " " Sir, I can tell you no more what they do intend; but I will inquire here among these gentlemen of a special friend of mine who is chief of all their counsel."

With that I repaired unto the said Sir Roger Lassels knight, desiring him most earnestly that he would vouchsafe to show me, whither my lord should go to be lodged that night ; who answered me again that my lord should be lodged within the Abbey of Pomfret, and in none other place ; and so I reported to my lord, who was glad thereof; so that within night we came to Pomfret Abbey, and there lodged.

And the earl remained still all that night in Cawood Castle, to see the dispatch of the household, and to establish all the stuff in some surety within the same.

The next day they removed with my lord towards Doncaster, desiring that he might come thither by night, because the people followed him weeping and lamenting, and so they did nevertheless although he came in by torchlight, crying, " God save your Grace,

II 2

God save your Grace, my good Lord Cardinal," running
before him with candles in their hands, who caused
me therefore to ride hard by his mule to shadow him
from the people, and yet they perceived him, cursing
his enemies.   And thus they brought him to the
Blackfriars, within the which they lodged him that
night.

And the next day we removed to Sheffield Park,
where the Earl of Shrewsbury lay within the lodge,
and all the way thitherward the people cried and
lamented as they did in all places as we rode before.
And when we came into the park of Sheffield, nigh to
the lodge, my Lord of Shrewsbury, with my lady his
wife, a train of gentlewomen, and all my lord's gentlemen and yeomen standing without the gates of the
lodge to attend my lord's coming, to receive him with
much honour; whom the earl embraced, saying these
words : " My lord," quoth he, " your Grace is most
heartily welcome unto me, and I am glad to see you
in my poor lodge, the which I have often desired ; and
should have been much more gladder, if you had come
after another sort."   " Ah, my gentle Lord of Shrewsbury," quoth my lord, " I heartily thank you : and
although I have no cause to rejoice, yet, as a sorrowful
heart may joy, I rejoice, my chance which is so good
to come unto the hands and custody of so noble a
person, whose approved honour and wisdom hath been
always right well known to all noble estates.   And,
Sir, howsoever my ungentle accusers have used their
accusations against me, yet I assure you, and so before

your lordship, and all the world, I do protest, that my demeanour and proceedings hath been just and loyal towards my sovereign and liege lord; of whose behaviour and doings your lordship hath had good experience; and even according to my truth and faithfulness so I beseech God to help me in this my calamity." "I doubt nothing of your truth," quoth the earl, "therefore, my lord, I beseech you, be of good cheer, and fear not; for I have received letters from the king of his own hand in your favour and entertaining, the which ye shall see. Sir, I am nothing sorry, but that I have not wherewith worthily to receive you, and to entertain you, according to your honour and my good will; but such as I have, ye are most heartily welcome thereto, desiring you to accept my good will accordingly, for I will not receive you as a prisoner, but as my good lord, and the king's true faithful subject; and here is my wife come to salute you." Whom my lord kissed bareheaded, and all her gentle-women; and took my lord's servants by the hands, as well gentlemen and yeomen as other. Then these two lords went arm and arm into the lodge, conducting my lord into a fair chamber at the end of a goodly gallery, within a new tower where my lord was lodged. There was also in the midst of the same gallery a traverse of sarsenet drawn; so that the one part was preserved for my lord, and the other part for the earl.

Then departed all the great number of gentlemen and other that conducted my lord to the Earl of

Shrewsbury's. And my lord being there, continued there eighteen days after; upon whom the earl appointed divers gentlemen of his servants to serve my lord, forasmuch as he had a small number of servants there to serve; and also to see that he lacked nothing that he would desire, being served in his own chamber at dinner and supper, as honourably, and with as many dainty dishes, as he had most commonly in his own house being at liberty. And once every day the earl would resort unto him, and sit with him communing upon a bench in a great window in the gallery. And though the earl would right heartily comfort him, yet would he lament so piteously, that it would make the earl very sorry and heavy for his grief. " Sir," said he, " I have, and daily do receive letters from the king, commanding me to entertain you as one that he loveth, and highly favoureth ; whereby I perceive ye do lament without any great cause much more than ye need to do. And though ye be accused (as I think in good faith unjustly), yet the king can do no less but put you to your trial, the which is more for the satisfying of some persons, than for any mistrust that he hath in your doings." " Alas ! " quoth my lord to the earl, " is it not a piteous case, that any man should so wrongfully accuse me unto the king's person, and not to come to mine answer before his majesty ? For I am well assured, my lord, that there is no man alive or dead that looketh in this face of mine, who is able to accuse me of any disloyalty toward the king. Oh ! how much it grieveth me that the king should have

any suspicious opinion in me, to think that I would
be false or conspire any evil to his royal person ; who
may well consider, that I have no assured friend in all
the world in whom I put my trust but only in his
grace ; for if I should go about to betray my sovereign
lord and prince, in whom is all my trust and confidence before all other persons, all men might justly
think and report, that I lacked not only grace, but
also both wit and discretion. Nay, nay, my lord, I
would rather adventure to shed my heart's blood in
his defence, as I am bound to do, by mine allegiance
and also for the safeguard of myself, than to imagine
his destruction ; for he is my staff that supporteth me,
and the wall that defendeth me against my malignant
enemies, and all other ; who knoweth best my truth
before all men, and hath had thereof best and longest
experience. Therefore to conclude, it is not to be
thought that ever I would go about or intend mali-
ciously or traitorously to travel or wish any prejudice
or damage to his royal person or imperial dignity ; but,
as I said, defend it with the shedding of my heart
blood, and procure all men so to do, and it were but
only for the defence of mine own person and simple
estate, the which mine enemies think I do so much
esteem ; having none other refuge to flee to for defence
or succour, in all adversity, but under the shadow of
his majesty's wing. Alas ! my lord, I was in a good
estate now, and in case of a quiet living right well
content therewith ; but the enemy that never sleepeth,
but studieth and continually imagineth, both sleeping

and waking, my utter destruction, perceiving the contentation of my mind, doubted that their malicious
and cruel dealings would at length grow to their shame
and rebuke, goeth about therefore to prevent the same
with shedding of my blood.   But from God, that
knoweth the secrets of their hearts and of all others,
it cannot be hid, nor yet unrewarded, when he shall
see opportunity.   For, my good lord, if you will show
yourself so much my good friend as to require the
king's majesty, by your letters, that my accusers may
come before my face in his presence, and there that I
may make answer, I doubt not but ye shall see me
acquit myself of all their malicious accusations, and
utterly confound them ; for they shall never be able
to prove, by any due probations, that ever I offended
the king in will, thought, and deed.   Therefore I
desire you and most heartily require your good lordship, to be a mean for me, that I may answer unto my
accusers before the king's majesty.   The case is his ;
and if their accusations should be true, then should it
touch no man but him most earnestly ; wherefore it
were most convenient that he should hear it himself
in proper person.   But I fear me, that they do intend
rather to dispatch me than I should come before him
in his presence ; for they be well assured, and very
certain, that my truth should vanquish all their untruth and surmised accusations ; which is the special
cause that moveth me so earnestly to desire to make
mine answer before the king's majesty.   The loss of
goods, the slander of my name, nor yet all my trouble

grieveth me nothing so much as the loss of the king's favour, and that he should have in me such an opinion, without desert, of untruth, that have with such travail and pains served his highness so justly, so painfully, and with so faithful a heart, to his profit and honour at all times. And also again, the truth of my doings against their unjust accusations proved most just and loyal should be much to my honesty, and do me more good than to attain great treasure ; as I doubt not but it will if the case might be indifferently heard. Now, my good lord, weigh ye my reasonable request, and let charity and truth move your noble heart with pity, to help me in all this my truth, wherein ye shall take no manner of slander or rebuke, by the grace of God." " Well then," quoth my Lord of Shrewsbury, " I will write to the king's majesty in your behalf, declaring to him by my letters how grievously ye lament his displeasure and indignation ; and what request ye make for the trial of your truth towards his highness." Thus after these communications, and divers others, as between them daily was accustomed, they departed asunder.

Where my lord continued the space after of a fortnight, having goodly and honourable entertainment, whom the earl would often require to kill a doe or two there in the park, who always refused all manner of earthly pleasures and disports either in hunting or in other games, but applied his prayers continually very devoutly ; so that it came to pass at a certain season sitting at dinner in his own chamber, having at his

board's end that same day, as he divers times had to
accompany him, a mess of the earl's gentlemen and
chaplains, and eating of roasted wardens at the end of
his dinner, before whom I stood at the table, dressing
of those wardens for him: beholding of him I perceived
his colour often to change, and alter divers times,
whereby I judged him not to be in health. Which
caused me to lean over the table, saying unto him
softly, " Sir, me seemeth your Grace is not well at
ease." He answered again and said, " Forsooth, no
more I am ; for I am," quoth he, " suddenly taken
about my stomach, with a thing that lieth overthwart
my breast as cold as a whetstone; the which is but
wind ; therefore I pray you take up the cloth, and
make ye a short dinner, and resort shortly again unto
me." And after that the table was taken up, I went
and sat the waiters to dinner, without in the gallery,
and resorted again to my lord, where I found him still
sitting where I left him very ill at ease; notwithstanding he was in communication with the gentlemen
sitting at the board's end. And as soon as I was
entered the chamber, he desired me to go down to the
apothecary, and to inquire of him whether he had any
thing that would break wind upward, and according
to his commandment I went my way towards the
apothecary. And by the way I remembered one
article of mine oath before made unto Master Walshe,
which caused me first to go to the earl, and showed
him both what estate he was in, and also what he
desired at the apothecary's hand for his relief. With

that the earl caused the apothecary to be called incontinent before him; of whom he demanded whether he had any thing to break wind that troubleth one in his breast; and he answered that he had such gear. " Then," quoth the earl, " fetch me some hither." The which the apothecary brought in a white paper, a certain white confection unto the earl, who commanded me to give the assay thereof to the apothecary, and so I did before him. And then I departed therewith bringing it to my lord, before whom I took also the assay thereof, and delivered the same to my lord, who received the same wholly altogether at once. And immediately after he had received the same, surely he voided exceeding much wind upward. " Lo," quoth he, " now you may see that it was but wind; but by the means of this receipt I am, I thank God, well eased:" and so he rose from the table, and went to his prayers, as he accustomedly did after dinner. And being at his prayers, there came upon him such a laske, that it caused him to go to his stool; and being there the earl sent for me, and at my coming he said, " Forasmuch as I have always perceived you to be a man, in whom my lord your master hath great affiance; and for my experience, knowing you to be an honest man " (with many more words of commendation than need here to be rehearsed), said, " It is so, that my lord, your lamentable master, hath often desired me to write to the king's majesty that he might come unto his presence, to make answer to his accusations; and even so have I done; for this day have I received letters from his Grace, by Sir William Kingston, knight, whereby I do perceive that the king hath in him a very good opinion ; and upon my often request, he hath sent for him, by the said Sir William, to come up to answer, according to his own desire : who is in his chamber.   Wherefore now is the time come that my lord hath often desired to try himself and his truth, as I trust much to his honour ; and I put no doubt in so doing, that it shall be for him the best journey that ever he made in all his life.   Therefore now would I have you to play the part of a wise man, to break first this matter unto him so wittily, and in such sort, that he might take it quietly in good part : for he is ever so full of sorrow and dolor in my company, that I fear me he will take it in evil part, and then he doth not well : for I assure you, and so show him that the king is his good lord, and hath given me the most worthy thanks for his entertainment, desiring and commanding me so to continue, not doubting but that he will right nobly acquit himself towards his highness.   Therefore, go your ways to him, and so persuade with him that I may find him in good quiet at my coming, for I will not tarry long after you."   " Sir," quoth I, " I shall, if it please your lordship, endeavour me to accomplish your commandment to the best of my power.   But, Sir, I doubt one thing, that when I shall name Sir William Kingston, he will mistrust that all is not well ; because he is constable of the Tower, and captain of the guard, having twenty-four of the guard to attend upon him."   " Marry it is truth," quoth the earl ;

" what thereof, though he be constable of the Tower? yet he is the most meetest man for his wisdom and discretion to be sent about any such message. And for the guard, it is for none other purpose but only to defend him against all them that would intend him any evil, either in word or deed; and also they be all, or for the most part, such of his old servants as the king took of late into his service, to the intent that they should attend upon him most justly, and doth know best how to serve him." " Well, Sir," said I, " I will do what I can," and so departed toward my lord.

And at my repair I found him sitting at the upper end of the gallery, upon a trussing chest of his own, with his beads and staff in his hands. And espying me coming from the earl, he demanded of me what news. " Forsooth, Sir," quoth I, " the best news that ever came to you; if your Grace can take it well." " I pray God it be," quoth he, " what is it? " " Forsooth, Sir," quoth I, " my Lord of Shrewsbury, perceiving by your often communication that ye were always desirous to come before the king's majesty, and now as your most assured friend, hath travailed so with his letters unto the king, that the king hath sent for you by Master Kingston and twenty-four of the guard, to conduct you to his highness." " Master Kingston," quoth he, rehearsing his name one or twice; and with that clapped his hand on his thigh, and gave a great sigh. " Sir," quoth I, " if your Grace could or would take all things in good part, it should be much better for you. Content yourself for God's sake, and think that God and your friends have wrought for you, according to your own desire. Did ye not always wish that ye might clear yourself before the king's person, now that God and your friends hath brought your desire to pass, ye will not take it thankfully. If ye consider your truth and loyalty unto our sovereign lord, against the which your enemies cannot prevail, the king being your good lord as he is, you know well, that the king can do no less than he doth, you being to his highness accused of some heinous crime, but cause you to be brought to your trial, and there to receive according to your demerits; the which his highness trusteth, and saith no less but that you shall prove yourself a just man to his majesty, wherein ye have more cause to rejoice than thus to lament, or mistrust his favourable justice. For I assure you, your enemies be more in doubt and fear of you, than you of them; that they wish that thing, that I trust they shall never be able to bring to pass with all their wits, the king (as I said before) being your indifferent and singular good lord and friend. And to prove that he so is, see you not how he hath sent gentle Master Kingston for you, with such men as were your old true servants, and yet be as far as it becometh them to be only to attend upon you, for the want of your own servants, willing also Master Kingston to remove you with as much honour as was due to you in your high estate; and to convey you by such easy journeys as ye shall command him to do; and that ye shall

have all your desires and commandments by the way
in every place, to your Grace's contentation and honour.
Wherefore, Sir, I humbly beseech your Grace, to imprint
all these just persuasions with many other imminent
occasions in your discretion, and be of good cheer; I
most humbly with my faithful heart require your Grace,
wherewith ye shall principally comfort yourself, and
next give all your friends and to me and other of your
servants good hope of your good speed." "Well, well,
then," quoth he, "I perceive more than ye can imagine,
or do know. Experience of old hath taught me."
And therewith he rose up, and went into his chamber,
to his close stool, the flux troubled him so sore; and
when he had done he came out again; and immediately my Lord of Shrewsbury came into the gallery
unto him, with whom my lord met, and then they both
sitting down upon a bench in a great window, the earl
asked him how he did, and he most lamentably, as he
was accustomed, answered, thanking him for his gentle
entertainment. "Sir," quoth the earl, "if ye remember
ye have often wished in my company to make answer
before the king; and I as desirous to help your request,
as you to wish, bearing towards you my good will,
have written especially to the king in your behalf;
making him also privy of your lamentable sorrow, that
ye inwardly receive for his high displeasure; who
accepteth all things and your doings therein, as friends
be accustomed to do in such cases. Wherefore I would
advise you to pluck up your heart, and be not aghast
of your enemies, who I assure you have you in more

doubt than ye would think, perceiving that the king is fully minded to have the hearing of your case before his own person. Now, Sir, if you can be of good cheer, I doubt not but this journey which ye shall take towards his highness shall be much to your advancement, and an overthrow of your enemies. The king hath sent for you by that worshipful knight Master Kingston, and with him twenty-four of your old servants, who be now of the guard, to defend you against your unknown enemies, to the intent that ye may safely come unto his majesty." "Sir," quoth my lord, "as I suppose Master Kingston is constable of the Tower." "Yea, what of that ?" quoth the earl, "I assure you he is only appointed by the king for one of your friends, and for a discreet gentleman, as most worthy to take upon him the safe conduct of your person ; for without fail the king favoureth you much more, and beareth towards you a secret special favour, far otherwise than ye do take it." "Well, Sir," quoth my lord, "as God will, so be it. I am subject to fortune, and to fortune I submit myself, being a true man ready to accept such ordinances as God hath provided for me, and there an end : Sir, I pray you, where is Master Kingston ?" "Marry," quoth the earl, "if ye will, I will send for him, who would most gladly see you." "I pray you then," quoth my lord, "send for him." At whose message he came incontinent, and as soon as my lord espied him coming into the gallery, he made haste to encounter him. Master Kingston came towards him with much reverence ; and at his approach he kneeled

down and saluted him on the king's behalf; whom my
lord bareheaded offered to take up, but he still kneeled.
" Then," quoth my lord, " Master Kingston, I pray you
stand up, and leave your kneeling unto a very wretch
replete with misery, not worthy to be esteemed, but
for a vile abject utterly cast away, without desert; and
therefore, good Master Kingston, stand up, or I will
myself kneel down by you." With that Master
Kingston stood up, saying, with humble reverence,
" Sir, the king's majesty hath him commended unto
you." " I thank his highness," quoth my lord, " I
trust he be in health, and merry, the which I beseech
God long continue." " Yea, without doubt," quoth
Master Kingston: " and so hath he commanded me
first to say unto you, that you should assure yourself
that he beareth you as much good will and favour as
ever he did; and willeth you to be of good cheer. And
where report hath been made unto him, that ye should
commit against his royal majesty certain heinous
crimes, which he thinketh to be untrue, yet for the
ministration of justice, in such cases requisite, and to
avoid all suspect of partiality he can do no less at the
least than to send for you to your trial, mistrusting
nothing your truth and wisdom, but that ye shall be
able to acquit yourself against all complaints and
accusations exhibited against you ; and to take your
journey towards him at your own pleasure, commanding me to be attendant upon you with ministration of
due reverence, and to see your person preserved from
all damage and inconveniences that might ensue ; and

to elect all such your old servants, now his, to serve
you by the way, who have most experience of your
diet.   Therefore, Sir, I beseech your Grace to be of
good cheer; and when it shall be your good pleasure
to take your journey, I shall give mine attendance."
" Master Kingston," quoth my lord, " I thank you for
your good news: and, Sir, hereof assure yourself, that
if I were as able and as lusty as I have been but of
late, I would not fail to ride with you in post: but,
Sir, I am diseased with a flux that maketh me very
weak.   But, Master Kingston, all these comfortable
words which ye have spoken be but for a purpose to
bring me into a fool's paradise : I know what is provided for me.   Notwithstanding, I thank you for your
good will and pains taken about me ; and I shall with
all speed make me ready to ride with you to-morrow."
And thus they fell into other communication, both the
earl and Master Kingston with my lord; who commanded me to foresee and provide that all things might
be made ready to depart the morrow after.   I caused
all things to be trussed up, and made in a readiness as
fast as they could conveniently.

When night came that we should go to bed, my
lord waxed very sick through his new disease, the
which caused him still continually from time to time
to go to the stool all that night ; insomuch from the
time that his disease took him, unto the next day, he
had above fifty stools, so that he was that day very
weak.   The matter that he voided was wondrous black,
the which physicians call choler adustine ; and when

he perceived it, he said to me, "If I have not some help shortly, it will cost me my life." With that I caused one Doctor Nicholas, a physician, being with the earl, to look upon the gross matter that he voided : upon sight whereof he determined how he should not live past four or five days ; yet notwithstanding he would have ridden with Master Kingston that same day, if the Earl of Shrewsbury had not been. Therefore, in consideration of his infirmity, they caused him to tarry all that day.

And the next day he took his journey with Master Kingston and the guard. And as soon as they espied their old master, in such a lamentable estate, they lamented him with weeping eyes. Whom my lord took by the hands, and divers times, by the way, as he rode, he would talk with them, sometime with one, and sometime with another; at night he was lodged at a house of the Earl of Shrewsbury's, called Hardwick Hall,* very evil at ease. The next day he rode to Nottingham, and there lodged that night, more sicker, and the next day we rode to Leicester Abbey ; and by the way he waxed so sick that he was divers times likely to have fallen from his mule ; and being night before we came to the Abbey of Leicester, where at his coming in at the gates the abbot of the place with all his convent met him with the light of many torches ; whom they right honourably received with great reverence. To whom my lord said, " Father Abbot, I

---

* This was Hardwick-upon-Line in Nottinghamshire, not Hardwick in Derbyshire.

am come hither to leave my bones among you," whom they brought on his mule to the stairs foot of his chamber, and there alighted, and Master Kingston then took him by the arm, and led him up the stairs; who told me afterwards that he never carried so heavy a burden in all his life. And as soon as he was in his chamber, he went incontinent to his bed, very sick. This was upon Saturday at night; and there he continued sicker and sicker.

Upon Monday in the morning, as I stood by his bedside, about eight of the clock, the windows being close shut, having wax lights burning upon the cupboard, I beheld him, as me seemed, drawing fast to his end. He perceiving my shadow upon the wall by his bedside, asked who was there? "Sir, I am here," quoth I. "How do you?" quoth he to me. "Very well, Sir," quoth I, "if I might see your Grace well." "What is it of the clock?" said he to me. "Forsooth, Sir," said I, "it is past eight of the clock in the morning." "Eight of the clock?" quoth he, "that cannot be," rehearsing divers times, "eight of the clock, eight of the clock, nay, nay," quoth he at the last, "it cannot be eight of the clock: for by eight of the clock ye shall lose your master: for my time draweth near that I must depart out of this world." With that Master Doctor Palmes, a worshipful gentleman, being his chaplain and ghostly father, standing by, bade me secretly demand of him if he would be shriven, and to be in a readiness towards God, whatsoever should chance. At whose desire I asked him that question.

" What have you to do to ask me any such question ? " quoth he, and began to be very angry with me for my presumption; until at the last Master Doctor took my part, and talked with him in Latin, and so pacified him.

And after dinner, Master Kingston sent for me into his chamber, and at my being there, said to me, " So it is, that the king hath sent me letters by this gentleman Master Vincent, one of your old companions, who hath been of late in trouble in the Tower of London for money that my lord should have at his last departing from him, which now cannot be found. Wherefore the king, at this gentleman's request, for the declaration of his truth hath sent him hither with his Grace's letters directed unto me, commanding me by virtue thereof to examine my lord in that behalf, and to have your counsel herein, how it may be done, that he may take it well and in good part. This is the chief cause of my sending for you ; therefore I pray you what is your best counsel to use in this matter for the true acquittal of this gentleman ? " " Sir," quoth I, " as touching that matter, my simple advice shall be this, that your own person shall resort unto him and visit him, and in communication break the matter unto him ; and if he will not tell the truth, there be that can satisfy the king's pleasure therein ; and in anywise speak nothing of my fellow Vincent. And I would not advise you to tract the time with him ; for he is very sick, and I fear me he will not live past to-morrow in the morning." Then went Master Kingston unto him ; and asked first how he did, and so forth proceeded in communication, wherein Master Kingston demanded of him the said money, saying, "that my lord of Northumberland hath found a book at Cawood that reporteth how ye had but late fifteen hundred pounds in ready money, and one penny thereof will not be found, who hath made the king privy by his letters thereof. Wherefore the king hath written unto me, to demand of you if you know where it is become; for it were pity that it should be embezzled from you both. Therefore I shall require you, in the king's name, to tell me the truth herein, to the intent that I may make just report unto his majesty what answer ye make therein." With that my lord paused a while and said, " Ah, good Lord! how much doth it grieve me that the king should think in me such deceit, wherein I should deceive him of any one penny that I have. Rather than I would, Master Kingston, embezzle, or deceive him of a mite, I would it were moult, and put in my mouth; " which words he spake twice or thrice very vehemently. " I have nothing, nor never had (God being my judge), that I esteemed, or had in it any such delight or pleasure, but that I took it for the king's goods, having but the bare use of the same during my life, and after my death to leave it to the king; wherein he hath but prevented my intent and purpose. And for this money that ye demand of me, I assure you it is none of mine; for I borrowed it of divers of my friends to bury me, and to bestow among my servants, who have taken great pains about me, like true and faithful men. Notwithstanding if it be his pleasure to take this money from me

I must hold me therewith content. Yet I would most humbly beseech his majesty to see them satisfied, of whom I borrowed the same for the discharge of my conscience." "Who be they ?" quoth Master Kingston. "That shall I show you," said my lord. "I borrowed two hundred pounds thereof of Sir John Allen of London ; and two hundred pounds of Sir Richard Gresham ; and two hundred pounds of the Master of the Savoy : and two hundred pounds of Doctor Hickden, dean of my college in Oxford ; and two hundred pounds of the treasurer of the church of York ; and two hundred pounds of the dean of York ; and two hundred pounds of parson Ellis my chaplain ; and a hundred pounds of my steward, whose name I have forgotten ; trusting that the king will restore them again their money, for it is none of mine." " Sir," quoth Master Kingston, " there is no doubt in the king ; ye need not to mistrust that, but when the king shall be advertised thereof, to whom I shall make report of your request, that his Grace will do as shall become him. But, Sir, I pray you, where is this money ? " " Master Kingston," quoth he " I will not conceal it from the king ; I will declare it to you, or I die, by the grace of God. Take a little patience with me, I pray you." " Well, Sir, then will I trouble you no more at this time, trusting that ye will show me to-morrow." " Yea, that I will, Master Kingston, for the money is safe enough, and in an honest man's keeping ; who will not keep one penny from the king." And then Master Kingston went to his chamber to supper.

Howbeit my lord waxed very sick, most likeliest to die that night, and often swooned, and as me thought drew fast toward his end, until it was four of the clock in the morning, at which time I asked him how he did. " Well," quoth he, " if I had any meat; I pray you give me some." " Sir, there is none ready," said I. " I wis," quoth he, " ye be the more to blame, for you should have always some meat for me in a readiness, to eat when my stomach serveth me; therefore I pray you get me some; for I intend this day, God willing, to make me strong, to the intent I may occupy myself in confession, and make me ready to God." "Then, Sir," quoth I, " I will call up the cook to provide some meat for you; and will also, if it be your pleasure, call for Master Palmes, that ye may commune with him, until your meat be ready." " With a good will," quoth he. And therewith I went first, and called up the cook, commanding him to prepare some meat for my lord; and then I went to Master Palmes and told him what case my lord was in; willing him to rise, and to resort to him with speed. And then I went to Master Kingston, and gave him warning, that, as I thought, he would not live; advertising him that if he had any thing to say to him, that he should make haste, for he was in great danger. " In good faith," quoth Master Kingston, " ye be to blame: for ye make him believe that he is sicker, and in more danger than he is." " Well, Sir," quoth I, " ye shall not say another day but that I gave you warning, as I am bound to do, in discharge of my duty. Therefore, I pray you, whatsoever shall chance, let no negligence be ascribed to me herein; for I assure you his life is very short. Do therefore now as ye think best." Yet nevertheless he arose, and made him ready, and came to him. After he had eaten of a cullis made of a chicken, a spoonful or two; at the last quoth he, "Whereof was this cullis made?" "Forsooth, Sir," quoth I, "of a chicken." "Why," quoth he, "it is fasting day, and St. Andrew's Eve." "What though it be, Sir," quoth Doctor Palmes, "ye be excused by reason of your sickness." "Yea," quoth he, "what though? I will eat no more."

Then was he in confession the space of an hour. And when he had ended his confession, Master Kingston bade him good-morrow (for it was about seven of the clock in the morning); and asked him how he did. "Sir," quoth he, "I tarry but the will and pleasure of God, to render unto him my simple soul into his divine hands. "Not yet so, Sir," quoth Master Kingston; "with the grace of God, ye shall live, and do very well, if ye will be of good cheer." "Master Kingston, my disease is such that I cannot live; I have had some experience in my disease, and thus it is: I have a flux with a continual fever; the nature whereof is this, that if there be no alteration with me of the same within eight days, then must either ensue excoriation of the entrails, or frenzy, or else present death; and the best thereof is death. And, as I suppose, this is the eighth day: and if ye

see in me no alteration, then is there no remedy
(although I may live a day or twain), but death, which
is the best remedy of the three." "Nay, Sir, in good
faith," quoth Master Kingston, "you be in such dolor
and pensiveness, doubting that thing that indeed ye
need not to fear, which maketh you much worse than
ye should be." "Well, well, Master Kingston," quoth
he, "I see the matter against me how it is framed;
but if I had served God as diligently as I have done
the king, he would not have given me over in my
grey hairs. Howbeit this is the just reward that I
must receive for my worldly diligence and pains that
I have had to do him service; only to satisfy his vain
pleasure, not regarding my godly duty. Wherefore, I
pray you, with all my heart, to have me most humbly
commended unto his royal majesty; beseeching him in
my behalf to call to his most gracious remembrance
all matters proceeding between him and me from the
beginning of the world unto this day, and the progress
of the same: and most chiefly in the weighty matter
yet depending (meaning the matter newly began
between him and good Queen Katherine); then
shall his conscience declare, whether I have offended
him or no. He is sure a prince of a royal courage, and
hath a princely heart; and rather than he will either
miss or want any part of his will or appetite, he will
put the loss of one half of his realm in danger. For
I assure you I have often kneeled before him in his
privy chamber on my knees, the space of an hour or
two, to persuade him from his will and appetite: but

I could never bring to pass to dissuade him therefrom. Therefore, Master Kingston, if it chance hereafter you to be one of his privy council, as for your wisdom and other qualities ye are meet to be, I warn you to be well advised and assured what matter ye put in his head, for ye shall never put it out again.

"And say furthermore, that I request his Grace, in God's name, that he have a vigilant eye to depress this new pernicious sect of Lutherans, that it do not increase within his dominions through his negligence, in such a sort, as that he shall be fain at length to put harness upon his back to subdue them; as the King of Bohemia did, who had good game, to see his rude commons (then infected with Wickliffe's heresies) to spoil and murder the spiritual men and religious persons of his realm; the which fled to the king and his nobles for succour against their frantic rage; of whom they could get no help of defence or refuge, but they laughed them to scorn, having good game at their spoil and consumption, not regarding their duties nor their own defence. And when these erroneous heretics had subdued all the clergy and spiritual persons, taking the spoil of their riches, both of churches, monasteries, and all other spiritual things, having no more to spoil, they caught such a courage of their former liberty that then they disdained their prince and sovereign lord with all other noble personages, and the head governors of the country, and began to fall in hand with the temporal lords to slay and spoil them, without pity or mercy, most cruelly. Insomuch that the king and other his nobles were constrained to put harness upon their backs, to resist the ungodly powers of those traitorous heretics, and to defend their lives and liberties, who pitched a field royal against them; in which field these traitors so stoutly encountered, the party of them was so cruel and vehement, that in fine they were victors, and slew the king, the lords, and all the gentlemen of the realm, leaving not one person that bare the name or port of a gentleman alive, or of any person that had any rule or authority in the commonweal. By means of which slaughter they have lived ever since in great misery and poverty without a head or governor, living all in common like wild beasts abhorred of all Christian nations. Let this be to him an evident example to avoid the like danger, I pray you. Good Master Kingston, there is no trust in routs, or unlawful assemblies of the common people; for when the riotous multitude be assembled, there is among them no mercy or consideration of their bounden duty; as in the history of King Richard the Second, one of his noble progenitors, which lived in that same time of Wickliffe's seditious opinions. Did not the commons, I pray you, rise against the king and the nobles of the realm of England; whereof some they apprehended, whom they without mercy or justice put to death? and did they not fall to spoiling and robbery, to the intent they might bring all things in common; and at the last, without discretion or reverence, spared not in their rage to take the king's most royal person out of the

Tower of London, and carried him about the city
most presumptuously, causing him, for the preservation of his life, to be agreeable to their lewd pro-
clamations? Did not also the traitorous heretic, Sir
John Oldcastle, pitch a field against King Henry the
Fifth, against whom the king was constrained to
encounter in his royal person, to whom God gave the
victory? Alas! Master Kingston, if these be not
plain precedents, and sufficient persuasions to ad-
monish a prince to be circumspect against the sem-
bable mischief; and if he be so negligent, then will
God strike and take from him his power, and diminish
his regality, taking from him his prudent counsellors
and valiant captains, and leave us in our own hands
without his help and aid; and then will ensue mischief upon mischief, inconvenience upon inconvenience,
barrenness and scarcity of all things for lack of good
order in the commonwealth, to the utter destruction
and desolation of this noble realm, from the which
mischief God of his tender mercy defend us.

"Master Kingston, farewell. I can no more, but
wish all things to have good success. My time
draweth on fast. I may not tarry with you. And
forget not, I pray you, what I have said and charged
you withal: for when I am dead, ye shall peradventure remember my words much better." And even
with these words he began to draw his speech at
length, and his tongue to fail; his eyes being set in
his head, whose sight failed him. Then we began to
put him in remembrance of Christ's passion; and sent

for the abbot of the place to anneal him, who came with all speed, and ministered unto him all the service to the same belonging; and caused also the guard to stand by, both to hear him talk before his death, and also to witness of the same; and incontinent the clock struck eight, at which time he gave up the ghost, and thus departed he this present life. And calling to our remembrance his words, the day before, how he said that at eight of the clock we should lose our master, one of us looking upon another, supposing that he prophesied of his departure.

Here is the end and fall of pride and arrogancy of such men, exalted by fortune to honours and high dignities; for I assure you, in his time of authority and glory, he was the haughtiest man in all his proceedings that then lived, having more respect to the worldly honour of his person than he had to his spiritual profession; wherein should be all meekness, humility, and charity; the process whereof I leave to them that be learned and seen in divine laws.

After that he was thus departed, Master Kingston sent an empost to the king, to advertise him of the death of the late Cardinal of York by one of the guard, that both saw and heard him talk and die. And then Master Kingston calling me unto him and to the abbot, went to consultation for the order of his burial.

After divers communications, it was thought good that he should be buried the next day following; for Master Kingston would not tarry the return of the

empost. And it was further thought good that the
mayor of Leicester and his brethren should be sent for,
to see him personally dead, in avoiding of false
rumours that might hap to say that he was not dead,
but still living. Then was the mayor and his brethren
sent for ; and in the mean time the body was taken out
of the bed where he lay dead ; who had upon him, next
his body, a shirt of hair, besides his other shirt, which
was of very fine linen holland cloth ; this shirt of hair
was unknown to all his servants being continually
attending upon him in his bedchamber, except to his
chaplain, which was his ghostly father; wherein he
was buried, and laid in a coffin of boards, having upon
his dead corpse all such vestures and ornaments as he
was professed in when he was consecrated bishop and
archbishop, as mitre, crosses, ring, and pall, with all
other things appurtenant to his profession. And lying
thus all day in his coffin open and barefaced, that all
men might see him lie there dead without feigning ;
then when the mayor, his brethren, and all other had
seen him, lying thus until four or five of the clock at
night, he was carried so down into the church with
great solemnity by the abbot and convent, with many
torches light, singing such service as is done for such
funerals.

And being in the church the corpse was set in our
lady chapel, with many and divers tapers of wax
burning about the hearse, and divers poor men sitting
about the same, holding of torches light in their hands,
who watched about the dead body all night, whilst the

canons sang dirige, and other devout orisons. And about four of the clock in the morning they sang mass. And that done, and the body interred, Master Kingston with us, being his servants, were present at his said funeral, and offered at his mass. And by that time that all things were finished, and all ceremonies that to such a person were decent and convenient, it was about six of the clock in the morning.

Then prepared we to horseback, being St. Andrew's Day the Apostle, and so took our journey towards the court, being at Hampton Court; where the king then lay. And after we came thither, which was upon St. Nicholas' Eve, we gave attendance upon the council for our depeche.

Upon the morrow I was sent for by the king to come to his Grace; and being in Master Kingston's chamber in the court, had knowledge thereof, and repairing to the king, I found him shooting at the rounds in the park, on the backside of the garden. And perceiving him occupied in shooting, thought it not my duty to trouble him : but leaned to a tree, intending to stand there, and to attend his gracious pleasure. Being in a great study, at the last the king came suddenly behind me, where I stood, and clapped his hand upon my shoulder ; and when I perceived him, I fell upon my knee. To whom he said, calling me by name, " I will," quoth he, " make an end of my game, and then will I talk with you ; " and so departed to his mark, whereat the game was ended.

Then the king delivered his bow unto the yeoman

of his bows, and went his way inward to the palace, whom I followed; howbeit he called for Sir John Gage, with whom he talked, until he came at the garden postern gate, and there entered; the gate being shut after him, which caused me to go my ways.

And being gone but a little distance the gate was opened again, and there Sir Harry Norris called me again, commanding me to come in to the king, who stood behind the door in a night-gown of russet velvet furred with sables; before whom I kneeled down, being with him there all alone the space of an hour and more, during which time he examined me of divers weighty matters, concerning my lord, wishing that liever than twenty thousand pounds that he had lived. Then he asked me for the fifteen hundred pounds, which Master Kingston moved to my lord before his death. " Sir," said I, " I think that I can tell your Grace partly where it is." " Yea, can you ? " quoth the king; " then I pray you tell me, and you shall do us much pleasure, nor it shall not be unrewarded." " Sir," said I, " if it please your highness, after the departure of David Vincent from my lord at Scroby, who had then the custody thereof, leaving the same with my lord in divers bags, sealed with my lord's seal, he delivered the same money in the same bags sealed unto a certain priest (whom I named to the king), safely to keep to his use." " Is this true ? " quoth the king. " Yea, Sir," quoth I, " without all doubt. The priest shall not be able to deny it in my presence, for I was at the delivery thereof." ' Well then," quoth the king, " let me alone, and keep this gear secret between yourself and me, and let no man be privy thereof; for if I hear any more of it, then I know by whom it is come to knowledge." " Three may," quoth he, " keep counsel, if two be away ; and if I thought that my cap knew my counsel, I would cast it into the fire and burn it. And for your truth and honesty ye shall be one of our servants, and in that same room with us, that ye were with your old master. Therefore go to Sir John Gage our vice-chamberlain, to whom I have spoken already to give you your oath, and to admit you our servant in the same room ; and then go to my Lord of Norfolk, and he shall pay you all your whole year's wages, which is ten pounds, is it not so ? " quoth the king. " Yes, for-sooth, Sire," quoth I, " and I am behind thereof for three quarters of a year." " That is true," quoth the king, " for so we be informed, therefore ye shall have your whole year's wages, with our reward delivered you by the Duke of Norfolk." The king also promised me furthermore, to be my singular good and gracious lord, whensoever occasion should serve. And thus I departed from him.

And as I went I met with Master Kingston coming from the council, who commanded me in their names to go straight unto them, whom they had sent for by him. " And in anywise," quoth he, " for God's sake, take good heed what ye say ; for ye shall be examined of such certain words as my lord your late master had at his departure, and if you tell them the truth," quoth he, " what he said, you shall undo yourself; for in anywise they would not hear of it: therefore be circumspect what answer ye make to their demands." " Why, Sir," quoth I, " how have ye done therein yourself ? " " Marry," quoth he, " I have utterly denied that ever I heard any such words ; and he that opened the matter first is fled for fear ; which was the yeoman of the guard that rode empost to the king from Leicester. Therefore go your ways, God send you good speed; and when you have done, come to me into the chamber of presence, where I shall tarry your coming to see how you speed, and to know how ye have done with the king."

Thus I departed, and went directly to the council chamber door ; and as soon as I was come, I was called in among them. And being there, my Lord of Norfolk spake to me first, and bade me welcome to the court, and said, " My lords, this gentleman hath both justly and painfully served the cardinal his master like an honest and diligent servant; therefore I doubt not but of such questions as ye shall demand of him, he will make just report, I dare undertake the same for him. How say ye, it is reported that your master spake certain words, even before his departure out of this life; the truth whereof I doubt not ye know ; and as ye know, I pray you report; and fear not for no man. Ye shall not need to swear him, therefore go to, how say you, is it true that is reported ? " " Forsooth, Sir," quoth I, " I was so diligent attending more to the preservation of his life than I was to note and mark every word that he spake : and, Sir, indeed, he spake

I 2

many idle words, as men in such extremities do, the which I cannot now remember. If it please your lordships to call before you Master Kingston, he will not fail to show you the truth." "Marry, so have we done already," quoth they, "who hath been here presently before us, and hath denied utterly that ever he heard any such words spoken by your master at the time of his death, or at any time before." "Forsooth, my lords," quoth I, "then I can say no more; for if he heard them not, I could not hear them; for he heard as much as I, and I as much as he. Therefore, my lords, it were much folly for me to declare any thing of untruth, which I am not able to justify." "Lo!" quoth my Lord of Norfolk, "I told you as much before; therefore go your ways," quoth he to me, "you are dismissed, and come again to my chamber anon, for I must needs talk with you."

I most humbly thanked them, and so departed; and went into the chamber of presence to meet with Master Kingston, whom I found standing in communication with an ancient gentleman, usher of the king's privy chamber, called Master Radcliffe. And at my coming, Master Kingston demanded of me, if I had been with the council; and what answer I made them, I said again, that I had satisfied them sufficiently with my answer; and told him the manner of it. And then he asked me how I sped with the king; and I told him partly of our communication; and of his Grace's benevolence and princely liberality; and how he commanded me to go to my Lord of Norfolk. As we were speaking of him, he came from the council into the chamber of presence; as soon as he espied me, he came unto the window, where I stood with Master Kingston and Master Radcliffe; to whom I declared the king's pleasure. These two gentlemen desired him to be my good lord. "Nay," quoth he, "I will be better unto him than ye ween; for if I could have spoken with him before he came to the king, I would have had him to my service; (the king excepted) he should have done no man service in all England but only me. And look, what I may do for you, I will do it with right good will." "Sir, then," quoth I, "would it please your Grace to move the king's majesty in my behalf, to give me one of the carts and horses that brought up my stuff with my lord's (which is now in the Tower), to carry it into my country." "Yea, marry, will I," quoth he, and returned again to the king; for whom I tarried still with Master Kingston. And Master Radcliffe, who said that he would go in and help my lord in my suit with the king. And incontinent my lord came forth, and showed me how the king was my good and gracious lord; and had given me six of the best horses that I could choose amongst all my lord's cart horses, with a cart to carry my stuff, and five marks for my costs homewards; and "hath commanded me," quoth he, "to deliver you ten pounds for your wages, being behind unpaid; and twenty pounds for a reward;" who commanded to call for Master Secretary to make a warrant for all these things. Then was it told him, that

Master Secretary was gone to Hanworth for that night. Then commanded he one of the messengers of the chamber to ride unto him in all haste for those warrants; and willed me to meet with him the next day at London; and there to receive both my money, my stuff, and horses, that the king gave me: and so I did; of whom I received all things according, and then I returned into my country.

And thus ended the life of my late lord and master, the rich and triumphant Legate and Cardinal of England, on whose soul Jesu have mercy! Amen.

Finis quod G. C.

Who list to read and consider, with an indifferent eye, this history, may behold the wondrous mutability of vain honours, the brittle assurance of abundance; the uncertainty of dignities, the flattering of feigned friends, and the tickle trust to worldly princes. Whereof this lord cardinal hath felt both of the sweet and the sour in each degree; as fleeting from honours, losing of riches, deposed from dignities, forsaken of friends, and the inconstantness of princes' favour; of all which things he hath had in this world the full felicity, as long as Fortune smiled upon him : but when she began to frown, how soon was he deprived of all these dreaming joys and vain pleasures. The which in twenty years with great travail, study, and pains, obtained, were in one year and less, with heaviness, care, and sorrow, lost and consumed. O madness! O foolish desire! O fond hope! O greedy desire of vain honours, dignities, and riches! O what inconstant trust and assurance is in rolling fortune! Wherefore the prophet said full well, *Thesaurizat, et ignorat, cui congregabit ea.* Who is certain to whom he shall leave his treasure and riches that he hath gathered together in this world, it may chance him to leave it unto such as he hath purposed? But the wise man saith, *That another person, who peradventure he hated in his life, shall spend it out, and consume it.*

THE TRAGEDY

OF

CARDINAL WOLSEY

BY

THOMAS CHURCHYARD.

.

TRAGEDY OF CARDINAL WOLSEY.

SHALL I look on, when States step on the stage,
And play their parts before the people's face?
Some men live now, scarce fourscore years of age,
Who in time past, did know the Cardinal's Grace:
A gamesome world, when bishops run at base,
    Yea, get a fall, in striving for the goal,
    And body lose, and hazard silly soul.

Ambitious mind, a world of wealth would have,
So scrats and scrapes for scarce and scorny dross:
And till the flesh and bones be hid in grave,
Wit never rests to grope for muck and moss.
Fie on proud pomp, and gilded bridle's boss!
    O glorious gold, the gaping after thee,
    So blinds mine eyes, they can no danger see.

Now note my birth, and mark how I began,
Behold from whence rose all this pride of mine,
My father but a plain poor honest man,
And I his son, of wit and judgment fine,
Brought up at school, and proved a good divine:
    For which great gifts, degree of school I had
    And Bachelor was, and I a little lad.

So, tasting some of Fortune's sweet conceits,
I clapt the hood on shoulder, brave as sun,
And hoped at length to bite at better baits,
And fill my mouth, ere banquet half were done.
Thus holding on, the course I thought to run,
   By many a feast my belly grew so big,
   That Wolsey straight became a wanton twig.

Lo what it is, to feed on dainty meat,
And pamper up the gorge with sugar plate :
Nay, see how lads, in hope of higher seat
Rise early up, and study learning late.
But he thrives best that hath a blessed fate ;
   And he speeds worst, that world will ne'er advance,
   Nor never knows what means good luck nor chance.

My chance was great, for from a poor man's son,
I rose aloft, and chopped and changed degree :
In Oxford first, my famous name begun,
Where many a day the scholars honour'd me,
Then thought I how I might a courtier be :
   So came to Court, and feathered there my wing,
   With Henry the Eighth, who was a worthy king.

He did with words assay me once or twice,
To see what wit and ready sprite I had :
And when he saw I was both grave and wise,
For some good cause the king was wondrous glad.
Then down I looked, with sober countenance sad,
   But heart was up as high as hope could go,
   That subtle fox might win some favour so.

We work with wiles the minds of men like wax,
The fawning whelp gets many a piece of bread :
We follow kings with many cunning knacks,
By searching out how are their humours fed.
He haunts no Court, that hath a doltish head :
　　For as in gold the precious stone is set,
　　So finest wits in Court the credit get.

I quickly learned to kneel and kiss the hand,
To wait at heel, and turn like top about,
To stretch out neck, and like an image stand,
To taunt, to scoff, and face the matter out,
To press in place among the greatest rout :
　　Yet like a priest myself did well behave,
　　In fair long gown, and goodly garments grave.

Where Wolsey went the world like bees would swarm,
To hear my speech and note my nature well.
I could with tongue use such a kind of charm,
That voice full clear should sound like silver bell.
When head devised a long discourse to tell,
　　With stories strange my speech should spicéd be,
　　To make the world to muse the more on me.

Each tale was sweet, each word a sentence weighed,
Each ear I pleased, each eye gave me the view,
Each judgment marked and paused on what I said,
Each mind I fed with matter rare and new,
Each day and hour my grace and credit grew :
　　So that the king, in hearing of this news,
　　Devised how he might my service use.

He made me then his Chaplain, to say Mass
Before his grace, yea twice or thrice a week :
Now had I time to trim myself by glass,
Now found I mean some living for to seek,
Now I became both humble, mild, and meek,
    Now I applied my wit and senses through
    .To reap some corn, if God would speed the plough.

Whom most I saw in favour with the king,
I followed fast, to get some hap thereby :
But I observed another finer thing,
That was, to keep me still in Prince's eye.
As under wing the hawk in wind doth lie,
    So for a prey I prowléd here and there,
    And triéd friends and fortune everywhere.

The king at length sent me beyond the seas,
Ambassador then, with message good and great :
And in that time I did the king so please
By short dispatch, and wrought so fine a feat,
That did advance myself to higher seat,
    The Deanery then of Lincoln he me gave :
    And bounty showed, before I 'gan to crave.

His Almoner too, he made me all in haste,
And threefold gifts he threw upon me still :
His counsellor straight likewise was Wolsey placed.
Thus, in short time, I had the world at will :
Which passed far man's reason, wit, and skill.
    O hap, thou hast great secrets in thy might,
    Which long lie hid from wily worldlings' sight.

As showers of rain fall quickly on the grass,
That fading flowers are soon refreshed thereby :
Or as with sun the morning dew doth pass,
And quiet calm makes clear a troubled sky :
So princes' power, at twinkling of an eye
  Sets up aloft a favourite on the wheel,
  When giddy brains about the streets do reel.

They are but blind that wake where fortune sleeps,
They work in vain that strive with stream and tide :
In double guard they dwell that destiny keeps,
In simple sort they live that lack a guide :
They miss the mark that shoot their arrows wide,
  They hit the prick that make their flight to glance
  So near the white, that shaft may light on chance.

Such was my luck, I shot no shaft in vain,
My bow stood bent and bracéd all the year :
I waited hard, but never lost my pain,
Such wealth came in, to bear the charges clear.
And in the end, I was the greatest peer
  Among them all, for I so ruled the land,
  By king's consent, that all was in my hand

Within one year three bishoprics I had,
And in small space a Cardinal I was made :
With long red robes rich Wolsey then was clad,
I walked in sun when others sate in shade :
I went abroad, with such a train and trade,
  With crosses borne before me where I past,
  That man was thought to be some god at last.

With sons of earls and lords I servéd was,
An hundred chains at least were in my train :
I daily drank in gold, but not in glass,
My bread was made of finest flour and grain :
My dainty mouth did common meats disdain,
    I fed like prince, on fowls most dear and strange,
    And banquets made of fine conceits for change.

My hall was full of knights and squires of name,
And gentlemen, two hundred told by poll :
Tall yeomen, too, did hourly serve the same,
Whose names each week I saw within check roll ;
All went to church, when service bell did knoll,
    All dined and supped and slept, at Cardinal's charge,
    And all would wait, when Wolsey took his barge.

My household stuff, my wealth and silver plate,
Might well suffice a monarch at this day :
I never fed but under cloth of state,
Nor walked abroad till ushers cleared the way.
In house I had musicians for to play,
    In open street my trumpets loud did sound,
    Which pierced the skies and seemed to shake the
        ground.

My men most brave, marched two and two in rank,
Who held in length much more than half a mile :
Not one of these, but gave his master thank
For some good turn, or pleasure got some while.
I did not feed my servants with a smile,
    Or glosing words, that never bring forth fruit,
    But gave them gold, or else preferred their suit.

In surety so, whilst God was pleased, I stood,
I knew I must leave all my wealth behind :
I saw they loved me not for birth or blood,
But serv'd a space, to try my noble mind.
The more men give, the more indeed they find
  Of love, and troth, and service, every way :
  The more they spare, the more doth love decay.

I joyed to see my servants thrive so well,
And go so gay, with little that they got :
For as I did in honour still excel,
So would I oft the want of servants note :
Which made my men on master so to dote,
  That when I said, let such a thing be done,
  They would indeed through fire and water run.

I had in house so many officers still,
Which were obeyed and honoured for their place,
That careless I might sleep or walk at will,
Save that sometime I weigh'd a poor man's case,
And salved such sores whose grief might breed disgrace.
  Thus men did wait, and wicked world did gaze
  On me and them, that brought us all in maze.

For world was whisht, and durst not speak a word
Of that they saw, my credit curbed them so :
I waded far, and passéd o'er the ford,
And minded not for to return I trow ;
The world was wise, yet scarce itself did know
  When wonder made of men that rose by hap :
  For fortune rare falls not in each man's lap.

I climbed the clouds, by knowledge and good wit,
My men sought chance, by service or good luck,
The world walked low, when I above did sit
Or down did come to trample on this muck :
And I did swim as dainty as a duck
　　When water serves, to keep the body brave,
　　And to enjoy the gifts that fortune gave.

And though my pomp surpast all prelates now,
And like a prince I lived and pleasure took :
That was not, sure, so great a blur in brow,
If on my works indifferent eyes do look,—
I thought great scorn such livings here to brook,
　　Except I built some houses for the poor,
　　And order took, to give great alms at door.

A College fair in Oxford I did make,
A sumptuous house, a stately work indeed,
I gave great lands to that, for learning sake,
To bring up youth, and succour scholars' need.
That charge of mine full many a mouth did feed,
　　When I in Court was seeking some good turn
　　To mend my torch or make my candle burn.

More houses gay I built than thousands do
That have enough, yet will no goodness show :
And where I built, I did maintain it too,
With such great cost, as few bestow I trow.
Of buildings large, I could rehearse a row,
　　That by mischance this day have lost my name,
　　Whereof I do deserve the only fame.

And as for suits, about the king was none
So apt as I, to speak and purchase grace.
Though long before, some say Shore's wife was one,
That oft kneel'd down before the prince's face
For poor men's suits, and helped their woeful case,
    Yet she had not such credit as I gat,
    Although a king would hear the parrot prate.

My words were grave, and bore an equal poise,
In balance just, for many a weighty cause:
She pleas'd a prince with pretty merry toys,
And had no sight, in state, nor course of laws:
I could persuade, and make a prince to pause
    And take a breath, before he drew the sword,
    And spy the time to rule him with a word.

I will not say but fancy may do much,
Yet world will grant that wisdom may do more:
To wanton girls, affection is not such,
That princes wise will be abused therefore:
One suit of mine, was surely worth a score
    Of hers indeed, for she her time must watch,
    And at all hours I durst go draw the latch.

My voice but heard, the door was open straight,
She might not come till she were called or brought:
I ruled the king, by custom, art and sleight,
And knew full well the secrets of his thought.
Without my mind, all that was done was nought,
    In wars or peace, my counsel swayéd all,
    For still the king would for the Cardinal call.

I kept a court, myself, as great as his,
(I not compare unto my master here)
But look, my lords, what lively world was this,
That one poor man became so great a peer?
Yet though this tale be very strange to hear,
    Wit wins a world: and who hath hap and wit,
    With triumph long in princely throne may sit.

What man like me bare rule in any age?
I shone like sun, more clear than morning star:
Was never part so played in open stage
As mine, nor fame of man flew half so far.
I sate on bench, when thousands at the bar
    Did plead for right: for I in public weal
    Lord Chancellor was, and had the great broad seal.

Now have I told how I did rise aloft,
And sate with pride and pomp in golden hall,
And set my feet on costly carpets soft,
And played at goal with goodly golden ball:
But after, Lord, I must rehearse my fall.
    O trembling heart, thou canst not now for tears
    Present that tale unto the hearers' ears!

Best weep it out, and sudden silence keep,
Till privy pangs make pinchéd heart complain:
Or cast thyself into some slumbering sleep,
Till wakened wits remembrance bring again.
    When heavy tears do hollow cheeks distain,
        The world will think thy spirits are grown so weak,
        The feeble tongue hath sure no power to speak.

A tale by signs, with sighs and sobs set out,
Moves people's minds to pity plaguéd men :
With howling voice do rather cry and shout,
And so by art show forth thy sorrow then.
For if thou speak, some man will note with pen
    What Wolsey said, and what threw Wolsey down,
    And under foot flings Wolsey's great renown.

What force of that ?　My fall must needs be heard.
Before I fell, I had a time to rise,
As fatal chance and fortune me preferred,
So mischief came, and did my state despise.
If I might plead my case among the wise,
    I could excuse right much of mine offence :
    But leave a while such matter in suspense.

The Pope, or pride, or peevish parts of mine,
Made king to frown, and take the seal from me :
Now served no words, nor pleasant speeches fine,
Now Wolsey, lo, must needs disgracéd be.
Yet had I leave (as doleful prisoner free)
    To keep a house (God wot) with heavy cheer,
    Where that I found no wine, nor bread, nor beer.

My time was come, I could no longer live,
What should I make my sorrow further known :
Upon some cause, that king that all did give
Took all again, and so possessed his own.
My goods, my plate, and all was overthrown,
    And look, what I had gathered many a day,
    Within one hour was cleanly swept away.

But hearken now, how that my fortune fell.
To York I must, where I the bishop was :
Where I by right, in grace a while did dwell,
And was installed, with honour great to pass.
The priors then and abbots 'gan to smell
    How Cardinal must be honoured as he ought,
    And for that day was great provision brought.

At Cawood then, where I great buildings made,
And did, through cause, expect my stalling day,
The king devised a secret under shade,
How Cardinal should be wrest and brought away.
One Wealth, a knight, came down in good array,
    And seasoned sure, because from Court he came,
    On Wolsey wolf, that spoiléd many a lamb.

Then was I led, toward Court, like dog in string,
And brought as beef, that Butcher-row must see :
But still I hoped to come before the king,
And that repair was not denied to me.
But he that kept the Tower my guide must be.
    Ah there I saw what king thereby did mean,
    And so I searched if conscience now were clean.

Some spots I found, of pride and popish parts,
That might accuse a better man than I :
Now Oxford came to mind, with all their arts,
And Cambridge too, but all not worth a fly :
For schoolmen can no foul defects supply.
    My sauce was sour, though meat before was sweet,
    Now Wolsey lacked both cunning, wit, and spreet.

A deep conceit of that possessed my head,
So fell I sick, consumed as some did think.
So took in haste my chamber and my bed,
On which device, perhaps, the world might wink.
But in the heart sharp sorrow so did sink,
  That gladness sweet forsook my senses all,
  In those extremes did yield unto my fall.

O let me curse the popish Cardinal hat,
Those mitres big, beset with pearl and stones,
And all the rest of trash I know not what,
The saints enshrine their flesh and rotten bones,
The mask of monks, devisèd for the nonce,
  And all the flock of friars, whate'er they are,
  That brought me up, and left me there so bare.

O cursed priests, that prate for profits sake,
And follow flood and tide, where'er it flows :
O merchants fine, that do advantage take
Of every grain, however market goes.
O fie on wolves, that march in masking-clothes,
  For to devour the lambs, when shepherd sleeps,
  And woe to you, that promise never keeps.

You said I should be rescued if I need,
And you would curse, with candle, book and bell :
But when ye should now serve my turn indeed,
Ye have no house, I know not where ye dwell
O friars and monks, your harbour is in hell,
  For in this world ye have no rightful place,
  Nor dare not once in heaven show your face.

Your fault not half so great as was my pride,
For which offence fell Lucifer from skies :
Although I would that wilful folly hide,
The thing lies plain before the people's eyes,
On which high heart a hateful name doth rise.
 It hath been said of old, and daily will,
  Pride goes before, and shame comes after still.

Pride is a thing that God and man abhors,
A swelling toad, that poisons every place,
A stinking wound, that breedeth many sores,
A privy plague, found out in stately face,
A painted bird, that keeps a peacock's pace,
 A loathsome lout, that looks like tinker's dog,
  A hellish hound, a swinish hateful hog,

That grunts and groans at everything it sees,
And holds up snout like pig that comes from draff.
Why should I make of pride all these degrees,
That first took root from filthy dross and chaff,
And makes men stay upon a broken staff ?
 No weakness more, than think to stand upright,
  When stumbling-block makes men to fall downright.

He needs must fall that looks not where he goes,
And on the stars, walks staring gosling like :
On sudden oft a blustering tempest blows,
Then down great trees are tumbled in the dyke.
Who knows the time and hour when God will strike ?
 Then look about, and mark what steps ye take,
  Before you pace the pilgrimage ye make.

Run not on head, as all the world were yours,
Nor thrust them back that cannot bide a shock :
Who strives for place, his own decay procures :
Who always brawls, is sure to catch a knock :
Who beards a king, his head is near the block :
    But who doth stand in fear and worldly dread,
    Ere mischief comes, had need to take good heed.

I having hap, did make account of none
But such as fed my humour, good or bad.
To fawning dogs sometimes I gave a bone,
And flung some scraps to such as nothing had :
But in my hands still kept the golden gad,
    That serv'd my turn, and laughed the rest to scorn,
    As for himself was Cardinal Wolsey born.

No, no, good men, we live not for ourselves,
Though each one catch as much as he may get :
We ought to look to him that digs and delves,
That always dwells and lives in endless debt.
If in such sort we would our compass set,
    We should have love where now but hate we find,
    And headstrong will, with cruel hollow mind.

I thought no thing of duty, love, or fear,
I snatched up all, and always sought to climb :
I punished all, and would with no man bear,
I sought for all, and so could take the time.
I plied the prince whilst fortune was in prime,
    I filled the bags, and gold in hoard I heaped,
    Thought not on those that threshed the corn I reaped

So all I lost, and all I gat was nought,
And all my pride and pomp lay in the dust :
I ask you all, what man alive had thought,
That in this world had been so little trust ?
Why, all things here, with time decline they must,
    Then all is vain, so all not worth a fly,
    If all shall think that all are born to die.

If all be base, and of so small account,
Why do we all in folly so abound ?
Why do the mean and mighty seek to mount
Beyond all hope, where is no surety found,
And where the wheel is always turning round ?
    The case is plain, if all be understood,
    We are so vain, we know not what is good.

Yet some will say, when they have heaps of gold,
With flocks of friends, and servants at their call,
They live like gods, in pleasure treblefold,
And have no cause to find no fault at all.
O blind conceit, these glories are but small,
    And as for friends, they change their minds so much
    They stay not long, with neither poor nor rich.

With hope of friends ourselves we do deceive,
With fear of foes we threatened are in sleep :
But friends speak fair, yet men alone they leave
To sink or swim, to mourn, to laugh, or weep ;
Yet when foe smiles, the snake begins to creep :
    As world falls out these days, in compass just,
    We know not how the friend or foe to trust.

Both can betray the truest man alive,
Both are to doubt, in matters of great weight ;
Both will sometime for goods and honour strive,
Both seemeth plain, yet both can show great sleight ;
Both stoop full low, yet both can look on height ;
 And best of both not worth a cracked crown :
 Yet least of both may lose a walled town.

Talk not of friends, the name thereof is nought,
Then trust no foes, if friends their credit lose :
If foes and friends of one bare earth were wrought,
Blame ne'er of both, though both one nature shows ;
Grace passeth kind, where grace and virtue flows,
 But where grace wants, makes foe and friends alike.
 The one draws sword, the other sure will strike.

I proved that true, by trial twenty times,
When Wolsey stood on top of Fortune's wheel,
But such as to the height of ladder climbs,
Know not what lead lies hanging on their heel.
Tell me, my mates, that heavy fortune feel,
 If rising up, breed not a giddy brain,
 And falling down, be not a grievous pain.

I told you how from Cawood I was led,
And so fell sick, when I arrested was :
What needeth now more words herein be said,
I knew full well I must to prison pass,
And saw my state as brittle as a glass :
 So gave up ghost, and bade the world farewell,
 Wherein, God wot, I could no longer dwell.

Thus unto dust and ashes I returned,
When blaze of life and vital breath went out,
Like glowing coal, that is to cinders burned;
All flesh and blood so end, you need not doubt.
But when the bruit of this was blown about,
    The world was glad the Cardinal was in grave.
    This is of world, lo all the hope we have!

Full many a year the world looked for my fall,
And when I fell, I made as great a crack
As doth an oak, or mighty tottering wall,
That whirling wind doth bring to ruin and wrack;
Now babbling world will talk behind my back,
    A thousand things, to my reproach and shame,
    So will it too of others do the same.

But what of that? The best is, we are gone.
And worst of all, when we our tales have told,
Our open plagues will warning be to none;
Men are by hap and courage made so bold,
They think all is their own they have in hold.
    Well, let them say and think what thing they please,
    This weltering world both flows and ebbs like seas.

THE END.

BALLANTYNE PRESS: CHANDOS STREET, W.C.

Messrs. George Routledge & Sons'

LIST OF

ANNOUNCEMENTS.

Two Entirely New Copyright Volumes of Essays by the late R. W. Emerson. 5s. each.

An Entirely New Complete Copyright Edition of the Writings of R. W. Emerson. With Original Notes to all the Volumes by his LITERARY EXECUTORS. In Six Volumes. 5s. each.

MR. LONGFELLOW'S LAST POEM—COPYRIGHT.

Michael Angelo. By the late H. W. LONGFELLOW. With 17 full-page Original Illustrations and 20 Woodcuts, specially designed for this work. 184 pp. 4to, cloth, gilt edges. 21s.

A New Edition of the Works of W. H. Prescott. In 15 Vols. Crown 8vo, cloth. £2 12s. 6d.

Men of the Time. The Eleventh Edition, Revised to 1883. Crown 8vo, cloth. 15s.

Shakspere. Edited by CHARLES KNIGHT. With 340 Illustrations by Sir JOHN GILBERT, R.A. Super-royal 8vo, cloth. 15s.

The Imperial Natural History. By the Rev. J. G. WOOD, M.A. 1,000 pages, with 500 Woodcuts. Super-royal 8vo, cloth. 15s.

The Cream of Leicestershire : Eleven Seasons' Skim-mings, Notable Runs, and Incidents of the Chase. By Captain PENNELL-ELMHIRST ("Brooksby"). With Illustrations (Coloured and Plain) by JOHN STURGESS, and Portraits and Map. Medium 8vo, cloth. 12s. 6d.

The Birthday Book of Flower and Song. Edited by ALICIA A. LEITH. With full-page Illustrations printed in colours. 4to, cloth, gilt edges. 10s. 6d.

A New Large-Type Edition of Professor Henry Mor-
ley's Edition of "The Spectator." 800 pp. in each Volume. In
3 Vols. Crown 8vo, cloth. 10s. 6d.

The Works of William Hogarth. By JOHN IRELAND. With
88 Copper-Plate Engravings. Super-royal 8vo, cloth. 10s. 6d.

Bartlett's Familiar Quotations. Author's New, Revised, and
Enlarged Edition, printed from new American Electrotype Plates, on
highly finished paper. Crown 8vo, cloth. 7s. 6d.

A Dictionary of Statistics. Edited by M. G. MULHALL
Crown 8vo. 7s. 6d. Roxburghe.

Discoveries and Inventions of the Nineteenth Cen-
tury. By ROBERT ROUTLEDGE, B.Sc., F.C.S. With 400 Illustrations. Crown 8vo, cloth, gilt edges. New and Cheaper Edition.
7s. 6d.

A Popular History of Science. By ROBERT ROUTLEDGE,
B.Sc., F.C.S. With 333 Illustrations and full-page Plates. Crown
8vo, cloth, gilt edges. New and Cheaper Edition. 7s. 6d.

The Homes and Haunts of the British Poets. By WIL-
LIAM HOWITT. With Portraits and Illustrations. 7s. 6d.

Routledge's Every Boy's Annual for 1884. With many
Illustrations and 13 Coloured Plates. Twenty-second year of Publication. 6s.

Routledge's Every Girl's Annual for 1884. With many
Illustrations and 12 Coloured Plates. Sixth Year of Publication. 6s.

The Circus and Menagerie Book. Printed in Colours.
Fancy Boards, 6s.

The Imperial Natural History Picture Book. With 80
full-page Illustrations. 5s. (And in boards, 3s. 6d.)

Little Wideawake for 1884. By Mrs. SALE BARKER. With
Original Plain and Coloured Illustrations, by M. E. EDWARDS, M.
KERNS, CHARLOTTE WEEKS, and others. Crown 4to, cloth, gilt
edges. 5s. (And in boards, 3s. 6d.)

The Boy's Playbook of Science. By Professor J. H. PEPPER.
With 400 Illustrations. New and Cheaper Edition. 5s.

The Playbook of Metals. By JOHN HENRY PEPPER. With
300 Illustrations. New and Cheaper Edition. 5s.

The Young Lady's Book: A Manual of Amusements,
Exercises, Studies, and Pursuits. Edited by Mrs. HENRY MAC-
KARNESS. With 270 Illustrations. New and Cheaper Edition. 5s

Notable Voyages: From Columbus to Parry. By W. H. G. KINGSTON. With Illustrations. 5*s.*

Great African Travellers: From Mungo Park to Livingstone and Stanley. By W. H. G. KINGSTON. With Map and Illustrations. 5*s.*

Travelling About Over New and Old Ground. By Lady BARKER. With Maps and Illustrations. 5*s.*

Modern Magic: A Practical Treatise on the Art of Conjuring. By Professor HOFFMANN. With 318 Illustrations. 5*s.*

The Practical Family Lawyer. By W. A. HOLDSWORTH. Barrister-at-Law. A New and Revised Edition, embodying all the Legal Changes to June, 1883. 5*s.*

A New Volume of Randolph Caldecott's Picture Books, containing his four latest Shilling Toy Books. 5*s.*

Lamb's Tales From Shakspeare. With Illustrations by Sir JOHN GILBERT, R.A. Cloth gilt, 5*s.* (And in boards, 3*s.* 6*d.*)

Dodd's Beauties of Shakspeare. With Illustrations by Sir JOHN GILBERT, R.A. Cloth gilt, 5*s.* (And in boards, 3*s.* 6*d.*)

Robinson Crusoe. With Portrait and 100 Illustrations by J. D. WATSON. Cloth gilt, 5*s.* (And in boards, 3s. 6*d.*)

KATE GREENAWAY'S NEW CHRISTMAS BOOK.

Little Ann, and Other Poems. By JANE and ANN TAYLOR. With Original Illustrations, by KATE GREENAWAY. Printed in Colours, by EDMUND EVANS. 5*s.*

Mano: A Poetical History of the Time of the Close of the Tenth Century, concerning the Adventures of a Norman Knight. By RICHARD WATSON DIXON, Vicar of Hayton, Hon. Canon of Carlisle. 5*s.*

Little Tiny's Book. With many Illustrations. Fcap. 4to, cloth. 5s. (And in boards, 3*s.*)

King Arthur and His Knights of the Round Table. By HENRY FRITH. With 50 Illustrations, by F. A. FRASER. 3*s.* 6*d.*

Robin Hood: Ballads and Songs. Collected by JOSEPH RITSON. With 50 Original Illustrations, by GORDON BROWNE. (*Red Line Poets.*) 3*s.* 6*d.*

Mrs. Hemans's Poems. A New Edition. With 50 Illustrations, by HAL LUDLOW. (*Red Line Poets.*) 3*s.* 6*d.*

The Poems of James Russell Lowell. (*Red Line Poets.*) 3*s.* 6*d.*

Longfellow's Poems. New Edition, re-set from new type, contain-ing Eighty-six Copyright Poems. With 83 Illustrations in the Text by Sir JOHN GILBERT, R.A., and other Artists. (*Red Line Poets*) 3*s.* 6*d.*

Old Wives' Fables. By EDOUARD LABOULAYE. With many Illustrations. 3*s.* 6*d.*

Routledge's Juvenile Books for Boys. New Volumes. 3*s.* 6*d.* each.

> Boys. By Lady BARKER.
> Hunting Grounds of the Whole World. By the OLD SHE KARRY.
> Ascents and Adventures: A Record of Hardy Mountaineering. By HENRY FRITH.
> Mayrick's Promise; or, Little Fugitives from the Jamaica Rebellion in 1865. By E. C. PHILLIPS.
> Holiday Stories for Boys and Girls. By Lady BARKER.
> Foxholme Hall. By W. H. G. KINGSTON.
> With the Colours. By R. M. JEPHSON.
> The Roll of the Drum. By R. M. JEPHSON.
> Sir Edward Seaward's Narrative of His Shipwreck. Edited by JANE PORTER.
> Perrault's Fairy Tales. Translated by J. R. PLANCHÉ.
> D'Aulnoy's Fairy Tales. Translated by J. R. PLANCHÉ.

The Bible Emblem Anniversary Book. With 365 Illustra-tions by WILLIAM FOSTER. Printed in Colours by EDMUND EVANS. 3*s.* 6*d.* (And in boards, 2*s.* 6*d.*)

Phiz's Toy Book. With 44 pages of Coloured Plates. Cloth, 3*s.* 6*d.* (Boards, 2*s.* 6*d.*)

Routledge's Young Ladies' Library. New Volumes. 3*s.* 6*d.* each.

> The Old House in the Square. By ALICE WEBER.
> The Asheldon Schoolroom. By the Author of "Jeanette," &c.
> Tempest-Tossed, the Story of Seejungfer. By the Author of "Mademoiselle Mori."
> The Doctor's Little Daughter. By ELIZA METEYARD.
> Schoolgirls all the World Over. With numerous Illustrations.
> Mark Dennison's Charge. By G. M. CRAIK.
> Dora and Her Papa. By ELIZA METEYARD.

Lord Brabourne's Fairy Tales. New and Cheaper Edition. 3*s.* 6*d.* each.

> Stories for My Children. | Ferdinand's Adventure

www.ingramcontent.com/pod-product-compliance
Lightning Source LLC
Chambersburg PA
CBHW030625030726
47497CB00006B/1640